CW01637856

Peter D[illegible] by, teacher t[illegible] rts journalist [illegible] e, Radio 4 a[illegible] early thirties and [illegible]

Pluto Crime

Edited by Ronald Segal

Murder in the Central Committee	Manuel Vázquez Montalban
October Heat	Gordon De Marco
The China Option	Nancy Milton
Morbid Symptoms	Gillian Slovo
The Waste Remains	Judith Cook
Junk on the Hill	Jeremy Pikser
Dance Hall of the Dead	Tony Hillerman
Days Like These	Nigel Fountain
Watching the Detectives	Julian Rathbone
The Dark Red Star	Ivan Ruff
Operation Emerald	Dominic McCartan
Frisco Blues	Gordon DeMarco
The Anvil Agreement	Ken Begg
Strange Inheritance	Bob Biderman

'. . . Is there anything inherently illogical with the concept of socialist – or, at least, politically and socially aware – crime fiction? Pluto Press, publishers of serious left wing books, have inaugurated a crime list to prove that the two can mix . . . the first batch of pinko whodunits augurs well for the genre.' *The Times*

'. . . the most innovative publishing experiment of the crime-story year!' *The Guardian*

Peter Dunant

Exterminating Angels

Pluto Press

London Sydney Dover New Hampshire

First published in 1983 by André Deutsch Limited,
105 Great Russell Street, London
This edition published in 1986 by Pluto Press Limited,
The Works, 105a Torriano Avenue, London NW5 2RX
and Pluto Press Australia Limited, PO Box 199, Leichhardt,
New South Wales 2040, Australia. Also Pluto Press
51 Washington Street, Dover, New Hampshire 03820 USA

Copyright © 1983 Peter Dunant

7 6 5 4 3 2 1

90 89 88 87 86

Printed in Great Britain by Cox & Wyman Limited, Reading, Berks

British Library Cataloguing in Publication Data
Dunant, Peter
Exterminating angels: a novel.
I. Title
823′.914[F] PR6054.U45/

ISBN 0 7453 0034 0

The lines quoted on p. 191 are from
'Missing Dates' by William Empson, Chatto and Windus

PART ONE

We have said a hundred times or more that when modern revolutionaries carry out actions what is important is not solely the actions themselves, but also the propagandist effect that they are able to achieve. Hence we preach not only action for itself, but also action as propaganda.

Johann Most, 1885

Terrorism is an attack on the whole community. It undermines everyone's confidence in the security of their families and the stability of their society. Where will the gunman strike? Whom will the bomber choose? This is the tension that induces cold fear – the atmosphere which the terrorist seeks to create. If he can destroy our trust in a well-ordered society, if he can spread consternation and provoke retaliation – then he is on the way to achieving his ends. Even more – if he can gain some recognition for his cause and some sympathy for this aim – then he can strike a body blow at society's efforts to defeat him. That is why TV and Press have so great a responsibility. They must, of course, report the facts. Nothing would be more damaging than misinformation and lack of balance. Yet the line is hard to draw for terrorism needs publicity. Newspaper and television coverage can provoke the very reaction the terrorist seeks.

Margaret Thatcher, May 20th 1981

Prologue

The house where it begins, and where it will end, is a rich, confident building, set back from the road in its own drive, and built in an age when Britain seemed poised to conquer the world. By rights it should be the setting for a quite different story, one where realism bows out in favour of romance, and where the heroine's only problem is deciding which of her many suitors she should marry.

But this is not that kind of tale, and the woman who lies dozing in the master bedroom is not that kind of heroine. Neither is the man downstairs that kind of hero. For the moment, however, he is the centre of attention.

He is sitting by an open fire staring into the flames. The air is misty with woodsmoke. The room around him is wealthy and tasteful, but he seems unaware of the decor: maybe he lives here and it is all easy and familiar to him. Certainly he seems to know his way around. Breaking the silence, he gets up and crosses the room to pour himself another drink.

Liquor crackles over fresh ice cubes as he moves towards the telephone. He dials a number with too many digits to be local and waits while the ringing tone becomes monotonous. Minutes pass. He looks at his watch and replaces the receiver. He takes a slow sip of his drink and then puts the glass down on the oak surface. The condensation leaves a ring of water on a table lovingly polished. He does not seem to notice. Again he picks up the telephone and the pattern is repeated. No answer, although this time he waits longer.

From the table he crosses to an alcove and a gleaming chrome stereo. A few seconds later the opening notes of Mahler's Fifth explode into the silence. He looks up sharply and reduces the volume.

Upstairs the woman's eyelids flicker, her dream pattern disturbed. She rolls over, sighs, and readjusts her limbs. Her breathing regains the rhythm of sleep.

In the room below the man is holding a small, automatic pistol, black and solid. He cocks it and slips the safety catch, each action a reflex. He lets it lie for a moment in the palm of his hand, testing its weight, welcoming it home.

Then, with deliberate strides, he is out of the door and into the hall. The strains of Mahler follow him into the silence, covering the sounds of his footfall as he climbs the stairs. Outside the bedroom door he pauses for a second, then slowly, silently turns the handle. From the window cold shafts of moonlight slide across the room revealing the bed and the shape of the reclining figure under the covers. He walks softly across the thick pile carpet until he is standing by the bedside staring down at her. Her dark hair is splayed out against the pillow. Caught in sleep there is a kind of innocence about her face, a hint of a pout around the corners of the mouth as the muscles slacken, a soft babyflesh quality to the skin. The man seems unaffected by her vulnerability. He moves the gun to the back of her skull. It is an almost matter-of-fact gesture. But even as the muzzle touches her hair her eyes flick open, alert immediately. He puts out his free hand and touches her cheek. It is almost a caress.

'Close your eyes, Anna. Go back to sleep.'

'You shouldn't do this.' Her voice is clean and steady, without fear. 'You shouldn't do this. It can't change anything.'

There is the sound of a shot.

Downstairs the last chords die away, and the arm lifts smoothly off the record. Soon the only sound left in the house is the gentle hum of one of the most expensive sound systems in Hampshire.

Chapter One

The Times March 6th

Authorities predict massive oil slick

BRITISH TANKER AGROUND OFF DEVON COAST

A supertanker loaded with 200,000 tonnes of crude oil ran aground and exploded in Lyme Bay last night, killing three of her crew of forty-two. There are fears of a pollution disaster on the scale of that caused by the sinking of the *Torrey Canyon* off Cornwall in 1967.

The *Mt McKinley*, which is owned by Lindop Oil International Ltd, was en route from the Persian Gulf to the Lindop refinery in the Isle of Grain. It had entered Lyme Bay to be lightered – a routine operation in which cargo is transferred to smaller tankers. At 8.47, in conditions of extremely poor visibility, the supertanker ran aground on a sand bank twenty miles off shore. The resulting explosion caused an outbreak of fire, which the crew succeeded in containing. No other vessels were involved.

At least two of the *Mt McKinley's* sixteen tanks are known to have been breached. Experts estimate the oil slick could reach the coast of Devon and Dorset in a matter of hours.

Harold Akeroyd, chairman of Lindop Oil International, had for many years followed a strict routine on rising for the day. He woke, without an alarm, at 6.30 a.m., washed and dressed immediately, and ate a grapefruit while reading the morning papers. At around 7.30 it was his habit to take a quick stroll outside the house for a little fresh air and to survey his modest but satisfying estate. His wife (they slept separately) would join him at eight for a leisurely breakfast cooked by the live-in maid, and soon afterwards his chauffeur would drive him to the Lindop offices in the City.

On the morning of March 6th that routine was interrupted when Akeroyd was woken in the middle of the night with the news of the *Mt McKinley* accident. He dealt with the immediate problems, such as briefing the press office on the official line, then lay in bed dozing until 6 a.m. He ordered his car for 7.30, but despite the earlier start, he determined to take his morning walk as always, and, just after 7.00, with a heavy frost still crisp on the grass, he put on his overcoat and went outside.

He walked down to the edge of the long garden which bordered on the farm estate, his steps crunching in the still air. To the left stretched a long greenhouse, to the right a beech hedge lining a swimming pool. He chose the right hand path, wanting to check that the gardener had raked away the final flurry of winter leaves before the water was changed for the spring.

Crossing through the trees he reached the edge of the pool. There were no leaves. Instead, a thick glutinous sheet of black slime covered the surface, pushing sluggishly against the walls and staining the tiles with a sticky, shiny tar. Harold Akeroyd's swimming pool was filled with crude oil.

He stood for a moment, transfixed by the sight, his nostrils filled with the pungent, nauseating smell rising off the surface. Then he turned, walked quickly back to the house, and made a few rapid telephone calls. By noon he was at Heathrow Airport, waiting to board the BA 5614 to Aberdeen. It was time, he decided, to lie low for a while.

Later that same morning a man was feeding the ducks from the white bridge in the centre of St James's Park. He was tall, not quite fleshed out enough for his height; and the set of his face and the hair greying at the temples gave the impression of a middle age he had not yet reached. He leant on the parapet, an old-fashioned black briefcase at his feet, a smart blue raincoat thrown carelessly over his shoulder as a talisman against the heavy grey skies.

Feeding ducks is no easy matter. If you throw in the bread carelessly, along come the mallards, the bullies of the wildfowl world, and swipe the lot. He put, therefore, all his concentration into tossing the crumbs where only his favourite ducks could reach them. He was totally absorbed in his task. If you had approached and addressed him he would have jumped a mile, surely.

'Hello, Daniel.'

'Hello, Anna.'

Daniel did not jump, nor did he turn. He continued the feeding, ignoring his new companion. The woman stood beside him, giving her full attention to the murky water beneath.

'Yuk,' she said. 'This water's filthy.'

'Not as polluted as some, I hear.'

'Oh, really?'

'Yes. Word from a country estate.'

'The swimming pool?'

'In roughly the same condition as the beach at Lyme Bay.'

Anna turned to face the centre of the bridge. She stood six inches shorter than him, dark-haired, dark-eyed, attractive and immaculate in both dress and make-up. There was character in her face, and a deliberate intelligence in the eyes, but these needed to be discerned beneath the meticulous artificiality of her turn-out. Like that of the ducks, her appearance was designed to attract a mate and repel predators.

'And what else from your informant, Daniel?'

'Akeroyd is somewhat shaken by the night's developments. Just as you predicted, Anna.'

'Good.'

'And he has decided for the sake of his peace of mind and the good of the company to pay a visit to Scotland.'

'To inspect North Sea oil installations?'

'Exactly. He will take the BA 5614 reaching Aberdeen at 2.35.'

'And the others?'

'They're all looking forward to his arrival.'

On the parapet a sparrow darted in and lifted a few spare crumbs from the stonework, making a fast getaway. Daniel regarded the heist with an unblinking stare. Then he turned back to the woman.

'I must say, Anna, your information has been first class. How did you manage it?'

She smiled, accepting the compliment but acknowledging the patronizing edge.

'Oh, it was nothing, Daniel,' she said softly. 'Akeroyd's sister is one of my clients. I recently helped her to augment her collection of eighteenth-century watercolours. She's very talkative and is extremely fond of her family, especially her famous brother. She'll be so upset to hear of the danger he's about to be in.'

'Well, you can reassure her that it's only his reputation that's at stake. There are bigger fish to fry.'

'You mean Global?'

'That, and other things. But let's nail Lindop first.'

He resumed his appraisal of the ducks. The bread in the brown paper bag was almost finished. He tipped the bag upside down and scattered the last of the crumbs onto the water. The ducks went wild, snapping and pecking one another out of the way in the race for food. Daniel shook his head, as if dismayed by this sudden display of selfish anarchy.

When he looked up again the woman had gone. He crumpled the bag deliberately in his hand and deposited it neatly into the litter bin on his way out of the park.

Chapter Two

At three that afternoon, a few miles outside Aberdeen on the main road to Turriff, a dark blue Cortina stood parked in a lay-by. On its rear wing a slim short-wave aerial waved slightly in the bitter east wind. Inside the car were two police officers. The passenger, in the uniform of a sergeant, sprawled in his seat, his manner casual but his gaze intent on the road ahead. He had clean-cut good looks, a full but neatly trimmed beard, dark curly hair and deep brown eyes. Beside him sat a less reputable figure with a crumpled face and fleshy lips, a hand-rolled cigarette held between thumb and forefinger. He flicked his wrist to look at his watch.

Two hundred yards ahead a metallic grey Renault 30TX pulled out from the airport car park, turned right and headed slowly towards them.

Harold Akeroyd was fumbling impatiently with the Renault's safety belt. 'Well, who knows, Jim? It could have been Exterminating Angel. It's their kind of theatrics. But whoever it was, I wasn't just going to wait for the press to come hammering at my door to ask.'

‘What instructions have you left with the press office?’ asked Jim Fennaway, head of Lindop Oil’s North Sea operations.

‘None. Let the newshounds sniff it out for themselves. But if they start poking their noses round the house there’ll be trouble. I’ve brought in some of our security men to keep them out.’

There was an hysterical edge to Akeroyd’s voice, and Fennaway glanced across at him anxiously. As he did so, his attention was distracted from the driving mirror and he failed to notice the Cortina do a U-turn and start to follow them.

‘But the real question is,’ Akeroyd continued, ‘how much else does the press know?’

‘What might they find out?’

‘That the radar was known to be dodgy when the *Mt McKinley* left port.’

Fennaway clicked his tongue. ‘Tricky,’ he murmured.

‘Good God!’ Akeroyd snapped. ‘You know what it costs a day to keep a full cargo and crew in port for repairs.’

The car reached a roundabout and Fennaway turned left up a side road leading to a quiet country restaurant which he knew would still be open for lunch. On their tail, now only fifty yards behind, came the Cortina.

‘What’s more,’ said Akeroyd, ‘there’s the question of that Health and Safety Executive report.’

‘Didn’t we manage to get that covered up?’

‘Yes, but it’s bound to come out now.’ Akeroyd relapsed into silence, massaging his temples. Then he returned to his original subject. ‘What gets me about these vandals is, how come they’re so well informed?’

His question was never answered. Both men started as the Cortina came alongside, its window down, and the police officer gestured Fennaway to pull over.

Parked on the grass verge, Akeroyd and Fennaway waited as the police sergeant walked evenly towards them. He approached the passenger door. Akeroyd pushed a button and the window slid down silently.

The policeman smiled politely. ‘Sorry to disturb you, sir, but there’s been a serious accident on the A947. I wonder if I could see your driving licence?’

Fennaway leaned forward to reach into the glove

compartment. Suddenly the passenger door was flung open to reveal an automatic pistol held low in the policeman's right hand. He jabbed the muzzle hard into Akeroyd's ribs, causing him to cry out in protest.

'O.K. Now do exactly as you're told. Move over.'

In a second he was inside, the door slammed. Akeroyd felt the warmth of the man's leg and the coldness of the steel pushing through his shirt. On the other side he sensed Fennaway's body harden in instinctive resistance.

'Please, Jim,' he begged. 'Do what he says.'

For a long, tense moment nobody moved. Then Fennaway's fist gradually unclenched. 'All right,' he said.

'Good. Eyes front, both of you.' The gunman's voice rasped. 'Now, Mr Driver, drive.' For good measure he poked with the gun again. Akeroyd yelped. The man waved to his accomplice in the Cortina, and they set off in convoy. No one spoke: the gun discouraged conversation.

Ten minutes later the two cars turned off the road up a track marked Forestry Commission. Four hundred metres up the track Fennaway was ordered to stop the car in a small clearing in the forest. Now the other gunman approached. Instead of the policeman's cap he wore over his head the trademark nylon stocking. He leant through the open window of the car and held his automatic on the mesmerized oilmen while the first gunman pulled on a similar disguise.

'Right, lads,' he said, opening the passenger door. 'Let's have you out.' With his left hand he seized Akeroyd's hair and yanked. Akeroyd howled, but he moved, fast, tipping out of the car off-balance, face down on the grass. The gun was directed at the back of his head. 'I want you to lie there completely still. As if you were dead.'

In a moment Fennaway had joined his boss on the ground. The gunmen produced hypodermic syringes and the businessmen's left arms were bared and injected. The two watched their victims in silence for a few moments. Then the driver crouched beside Akeroyd. He turned him over. Akeroyd's head lolled. He ground his knuckles hard into the breast bone. No response. He applied the same test to Fennaway. 'O.K.,' he said. 'They're out, Alex.'

They peeled off their stockings. Alex pulled at the corner of his beard. It came off in one clean movement. 'Shit!' he exclaimed, wincing and rubbing the smarting skin. 'All right, Wolf. Let's go.'

Picking up Fennaway, they hoisted him into the back of the Renault and covered him with blankets. Next, Alex fiddled around under the bonnet and came out with the distributor cap. He hurled it crashing into the undergrowth. They put the comatose Akeroyd into the Cortina and set off again down the track deeper into the forest.

In another clearing a helicopter stood waiting. As they approached, the pilot ran towards them. Alex jumped out of the car. 'O.K. So far, so good, Brian. Any problems your end?'

'Nope.'

As Brian strapped Akeroyd into a seat in the helicopter the two kidnappers changed their clothes. Alex put on denims and a polo neck, Wolf a business suit. He pulled a comb through his heavy fair hair, putting the finishing touches to a change of image, and grinned at Alex.'

'How do I look?'

'Ridiculous. I swear, Wolf, you make the worst-looking executive I've ever seen.'

'Well, we can't all be pretty. I've came across enough ugly businessmen in my time.'

Alex smiled and checked his watch. 'Let's go over it again.'

'I drive into Aberdeen. Leave the car in a multi-storey. Walk to the station. Take the 4.55 to Glasgow, then the 9.23 to Lockerbie. Livia picks me up at eleven.'

'Check. And take it easy, Wolf. We've got plenty of time. Don't get done for speeding.'

Wolf grinned. 'In a police car? Don't worry.'

They moved towards each other, embraced fiercely for a second, then Alex broke away, slapping his friend on the shoulder. 'All right,' he shouted. 'Let's go.' He ran to the helicopter and jumped in as the machine slowly lifted, smashing the foliage around it. It wheeled to the right and headed off, the pale March sunshine glinting on its blades.

Shielding his face with his arm, Wolf returned to the Cortina. As the chopper disappeared from view the car followed it down the track towards the open road. Silence was restored to the forest.

An hour later the whirling machine roared and spat its way down onto the moors of Dumfriesshire. A few sheep shuffled back, disturbed by the gale but too stupid to run from the danger. Then, as the wind died down, they returned their attention to the grass, their memories sifting and rejecting information not related to food. Fifty yards away a woman stood leaning against a land rover, one arm cupped over her head to protect herself from the snarling windspray.

As the blades slowed their rotation, she ran crouching towards the machine. The door opened and Alex leaped out, an arm raised in triumphant welcome. She returned a smaller, more guarded gesture and peered behind him to the passenger seat where Akeroyd was strapped in.

'O.K. Let's get him out and have a look at him.' Her voice held the touch of an accent, difficult to locate. It was a dark voice, stronger than her small-framed body. Kneeling by the unconscious man she became efficient, a professional. She checked heartbeat, pulse, pupils, studied the mark on his arm. She nodded. 'He's fine. Who gave him the jab?'

Alex smiled, bowing in exaggerated modesty.

She raised an eyebrow. 'It's a clean one, Alex. You're getting better at it.' She stood up. 'Let's get him into the car. Then Brian can get on his way.'

Alex stood there, poised to move, his weight resting on his toes. 'Aren't you going to ask how it went?'

She frowned slightly and shrugged. 'I can see how it went. Just according to plan. We can talk later. It's too exposed here.'

She walked back to the land rover. Alex watched her go, impatient for a moment with her efficiency. Then he let the irritation pass and called to Brian for help. Together they bundled the sleeping body of Akeroyd into the back of the vehicle. The woman started the engine, leaning over to open the passenger door. Her movements had a precise, almost brusque quality to them. She was obviously someone used to getting things done.

Outside the car Brian put his hand on the open window and bent to look at her.

'All right, Livia. You know where to contact me if you need to. I'll be there till the job finishes. Good luck, both of you.' He grinned, and she smiled back, her first smile, bright but contained.

'Keep the luck, Brian . . . We won't need it.' She put a hand on his. 'Take care.'

Thirty minutes later the land rover pulled up outside a small stone cottage cradled in a hollow of the landscape. Between them, she and Alex manoeuvred their captive into the house, humping his arms over their shoulders and dragging his leaden weight towards the door. Behind them lay an empty skyline chilled by the moorland winds. Inside, they left him sprawled on a bed in a tiny basement room. Livia carefully covered him with blankets. As they went upstairs, she put her arm through Alex's, her body relaxing against him.

'Now you can tell me what happened. I've got some food and drink ready.' She looked him in the eyes. 'Well done.'

Chapter Three

In London it was late afternoon before the Lindop executives began to realise that their chairman's leisurely lunch had lasted a little too long for comfort. Although officially Harold Akeroyd was unavailable for comment, he had been expected to contact his managing director on arrival at the Aberdeen office. Finally, Jim Fennaway's secretary managed to track down the Tarragon restaurant where her boss sometimes ate, and they confirmed that yes, Mr Fennaway had made a reservation, but no, he had never turned up.

Unpleasant though it was, Lindop executives had no alternative but to cancel their various dinner engagements and accept that their chairman was missing and all hell was about to break loose. At 6.30 they called the police, who called in Scotland Yard, and it was agreed that for the moment the press would not be informed. In Aberdeen, police reinforcements were called in and enquiries got under way, but nothing was discovered. Harold Akeroyd, it seemed, had disappeared.

The pattern was unmistakeable to both Lindop and the police. It was just six months since David Sloane, chairman of Ryder Hawkins Tobacco, had disappeared under similar circumstances, the day after the publication of a major, damning report on health and smoking. To get him back, Ryder Hawkins had submitted to the suggestion that they transfer £500,000 of their profits into a new cancer research project doing advanced work in chemotherapy. Remembering that incident, and reading the reports coming in of the oil slick damage, the Lindop directors began to speculate on what it was going to cost to get their chairman back.

Some hours later that evening, in her house just outside Winchester, the woman who had stood on the bridge in St James's Park now sat curled in an armchair by an open fire watching the television news.

She was less immaculate now, her face softer and more ghostly without the skillful structure of make-up, and her feet bare under a pair of faded jeans. To her many casual friends, Anna Weston, thirty-five, married, part-time art consultant, was a bright, fashionable woman who enjoyed money, never talked politics, and voted Conservative, or possibly Social Democrat. To the five people who knew her more intimately Anna Weston was a terrorist with a perfect cover.

The news ended and she got up from her seat to switch off the set. There had been nothing about Akeroyd's disappearance. Things were going exactly according to plan. She stood in the middle of the room for a moment, lost in thought. Outside, the grandfather clock struck half past ten. Half an hour to go. She walked to the other side of the room to an easel. On it was an old, cracked canvas, a picture of a farmcart in a country lane, its surface obscured by layers of thick, dark varnish. She stood back from the canvas, studying it carefully. Then, picking up a needle from a small table next to the easel, she approached one corner of the painting and stuck the end firmly into the built-up mass of paint. As she withdrew it, a minute quantity of sticky pigment stayed on the tip. This she transferred to a glass block on the table. She smiled. The painting, as she had suspected, was a fake.

She was moving towards the desk to consult her files when the clock struck eleven. She froze, listening to the chimes. As the eleventh one died away the telephone began to ring. She made no move to answer it. It rang five times, then stopped.

She put on a light raincoat and left the house. A quarter of a mile down the road the call box was empty. Inside, she took out a stopwatch and placed it on the directory in front of her. Then she stuffed a handkerchief into the mouthpiece and dialled.

'Hello?'

'Mrs Akeroyd?'

'This is her daughter. My mother is rest—'

'Be quiet and listen. Your father is being held by Exterminating Angel. He will be returned to you unhurt if you comply with our demands. These will be made known to you shortly.' It was a prepared statement and Anna delivered it without a falter.

'Please—'

Whatever the woman would have said was lost as Anna put the phone down. She looked at her stopwatch. Nineteen seconds. The police required at least half a minute to trace a call. She walked briskly home, methodically tearing up and scattering the piece of paper on which the Akeroyd number had been written. Inside, she poured herself a large brandy and returned to her place by the fire. She sat for a long time staring into the flames, thinking of the cold, stone cottage on the Scottish moors where her husband was spending the night. She raised the glass in silent toast and let the rich, dark liquid burn its way down her throat.

Chapter Four

On the moor the night had brought with it a freezing fog. Outside the cottage the air was heavy with the distinctive Scottish chill, damp and vicious. Alex was standing with his back against the wall, hunched inside his down jacket, staring into space, his cigarette end glowing sharply in the black air. There was a tightness behind his eyes, as if the muscles of his retina had been overstretched. He recognized the sensation of exhaustion brought on by the tension of the day. But it was not the kind of exhaustion that led to sleep. He rubbed his eyes hard with the heel of his palm. For a second his vision splintered into spark streams of light, then re-formed into solid darkness.

Behind him Livia appeared from the door. She came and stood next to him, small beside his large frame. There was a long silence between them. She broke it.

'Why don't you go to bed, Alex? Akeroyd will be unconscious till morning. Even Wolf's out cold. He was almost asleep in the car back from the station. Why don't you join him?'

Alex flexed his shoulders inside the warm down, shaking his head. 'I'm not sleepy.'

'It's a long way from being finished,' she insisted gently. 'Tomorrow will be the heaviest day. You need the rest.'

He said nothing, just stared outward into the foggy darkness. She dug her hands deeper into the pockets of her coat, trying to cut out the chill, moving slightly closer to him.

'You can't let it go, can you? Your stomach's still knotted around your nerve ends.'

He looked down at her intently. 'And you never feel it, do you, Livia? It never seems to touch you.'

She smiled, looking down at her feet, almost lost in the mist around them. 'It used to. A long time ago. But that kind of feeling doesn't help me now. It stops me thinking straight, makes me sick in my stomach.' She paused. 'But maybe it's right for you. It gives you an edge, makes you sharper . . . Tougher.' She added the word almost as an after-thought.

'We need to be tough.' He was defending himself.

She put a hand on his sleeve. 'Alex, I'm not criticizing you. I'm just saying that it doesn't work for me any more. Doesn't seduce me now, that's all. It's just a tool, the means to an end.'

He fell silent. After a moment she squeezed his arm, then withdrew her hand and turned to go inside. 'I'll wake you at six. He'll be coming round about then.'

He grunted a reply, taking a last drag at the cigarette before flicking the butt out into the darkness. Then he said: 'I'm O.K., Livia. I do let it out, you know. But afterwards, not during. That's the difference between us.'

She shrugged. 'Everyone has their own way. Don't worry. You're good at your job, Alex. No one would deny that.'

Leaving him alone with the night silence, she returned indoors, to a room where Wolf was asleep fully clothed on a mattress. In the corner was a long sofa strewn with a mound of blankets. She took off her coat, tucked her automatic under one of the sofa cushions, and slid underneath the covers, curling herself up to preserve her body warmth. She set her wristwatch for five o'clock, then closed her eyes. She would wake before it went off. Inside her head she moved a slow windscreen wiper deliberately across the surface of her mind. She was asleep before it had time to begin its return journey.

A begrudging winter dawn crept over the Scottish hills just before seven the next morning. In the back of the company Renault Jim Fennaway awoke to cramped limbs, a lost distributor cap and a long walk before breakfast. Some miles to the southwest the chairman of Lindop Oil opened his eyes onto a dingy basement room and the figure of a masked man sitting opposite him.

The relationship between Alex and his captive continued as it had begun the day before: abrupt and bordering on the brutal. The masked man gave the orders, and Akeroyd obeyed. Under instruction he got up, washed in a bowl of cold water, drank a cup of coffee and ate two slices of toast which he immediately threw up. Alex was unmoved, saying only: 'You should have taken it slower. Your system's still recovering from the sedative.' Then he left him to clean up the mess as best he could.

At 8.30 Akeroyd was brought upstairs. Daylight filtered

through shuttered windows into an empty room, furnished with just a single, hard chair in one corner and a barrage of spotlights trained on it. Alex prodded him towards the corner and he sat down.

Watching the man set up the video equipment, Akeroyd thought back to a play he had seen once in which a kidnapped executive somewhere in Latin America had established communication with his jailor and almost talked his way to freedom. When Alex approached him, carrying a piece of paper, Akeroyd swallowed hard, looking straight up at the slits in the mask.

'Have you told my family that I'm safe?'

'Shut up,' the voice said flatly. 'When you need to know something I'll tell you. Until then keep your mouth shut.'

Akeroyd did as he was told, feeling his tongue go dry against the roof of his mouth. Alex watched his captive's fear grow and felt himself harden in response to it. It was always like this: robbed of their status and power they always caved in. It made it easier to hate them. He pushed the piece of paper into Akeroyd's hand.

'Read this and read it well. In a few minutes you'll see the same words on the board straight above the camera, and you'd better make no mistakes. I want it right first time. Is that clear?'

He put his hand out towards Akeroyd's face. The businessman flinched, anticipating a blow, but none came. Instead, the hand smoothed Akeroyd's hair back over his head.

'Come now, Harold,' he said softly. 'You know the form. You've been on enough current affairs programmes worming your way out of corruption allegations to know that one has to look good for the cameras.' He stepped back. 'Now read it and read it well.'

Akeroyd turned his attention to the paper in front of him. What he read increased his fear tenfold. He looked up at the camera wondering how his wife would feel when the knighthood he had been promised was not forthcoming.

Chapter Five

In a darkened room of Tintagel House, headquarters of the Metropolitan Police Anti-Terrorist Branch, on the south bank of the Thames, three men were watching a video cassette recording. On the screen the stubbly, harassed face of Harold Akeroyd loomed strangely, his eyes avoiding the camera. When it finished Commander Johnson, Head of the Branch, stood up, turned off the set and flicked on the lights.

Bruce Macklin, managing director of Lindop Oil International, was the first to speak. 'I never heard him stutter before.'

Seated again, Johnson asked: 'How's his health?'

'He's sixty-four. Suffers from an ulcer.'

'Bad sign.' Johnson pursed his lips sympathetically.

Macklin nodded slowly. He spoke to the ceiling. 'We've been colleagues for thirty years.' There was silence in the room as the other two waited for Macklin to continue. He turned to Commander Johnson. 'Tell me. What chance do we have of finding these hoodlums?'

The Commander's gaze shifted round his scrupulously tidy office, taking in the signed photograph of Sir Robert Mark and other mementoes of forty years in the Force, before coming to rest on the troubled eyes of the oilman. 'I'll be honest,' he said. 'We're following up a few leads, but I can't promise anything. If we knew who Exterminating Angel were . . . You're still sure, Mr Macklin, you want to keep it out of the press?'

'Both the board and his family are adamant about that, at least at this stage.'

'Very well.' Johnson frowned: his good manners would not permit a shrug. 'You realize, of course, that without press coverage we can't expect any help from the general public?' The question was rhetorical: he had made his point. He continued: 'Kidnapping's the easiest crime in the world for professionals. The trouble with political crime is you're dealing with idealists. Ordinary criminals will always shop each other for money, and other reasons. But the politicals are different. It's a closed world.'

Seated in an easy chair in a corner by the window, the third man cleared his throat. He was a tall, thirteen-stone man in a Savile Row suit cut when he was a few pounds lighter. This was Jarvis, representing the Security Service. When he had his audience's attention he spoke:

'And you'll appreciate also, Mr Macklin, that since Exterminating Angel demand no money for themselves, this makes the police's task doubly difficult.'

'The kidnapper is at his most vulnerable when he tries to collect,' added the Commander.

Macklin nodded slowly. 'Yes . . . I see.'

'Can I ask what attitude your board might take to the ransom demands?' asked Jarvis.

Macklin sighed. 'They're certainly steep. A quarter of a million to Devon and Dorset County Councils, and more to various charities. The sums for the casualties are huge.'

'Surely insignificant compared to last year's profits. What was it, five hundred million?'

Macklin raised an eyebrow. 'Insignificant? That's not a view our shareholders would necessarily hold. But I take your point. Yes, if that's what it costs, that's what we'll pay. No question.'

Jarvis sat motionless, giving Macklin his full attention. 'And the press release?'

'Aye, there's the rub.' Macklin frowned, absent-mindedly smoothing down a few wispy hairs over his almost bald head. 'Did you hear what they want us to say? The *Mt McKinley* substandard, inadequate crew training, navigational equipment not maintained!' He gesticulated angrily. 'Accidents happen, damn it. It's preposterous!'

Jarvis remained calm. 'It's not true, then?'

'Of course it's not true!'

'I'm surprised to hear you say that, Mr Macklin.'

'And what the hell do you know about it!'

Jarvis blandly returned his stare.

Macklin snorted impatiently. 'Whose side are you people on, anyway?'

'Come, come, no need to take umbrage.' Jarvis took out a packet of small cigars and, after Macklin's impatient refusal, lit one for himself. 'I'm just being realistic. If it's not true, then you can deny it after Mr Akeroyd's release. There will, of course, be an official enquiry into the accident. You will be exonerated, and that will be the end of the matter with no harm done. However, if it is true . . .' He carefully inhaled from the cigar and blew out, watching the grey smoke drift up towards the neon light. 'If it is true, it will all come out in the end, so it might be better for public relations to announce it now.'

Macklin produced a cigarette of his own and, taking out his aggression on a box of matches, lit it. He glared at the Goya print, Disasters of War, which the Commander kept above the desk for inspiration.

'O.K.,' he said flatly, 'you've made your point.' He stood up. 'Thank you, gentlemen.' He spat out the words. 'If there's nothing else. I shall convey your views to the board. I wish you good day.' With that he strode out of the room and banged the door.

There was half a minute's silence as both men pondered Macklin's abrupt departure. Jarvis drew on his cigar while Johnson fingered his military moustache.

'Touchy, isn't he?' said Johnson at last.

'Well, it's understandable.'

'My advice is still the same – splash it all over the papers, refuse the demands, and see what happens. Exterminating Angel have never killed before.' He shrugged. 'But I suppose the family—'

'The terrorists wouldn't kill Akeroyd,' interrupted Jarvis.

'How can you be so sure?'

'It wouldn't make any sense to martyr him. They want to exploit him for propaganda purposes. What happens if Lindop refuse their demands? A dramatic, possibly protracted search for Akeroyd. The terrorists make periodic threats, issue communiqués, generally keep the publicity pot boiling. Lindop's name in the headlines for days, even weeks, that's the last thing they'd want. The press digging around doing background stories. Old scandals rehashed. The various corruptions the company's been implicated in. Reporters swarming all over their decrepit old tankers. It's no coincidence the terrorists went for Lindop, rather than some other oil company. Their record's terrible.'

'But all this would have come out, anyway.'

'Not nearly to the same extent. An oil slick rates an investigative article in the *Sunday Times*, but it takes a kidnapping to bring in the tabloids. No, I think Macklin will decide to settle for the honourable suicide rather than the public execution. All good Roman stuff. Get it over with as soon as possible, before too much mud gets stirred up.'

'That's all very well,' Johnson snapped. 'But we're here to fight crime, not protect the good name of Lindop Oil.'

'I couldn't agree more, Commander,' Jarvis reassured him. 'But there are larger issues we should take into account. Oil slicks are a very emotive subject. Imagine the scene – a newspaper hoarding – "Oil slick man kidnapped", and two people standing in a bus queue saying to each other, "Serves the bugger right!"?'

'I can. So what's your point?'

'My point is that given a confrontation between Harold Akeroyd, arch-polluter, corrupt businessman – and that is exactly how some sections of the media will present it – and Exterminating Angel, the terrorists will become heroes overnight. You recall, Commander, that a convicted terrorist was once elected to Parliament. When terrorists are perceived to be representing popular feeling – spuriously or not – it is essential to handle the matter most delicately.'

'For God's sake, Jarvis, is it our job to engage in this futile speculation?'

Jarvis let the question hang in the air. He got to his feet and picked up his briefcase and overcoat. 'Anyway, if they decide they don't want to risk Akeroyd's life, there's nothing you or I can do about it. And I think they will decide . . .' He turned in the doorway to shake hands with the policeman. 'They'll decide that one million pounds is a small price to pay for the life of their beloved chairman.'

The Guardian March 9th

AN EXPENSIVE LEAK

The cost of spilling oil is proving even higher than the cost of drilling it, as Lindop Oil International Ltd has discovered. Yesterday the company announced its intention to pay £1,000,000 in compensation for damage caused by its supertanker *Mt McKinley*, which ran aground in Lyme Bay just three days ago.

The size of the compensation and particularly the speed with which it has been offered are unprecedented. Lindop strenuously deny, however, that this is the result of threats by the Robin Hood terrorist group Exterminating Angel.

In a statement made at a news conference yesterday Lindop Managing Director Bruce Macklin insisted that the company had made this offer as 'It has always been Lindop's policy to be a friend to the environment and to accept responsibility for the unforeseen tragedies which happen in the name of progress.' Asked whether the decision had anything to do with Exterminating Angel, he added: 'This payment is entirely voluntary. We are deeply shocked at the damage to the environment and the tragic loss of lives. It is important the industry shows its concern. That is the only motivation behind this payment.'

Although the accident was 'unforeseen', it could, apparently, have been prevented, for Lindop admit that 'insufficient maintenance and crew training contributed to the disaster.' Pressed by reporters on his unusual candour, Mr Macklin criticized the 'cynicism' of the press, and said: 'We believe at Lindop that an atmosphere of frankness and trust is absolutely essential for good public relations.'

The Royal Society for the Protection of Birds, which stands to gain £200,000 from today's donation, said they were 'surprised and delighted at the generous offer'. They added: 'The extent of the damage is inestimably larger than money can help.'

Devon County Council expressed similar delight at their compensation of £250,000 to help clean up the polluted beaches, and Friends of the Earth, the environmentalist group, were 'frankly astounded' at the generosity. Widows and families of the three men killed will receive £100,000 each.

The Lindop Chairman Harold Akeroyd was not at the news conference. He is believed to be visiting the company's North Sea oil installations in Scotland. Mr Macklin said the Chairman had been kept in touch with developments and would be returning to London shortly to supervise payment of the compensation.

In his flat in North Kensington Daniel added the newspaper

clipping to a pile of others on his desk. He read them all, but in a cursory way, then gathered them together in a plain file which he locked in the bottom drawer of his desk.

Although he had not moved out of the city in the last few days, it was Daniel, more than any other of the terrorists, who was responsible for the triumph of the Lindop operation. The conception, planning and timing of the job had all been his. As he smoked a cigarette he looked out of his seventh floor window over the twinkling rooftops of the city. Success was not a particularly sweet taste for Daniel: he was more intoxicated by challenge. The Air India flight which had left London early that morning was the beginning of what would be their most spectacular exploit yet. Daniel was already looking forward.

PART TWO

The urban guerrilla must know how to live among the people, and must be careful not to appear strange and separated from ordinary city life.

The urban guerrilla has a certain advantage over the conventional military or the police. It is that the urban guerrilla defends a just cause, which is the people's cause. This moral superiority is what sustains the urban guerrilla.

Carlos Marighella, d. 1969

Chapter Six

In Bombay Airport the man loosened his tie and wiped away another coating of sweat from his forehead. His body was ready for sleep, but here, halfway across the world, the day was only half over. He stood watching the rickety baggage conveyor jog its way round for the twelfth time without disgorging his luggage. He wondered idly if they had lost it. It would hardly matter if they had: there was nothing in it by which he could be identified, but the loss might delay him unnecessarily, and make him more conspicuous. The thought dissolved as his smart leather case tumbled out of the grubby hole and began its slow, juddering journey towards him.

He contemplated moving to pick it up, but found his energy severely depleted. Half an hour later, after the Indian customs had laboriously checked him and his luggage ('Are you most certain now, sir, that you are having no electrical objects to declare?') he walked out into the blinding sunshine of a March afternoon. Technically it was winter, but the tarmac of Bombay Airport blistered under the sun's glare and he could feel the heat of the ground through the soles of his shoes. He watched in silent amazement as a half-naked figure tripped across the road on bare feet, supporting two planks on its wraithlike back. The authorities were rebuilding the airport.

He climbed into the back of a taxi and sat mesmerized for the next half hour as the magical horror of India defiantly unfolded itself to the visitor. Colour and activity exploded like fireworks around him. Shanty towns, which had sprung up overnight, littered the roadside from the airport, providing shelter for just a handful of Bombay's eight million population.

The women were tall and thin: graceful examples of malnutrition. Western women, he thought, spent a small fortune trying to achieve what Indian women couldn't avoid. The wasted bodies, swathed in bright, tattered saris, were standing by the roadside, with children slung along their hips, or squatting by the fires, blackened cooking pots all around them. A few men were lying on the ground, their rib bones moving rhythmically in sleep.

And the children. Hundreds of them, it seemed; some of them running and shouting, but more silent and still, sitting on the ground playing with the earth, or just staring out into the distance. The same look in their eyes. The man's memory played back older home movies. India had not changed. Those same neutral blinking eyes. India screamed her protest to the world without using words, without using sounds. It was a look that had been cheapened by acres of news footage and Oxfam posters, but in the flesh it was still a look which could pinpoint sudden guilt in the mind of the onlooker.

He turned away from the window, suppressing the desire to stop the car and empty his pockets into the hands of the nearest calm-eyed, bony mother. His body, through his light linen suit, was sticking to the plastic seat, and he could feel the sweat dribbling its way down the small of his back. He leaned back and closed his eyes.

When the car stopped a form of civilization had re-established itself. Towering above him stood the massive Imperial Hotel, its exterior unceasingly British in a country where the sun had set on the Empire almost half a century before. He got out of the car and walked through the doors into the air-conditioned lobby. Muzak played and women wore stockings. Money began to sing around him, blotting out the poverty just outside the door.

Chapter Seven

On the night that Harold Akeroyd arrived home from his involuntary sojourn in Scotland, Anna Weston was entertaining. In her large, elegant drawing room two couples sat sipping sherry and cocktails. The smell of perfume mingled with the woodsmoke from the open fire, and the muted lighting flattered faces no longer young.

Anna was perched on the edge of a sofa next to the fire, her face slightly flushed from the blaze. She was wearing a long, sculptured brown dress, expensive in its simplicity. Her guests all exhibited similarly rich tastes, although with a good deal less style.

Anna had known most of them almost five years now; they were part of a network of friends that she and Alex had consciously developed since moving to Winchester. They had been welcomed into the community as the perfect couple: attractive, comfortably wealthy, good company, intelligent but not too critical: an asset, in fact, to the neighbourhood. It was an image they had put a lot of energy into cultivating. Recently they had cut down on their socializing; their position established, they could afford to relax. But on the occasions when they did entertain,the food and drink always flowed abundantly. They were good hosts. The fact that they despised all their guests was something they both had to get used to. It was, after all, part of their job to fool some of the people all of the time.

The conversation in the pre-dinner stage that night, as at many such dinner parties, revolved round Lindop and their oil slick.

On the sofa a red-headed woman pushed a lock of hair back into a hair grip. 'Well, quite frankly, I think you're all fantasizing. You've got terrorism on the brain. I don't see why Lindop's announcement shouldn't be perfectly genuine. I think it's extremely philanthropic of them to pay up like this.'

'Yes, and it's also completely uncharacteristic,' said a man sitting opposite her, trim and dapper with a small moustache. 'It's obvious that there's been some pressure behind the scenes. The question is, what pressure, because we all know who's been applying it.'

'Who?' His wife, a lady with a voice as low-cut as her dress, cooed at him from a seat beside the fire.

'Oh, Erica, don't be naive. Exterminating Angel, of course.'

'But if it is them,' the redhead frowned, 'then why didn't they just come out and say so? Take the credit for what they've done.'

'Presumably because they don't need to any more. That's the whole point, surely,' the trim man called Colin explained patiently. 'After all, there we all are assuming it's them anyway. It's very interesting how they've become almost accepted as a kind of renegade pressure group, don't you think, Roland?'

On the sofa Roland looked very like his name. While other men approaching middle age took up squash or jogging to counter expanding waistlines, Roland obviously hadn't found it worth the effort. Talking, it seemed, was his favourite exercise.

'Of course,' he agreed. 'But I tell you what I think is even more interesting. And that's the way they've been glamorized. By everyone, press and public alike. We've been taken for a ride. Anyone would think this band of criminals was some kind of vigilante force. You're overlooking one very salient fact. They get what they want by using methods of terror. Mark my words, if they are responsible for Lindop's actions, then you can bet they used some kind of extortion. And in my book extortion equals terrorism, and terrorism is a crime against the State.'

'Do you really think it's that serious, Roland?' Anna asked quietly, sipping her drink. 'Are they that much of a threat?'

'Oh, of course not. He's just being stuffy,' Erica broke in. 'They don't do that much harm. I think they're rather entertaining.'

'And I suppose you thought the incident with Robert Granger was "entertaining" also?' retorted Roland. 'The man will be in a wheelchair for the rest of his life thanks to their summary justice.'

'Now to be fair that was partly his own fault, Roland.' His wife Helen's tone was deliberately placatory. 'I seem to remember that they gave him plenty of warning to get out of the house before they blew it up.'

Colin laughed softly. 'And you have to admit it was certainly a theatrical answer to property speculation – to blow up the speculator's own house. I gather he hasn't gone in for that kind of thing recently.'

Roland shook his head. 'It could have been murder.'

'Yes, but it wasn't. They're obviously very careful about how they operate. And Erica's got a point. They are entertaining. Rather surprising, isn't it? You don't expect the extreme left to have a sense of humour. They're usually relentlessly fierce and dull, like feminists.'

Anna choked softly on her sherry until Erica hit her on the back. 'All this politics,' Erica muttered. 'We're boring poor Anna to death. As far as I'm concerned I think it's all rather exciting, sexy almost.' It was traditional at such dinner parties that Erica and Roland would argue; she enjoyed baiting him. 'Frankly I'd rather relish the idea of Colin being a terrorist. What do you think, Anna, wouldn't you like Alex to come home masculine and triumphant with the latest scalp hanging from his belt?'

Anna, having regained her composure, laughed and got up from her seat. 'At this rate I'd be happy to see him come home at all. Can I get anyone a drink? Erica? Helen?'

Helen handed over her glass, 'Yes, thank you. By the way, where is Alex? Surely you're expecting him for dinner?'

'Oh, yes,' Anna had her back to them as she stood by the cocktail cabinet looking out into the thickening darkness of the drive. 'I was expecting him this afternoon. But he's driving down, and you know Alex. He's probably been delayed.'

'Where was he this time, Anna, Yorkshire wasn't it?' asked Roland.

'Yes, the moors somewhere.'

'What, not another guided tour of filthy rich Americans out to discover the original Wuthering Heights?'

Anna laughed. 'Something like that.'

'I don't know how he stands it,' said Erica. 'I mean, doesn't he find them all awfully boring?'

'Well, one can't get on with everyone, can one?' Anna smiled brightly, turning to her guests. 'Sometimes it's worth putting one's energies into pretending.'

She moved towards them with a tray of drinks and sat down again. The conversation turned to the gentle art of dissembling. Anna watched and listened, her mind continually elsewhere.

'All I can say is thank goodness for the friends one feels natural with!' Erica's voice lifted artificially above the chatter. 'Speaking of which, where *has* Alex got to? I think you should have a strict word with him about punctuality when he gets home, Anna.'

Anna, who knew full well that Erica had long been attracted to her husband, laughed and stood up. 'I promise, Erica, that you can do the chastizing. Meanwhile I think I'd better go and see how dinner is progressing.'

As she spoke there was the sound of a car on the gravel in front of the house. Her body tensed slightly, as if she had sensed somone coming up behind her.

'Ah ha,' muttered Roland. 'Talk of the devil.'

Anna went into the kitchen, through the pantry and out

towards the drive. She stopped by the side door, resting against the frame, and watched quietly as her husband got out of the car and leaned over into the back seat to pull out a suitcase. He looked up and saw her there, straight and quiet, caught in the orange glow of the outside light, and he smiled. It was a long look, each holding the other's eyes for a good ten seconds. Neither of them spoke or moved. Then the frame unfroze: he picked up his case and came towards her. As he passed her, his free hand brushed against her thigh, and he stopped and kissed her. He did not put down the case. In fact, anyone witnessing the scene might have mistaken it for a simple suburban 'hello, I'm home' gesture. It was, however, not at all suburban. It was too long a kiss for that, and although neither was properly touching the other, it was the kind of contact which has more to do with sex than casual affection. The air between them was charged. She kept her hands tight by her side and was the first to break, moving away from him with the single mouthed word: 'Guests.'

He darted his tongue into her mouth. 'Send them home,' he said softly.

She shook her head, smiling, bright-eyed. Touching his jacket with a small, manicured hand, she said in a deliberately social voice, a little louder than was necessary: 'Well, I hope you've got a good excuse. Investigating the cellar at Castle Howard?'

He went past her into the house, his facetious reply lost to her as he moved into the drawing room to be greeted by squeals of welcome. She turned back into the kitchen, sat suddenly and heavily on one of the kitchen chairs, for a split second out of control. A sound halfway between a laugh and a sob caught between her teeth and she pushed it back fiercely. She stood up again almost immediately. Under her breath she whispered sharply: 'Come on, Anna. It's just another day at the office. Pure routine.'

She took a padded cloth off the wall and opened the wall oven, releasing the heavy aroma of roast venison. Next door the chatter ebbed and flowed with the careless rhythms of the rich at play.

Chapter Eight

Meanwhile in London, at the Royal Festival Hall on the South Bank, Daniel and Livia were attending a concert of Italian baroque chamber music. Livia was enjoying the music very much. Daniel was not listening at all.

During the interval the audience crowded into the riverside bar, billing and cooing over the excellence of the performance. Livia found a table overlooking the river while Daniel went for the drinks, his long, thin figure picking a way through the crowd, inconspicuous in his dark suit and plain tie. One would have pinpointed him as an academic or perhaps a lawyer, at any rate a man who kept the peace.

He jostled his way across the room and sat down beside her. She picked up her drink and raised it to him, grinning over the top of her glass. The skin around her eyes broke into a lace pattern of lines. Her face was small and well defined, and her cropped hair heavily flecked with grey. She was the kind of woman who would not be bothered by unwanted advances. There was no careless sexuality here. Her intensity was of a quite different nature.

They began talking immediately, in normal tones which did not draw attention. The couple opposite were anyway deep into their own conversation. Daniel spoke first.

'So you think Alex still overreacts?'

'No, not overreacts, Daniel, that's the wrong word. It implies he makes mistakes – he doesn't. He never puts a foot wrong. It's just I think he internalizes the tension too much. It's like being near a tightly coiled spring. You never know when it's going to uncoil.'

'And Wolf?'

'Oh, Wolf is like he always is. More laconic. Not so mercurial. But, you know, for all that there's a violence at the heart of him that I think Alex finally lacks. Wolf's been around a long time. He understands himself very well. When Alex gets heavy it's always self-conscious, a kind of theatre. Effective, but finally it's

Wolf who I'd want on my side.' She shrugged. 'Together they make a good team.'

'They have a good leader.'

She laughed. 'Don't flatter me, Daniel. You know I find it patronizing.'

'That's why I do it, my dear. And the cottage? How was that? Any contact with the locals?'

'No, it was suitably remote. But, of course, in another way the more remote it is, the more you draw attention to yourself. In that part of Scotland they're not accustomed to seeing the English, let alone other foreigners. It wasn't my favourite place.' She had a way of jutting her chin forward as she watched someone. It was a gesture Daniel knew very well. 'You should come there sometime, see what it's really like.'

'Touché.'

She waited. He did not speak. She relaxed back against her seat, unperturbed by his silence. Other people hated Daniel for his reserve: his coldness, as they saw it. But for Livia it was a positive quality, something strong and fascinating.

It had always been thus between them: an intense and unique intellectual communication. For a while, at the beginning, they had been lovers, but both came to realize – perhaps they had always known – that the mainspring between them was not physical.

They had met during a turning point in both their lives, in 1973. She was alone and deliberately friendless in Britain, trying to bring order into the chaos of the previous four years of her life. Her first experience of street politics had been in America where she spent a year in medical school in 1969. Back home in Italy, filled with the enthusiasm for a new world, she had become increasingly involved in the radical left. Eventually, through a logic inevitable to many young Italians of the time, she became what they call an urban guerrilla.

That lasted two years; a lifetime she later thought. She remembered who she had been in those days. She thought of the intoxication of what they had been doing, and inevitably, the rashness and occasional stupidity of the way they had done it. She remembered the glamour – or so it had seemed – and the squalor of being on the run, the fervour of their ideological purity and the intense and hermetic atmosphere that somehow denied the world it sought to redeem.

Then, as with most of the groups, there had come the débâcle. With hers it had been Paulo's death, blown up by his own bomb in a crowded merchant bank in Milan. The group had disintegrated, their cover (all except Livia's) exposed, and she had come to London to be anonymous and try to reconcile the politics with personal despair. And it was there, after a long, solitary winter, that she had met Daniel. He was a different kind of dissident, with a different kind of anger, less impetuous, more sustained. His strength drew her immediately towards him. It was an equal partnership. He brought her out of despair and gave her another goal; she gave him the political experience necessary to transmute his ideas into reality.

Exterminating Angel had been their joint brainchild. But she soon stepped aside and let him take control. She was too interested in preserving the anonymity that had comforted her for so long. He designed the jobs, she orchestrated them. They were careful and meticulous. The formation of the cell was a deliberately painstaking operation, and it was years until they were ready to pull the first job. Daniel was scrupulous in recruiting people not known to the authorities. The whole point about Exterminating Angel was that it could move in the circles it was out to attack, and in that way avoid detection. It was that deliberate respectability which saved it from the fate that had befallen so many radical opposition groups of the late seventies and early eighties. While the Security Service and the Anti-Terrorist Branch went for the groups with potential riot connections, Exterminating Angel stayed off the streets. Their isolation made them less immediately effective, but their aims were longer term. Livia had learnt the lessons of the Italian failures well. There were no more arbitrary attacks on the centres of power, no more bankers or industrialists blown to smithereens and then mythologized by the press. Their aims were to expose capitalism theatrically, by the judicious use of force, and to take public opinion with them. And they had succeeded – as far as they had gone.

Livia watched Daniel in silence. She thought again with surprise how much she enjoyed his presence. She had slept with a lot of men when she was younger, and had forgotten most of them – forgotten even how it had been between her and Daniel. But her affair with his intellect still intoxicated her.

He turned to her abruptly. 'Shall we go? I want to talk about Global.'

She nodded. 'O.K.,' she said simply.

Chapter Nine

Wolfgang Mueller, a loner by trade, chose to relax after a job in a different environment. Three hours before, he had been sitting on a shuttle flight from Glasgow to Heathrow, besuited, bespectacled, and reading a copy of *The Economist*. Now he was lying half-dressed on a rumpled bed rolling a joint.

The bed, which took up most of the room, stood alongside a table with a bottle of Scotch on it. Across one wall there was a shelf of books, and on top of a chest of drawers a stereo system which had seen better days. The stylus was cutting its way through a quiet piece of Vivaldi. Wolf was not a man interested in his physical surroundings.

It was the kind of room which generations of students had passed through, asking, at various times, the same questions about the nature of life and society, before going out into the world to beget children and mortgages. For Wolf, however, it was at least ten years too late for such answers.

He tore off a strip of cardboard from the packet of cigarette papers and rolled it into a thin tube, teasing it carefully into the filter end of the joint. He brushed the remains of the tobacco off the album cover he was holding onto the floor, lay back and lit up the joint.

The air was thick with the smell of roasted hash, a close, familiar aroma reminiscent of past evenings of dislocated pleasure. He lay watching the night sky outside the window, yellow with the glow of street lights. He took another long drag and felt his balance slide a little. It was a comfortable, delightful feeling, as if someone were prising a fist open in his head, allowing something to fly free. For a while he simply lay still, watching the inside of his head re-forming, then he turned his attention to the bed, where about a dozen newspapers and magazines were scattered in front of him, a blaze of headlines proclaiming the latest anonymous triumph of Exterminating Angel. Wolf enjoyed his work enormously, and it was one of his particular pleasures after a job to get stoned and read other people's versions of his reality.

He flicked through a few leading articles and editorials, snorting at the more imaginative bits. There was, as always, a lot of newsprint dedicated to the sensational aspects of the story (photographs of oil-damaged birds and the like) and less about the issues it raised. The more Exterminating Angel sought to emphasize the politics, the more the popular press disregarded it.

In the London evening paper another headline caught his eye, under the picture of a golden girl, blow-dried hair and toothpaste smile. It read: *TERRORISTS FOR TV.* The report was by their gossip columnist.

> **Independent Television today announced their new surprise show scheduled for the spring which will bring the exploits of the notorious Exterminating Angel right into our homes at peak viewing time.**
>
> **Producer Ken Rodney said today at a special lunch to launch the series that the new show would 'attempt to strip the glamour from the world of terror. We see the men and women behind the action as they really are – loving, hating and fighting. The truth behind the mythology.'**
>
> **Star Belinda Bellman, who plays the chief woman terrorist and the gang leader's mistress, said: 'No, it's not meant to be based on anyone living, but of course I expect most of us will see certain parallels.' Although she was unwilling to disclose much about the character she will play, she did say: 'Viewers will definitely see the real woman behind the gun. The human, loving side, the person behind the politics. But,' she added with a smile, 'it's not all talking. There's a lot of action too.' Belinda, we can't wait. The only question is: will you-know-who be watching the series, and, if they are, what will they think of it?**

Wolf dropped the newspaper onto the floor, his stomach contracted by a spasm of laughter. He lay back weakly against the pillows, trying to catch his breath as the dope and the absurdity mingled in his brain, sending him reeling. His eyes, bright and dilated, focused on the other side of the room as a draught rattled the window frame and caught the curtain.

He lay without moving and thought about 'the loving, the hating and the fighting', and the smile on his face got broader and broader.

Chapter Ten

In Winchester the meal had passed in a gentle haze of civilized chatter and good wines. Some ate too much, and most drank too much. Anna drank very little. Conversation touched again on the habits of rich Americans, Colin's position with ICI since the merger, and various problems with new au pairs and Ceefax systems. No one told the whole truth about what they were thinking. But then no one ever does: dinner parties would be sorry affairs if people did.

Anna and Alex directed very few remarks at each other. Their contact was minimal. Once, as she was bringing out the cheese, she stood behind his chair, lingering for a moment, and he leaned back against her, putting a hand softly against the back of her leg. And there were the casual touches, such as befit a married but independent couple on show with their friends. The electricity between them had not ceased, but they were obviously very adept at turning down the voltage when necessary. After the last morsel had been crammed into overstuffed mouths they all sat in front of the fire sipping liqueurs. There was a muggy silence in the room, brains clouded with booze struggling to stay witty. Anna wished they would all go home. Alex caught her thought and smiled.

Colin led the last charge of the conversation, returning to the day's headlines. 'So, Alex, what's your opinion on the latest example of philanthropic terrorism? What do you think Exterminating Angel had on Lindop that made them pay?'

Alex smiled sheepishly. 'You know, Colin, I've been working so damned hard the last few days I'm not really in touch with all the details. Was it them behind it, do you think?'

'Of course it was them,' interjected Roland. 'And as usual everyone's treating the whole affair with kid gloves. I was saying before you got here – I'm bloody sick of the way this flagrant lawbreaking is being applauded by your average pundit.'

Alex stretched over and poured himself another port. 'Steady on, Roland. No one's proved it's them yet.'

'Of course it's them. Who else could it be?'

'Well, what do you expect from the press in any case? They've got nothing else to write about. Anyway, they're missing the point altogether.'

'Oh yes, old chap,' Roland drawled provocatively. 'And what is the point?'

'Surely it's obvious. Behind all this theatre these jokers, whoever they are, do have serious things to say.'

'My dear Alex,' broke in Colin, 'I know you think it's all meant to be some kind of challenge to the Government. But you're being as romantic as they are. All these shenanigans aren't going to change Government policies one jot. So what happens? Someone gets caught with their knickers down. A little money gets diverted into a charity under duress. A few rich men get singled out for public attention. Everyone enjoys the daring and humour of it all. But no more than that. And finally they'll get done. Like every other group Exterminating Angel will finally be crushed.'

'Do you really think so?' Anna's voice was quiet from her seat by the fire. 'It makes it all rather pointless, doesn't it?'

Colin shrugged. 'Terrorism always is. It can't change anything.'

'You've changed your tune, Colin.' Alex picked up the thread again. 'I remember after the first couple of escapades you thought they were going to be a genuine danger.'

'Well, you couldn't be sure how far things would go then. How far they themselves were willing to go, or how the Government would react. But it's obvious that no one's really concerned with their antics any more. The Government's not scared. In fact I wonder if it doesn't just keep the public's mind off other problems. A little light relief, a little sensationalism. That's fine by me. I prefer to live in a Britain which allows light relief and keeps the status quo, than one which is deadly serious and encourages lethal terrorism. But luckily, old chap, that's how the British are.'

'Natural conservatism and all that.' Alex mocked him slightly.

'Certainly. But would you and I really have it any different? Look around you, Alex.'

From across the room Alex felt Anna's eyes on him. He laughed. 'Not me. I like my comforts too much.'

'I'll drink to that,' mumbled Erica.

'You've drunk too much already,' said her husband, carefully removing the glass from her hand and getting to his feet.

Anna yawned and the hint turned into an exodus.

Later, in the warm light of the fire, she sat curled against his legs, his hand teasing her hair. She put her head back and closed her eyes. His hand slid down her neck, his fingers playing along the lines of her shoulder bone.

'Oh, Christ, I'm glad they've gone.' She let out a long breath through her teeth. 'Sometimes I think we've learnt to play our parts a little too well, don't you?'

'I don't know. At least it gives us a chance to hear what the other half are thinking. We wouldn't get that kind of insight elsewhere.'

'Oh, yes – "understanding fascism". What a way to spend one's spare time!'

His answer was to bend his head to the nape of her neck and run his tongue over her skin. 'Why don't we go to bed?'

She smiled, pulling herself gently away from his touch and turning round to face him. 'Not yet, I want to talk.'

'We've been talking all evening.'

'No, we haven't.' She shook her head fiercely. 'They were talking. We were just feeding them the lines. Anyway, it was rubbish, all of it. I want to hear about the job. Tell me how it went.'

He leaned back, relaxed and expansive. 'It went like a dream, Anna. So smoothly, not one slip. Akeroyd was scared stupid. Our reputation goes before us now.'

'Hmmm, for what it's worth,' she murmured, thinking back to Colin's comments. 'What did you think of Akeroyd?'

'Like all the others. It helps when you know so much about them, and they know nothing about you. It's a great moment, when they crumble. It still makes me high.'

Anna said nothing. She had always been less directly involved in the action than him, partly through choice, partly because that was how it had worked out. She helped to set things up, began the jobs, but was not usually in at the kill. Her satisfaction was more subtle, more intellectual than his. But through him she could share some of the excitement. They balanced each other.

Alex took another sip of brandy. 'Wolf and I were talking about Bombay. What's the state of play?'

'Daniel's got someone out there already. The Global Food conference begins there in ten days. We're meeting on Tuesday to discuss the job. I'm not sure about it, Alex. I think it's too big for us.'

Alex shrugged. 'Wolf thinks Daniel's got a second plan up his sleeve. Another way of pulling it off.'

Anna shook her head. 'It still doesn't feel right. We don't have the resources.'

'Well, Wolf's hunches aren't usually wrong.'

'Did you ask Livia?'

'What do you think? When did you last have a casual conversation with Livia? It's like getting an oracle to speak.'

Anna smiled. In the early days she had been intimidated by Livia, and had found her self-containment unnerving. Gradually they had grown easier with each other but they would never be really close: Livia didn't seem to need people in that way. 'Do you think she's different with Daniel? Maybe they chattter away nineteen to the dozen.'

'You mean like you and I?' He caught her eye, holding the gaze between them. Inside she felt something twist over in her stomach, a sweet tight knot; she recognized it as the beginnings of desire. She looked away, deliberately playing with the tension, letting it grow slowly.

He picked up the signals, following her pace. 'How are you feeling, Annie? How have you been?'

She looked down at the rug, tracing a pattern on the Turkish weave with her fingers. 'Oh, I'm O.K. Like always I'm a little nervous when you're out there doing it and I'm stuck at home playing normal.' She looked up at him. 'It feels very strange sometimes, to be living here relentlessly pretending. Spending time with the Ericas and Rolands of the world. Listening to their idiot complacencies.'

'But you're an expert at it. That's what's so amazing about you. It must have been all the practice you had at school. That's where you got the talent for it, isn't it? I still sometimes wonder how you coped.'

'I suppose the same way you did when you were at Oxford and hated all the people around you.'

'But I didn't try to fit in . . . Anyway, I was older. You were just a kid.'

'That probably made me more adaptable. You'd be surprised how quickly children adjust to schizophrenia; putting on the plummy voice and acting privileged during term time, and then sliding back into the world of the lower middle classes during the holidays.' She snorted. 'And you know, I still think he believed he was doing me a favour. That's what comes of giving illegitimate children their mother's class and their father's education.'

'It could have been worse. He could have just disappeared without making any provision for you.'

'That might have made it easier. At least my life would have been consistent.'

'But you wouldn't be here now.'

'Yes, that's true. There's nothing like first-hand experience of exploitation to breed anger. It's funny, you know . . .' She added, almost as an afterthought, 'I still hate him. It's ironic, really. The only thing his money did was to make my anger more articulate.'

'And it's your anger that makes you who you are, that makes you different from the Ericas and the Rolands,' he said, not taking his eyes off her. 'It's what makes you carry on.' His voice was very gentle, enveloping almost. 'And it's also what makes me love you.'

She let out a sigh, still looking at him. 'And you?' she said softly. 'How's it been with you?'

He shrugged. 'Oh, you know. Same old thing. For me it's more about doing than thinking.' He moved his foot towards her, rubbing it slowly against her thigh. 'I want to make love, Annie.'

She smiled. 'Do you think we have visitors deliberately, so that we can't go to bed straight away? Maybe it's some weird psychological need that we have.'

'Who knows? Aren't terrorism and sex supposed to be linked? Isn't that what Erica always says?'

'And what does Erica know about it?' Her voice was even, but the mischief was plain in her eyes. 'Why don't you tell me about the job?'

'Later. Now I want to make love, and so do you.'

She felt the spasm tighten in her stomach, sharper this time, like a muscle contracting. She let it grow freely now, blotting out the other thoughts from her mind like ink spreading over a sheet of paper. She lay back on the rug and smiled at him.

'O.K. You win. Fuck now, talk later.'

Chapter Eleven

The lights from the Embankment flickered across the black surface of the Thames, giving an oily, slimy quality to the dark moving waters. There was a sharp wind blowing as Daniel and Livia stood by the wall looking over at the grandly-lit facade of Somerset House. Daniel was talking.

'Oil companies are such easy meat, aren't they? Everybody loathes them. I always thought the PFLP kidnapping of the OPEC delegates in 1975 was a particularly botched affair. All that just for money! Think of the spectacular things they could have done . . .'

'They could have flown the delegates to one of the countries without oil, like Tanzania or Bangladesh, and shown them – and the world's media – how the other half lives,' said Livia.

'Or they could have insisted OPEC reduce the price of oil. That would have gone down big, particularly in the States.'

'You think OPEC would have agreed?'

'That wouldn't have mattered! It would have gained PFLP

a lot of good will, and may be they could have got people to think a bit more about oil economics and Middle Eastern politics. That's the beauty of this game. You play it so that whatever happens, you win.'

'Alex thought the Lindop job was great,' Livia said suddenly.

'Alex thinks tactically, not strategically.'

Daniel took out a crumpled pack of cigarettes. She waited for him to light one, cupping his hand around the match, and then she spoke.

'Well then, maestro . . .'

He stared at her, concentrating. 'O.K. Lindop was low key – we weren't obviously involved. Of course rumour about us was rife, everybody knows it was us, but since we never said anything, and neither did Lindop or the police, all the media could do was speculate. They didn't have to confront *us* as such. Next time . . .' He was talking fast now, animated. 'Next time they're going to have to do just that, and we're not going to make it easy. We're going to take a position that they'll find uncomfortable, to force them to take the issues seriously. Remember the Hansford kidnapping? After that they called us Robin Hood . . .'

'They loved us.'

Daniel snorted agreement with Livia's irony. 'They trivialized us. It was so predictable. What does the media do with something that challenges its narrow system of values? If it can it ignores it. If it's too big to ignore, it abuses it. If it's too popular to abuse, it trivializes it. We've been institutionalized, Livia. Transformed into instant entertainment.'

'But that was predictable. We knew it at the time.'

'Of course we did. And as far as it went it's no bad thing. A stage in the progression. It proves how successful we've been. But it's time to change that. To stop playing the good guys. To go for something more ambiguous, more ambitious. Collaborate with other groups abroad – we've wanted to do that for a long time.'

'Which is where Global comes in.' Livia picked up his thought. 'As you've said – the perfect target. They're international, so attacking them would move us out of the parochial realm of Britain. The press couldn't ignore that, we'd be world news.

And Global has more dirty linen ready for public washing than any other multinational operating in the Third World.' She paused, weighing up her words. 'But we still haven't worked out exactly how we attack them, Daniel. What's the angle? Global is just a name to people in the West. What the average European knows about Third World exploitation could be written on the back of a postage stamp. We still need an angle.'

'Exactly. Well, what have we already discarded? There's the dumping of surplus processed foods in underdeveloped countries . . . Too general. Marketing drugs which haven't passed safety regulations in the West? Too abstract, too technical. But there is one other issue, Livia, which we could make concrete and emotive.' He paused for a second. 'One of Global's most profitable enterprizes – selling powdered baby milk to the Third World. If we make a video showing the effects of that milk on the children, and the unscrupulous sales techniques used, and force the media to show it – then we could blow the lid off Global.'

Livia thought for a second. A cat whipped across her line of vision, disappearing into the darkness beyond the pool of the street light. 'O.K., as far as it goes,' she said quietly, then shook her head. 'But we've still got a problem. How do we apply the pressure? What lever do we use?'

'Listen, last week I met Reinhardt of the Swiss August 8th Movement. They've been interested in Global for a long time. The annual World Health Assembly meets in Geneva next month. An operation to coincide with that would get maximum worldwide exposure. We had this idea . . .'

She stared at him for a second and then smiled. 'All right . . . Tell me.'

'Let's walk.'

They walked quickly, the woman easily matching the man's long, nervous stride. From time to time they stopped and faced each other, her hands deep in her pockets, his all over the place seizing the air in heated argument. Some time later, near Lambeth Bridge, they stopped and looked across at the formidable bulk of Westminster.

'And can Mike handle the Bombay side of it?' she asked finally.

'I don't see why not. He knows the city well enough.'

She nodded slowly and smiled. 'O.K. then, I agree. You're right, it's a very powerful idea. But not everyone's going to like it.'

'I know.'

Chapter Twelve

In Bombay it was the middle of the night. In the city down below the heat had relaxed its vicious grip for a few precious hours, but, encased in the world of stale reconditioned air in the hotel room, Mike could not even share the relief of the rest of the population.

His anaesthetised isolation depressed him. He put down his book and poured himself another Scotch. The edge of his brain was frayed with tiredness, the words were beginning to swim on the page, but sleep refused to come. He ought to sleep. He looked at his watch: 4.30. In a few hours he would have to present himself to the hotel manager, fresh and efficient in the manner of the young executive, ready to begin his investigations into hotel security. He was amazed at how easy it had been until now. But then such things were always easy in India, especially if you were white and had a stuffed wallet. The Indians were eager to please. Why should they question credentials? If Global Food had seen fit to send out some executive whizz kid to check security, who were they to criticize? They would probably fall over themselves to give him all the information he needed.

He swung his legs off the bed and walked across to the window. The curtains were drawn back, and outside in the darkness he could just make out a few specks of light from the fishing boats at sea. In daylight, too, this seascape was calm, unlittered with the evidence of human debris which dominated the city streets. The crowds around the Gateway of India looked romantic rather than hungry from this height. In India money could even buy you a poverty-free view.

He pulled the curtains shut. He hated this confusion of identities which came with the job, the hypocrisies necessary to blend in with the people you were out to destroy. Ten years ago Mike had stayed in this city as a traveller. He had been part of its underbelly, sweating his way through the streets and markets, unprotected (relatively) by wealth. It was less comfortable, but more real. The antiseptic nature of his present environment was getting to him. But there was not long to go. These were always the worst moments. The periods of waiting, alone. He threw himself back on the bed. By his side was a crumpled copy of the *Bombay Times*. He picked it up. Half way down the front page was a report on the climax of the Lindop kidnapping. He smiled to himself, feeling the pleasure of anonymous fame, of being responsible for a kind of action, a kind of change.

The thought made him feel better. He took a last slug of whisky and started to undress.

Chapter Thirteen

'My God, Jarvis, if I didn't know better I'd say we'd trained them ourselves.'

In a dingy room above Curzon Street in Mayfair William Macclesfield looked up from his desk to face his two subordinates sitting opposite him. 'I suppose that is one possibility we can reject?'

Jarvis acknowledged the jest with a token burst of laughter. 'Yes sir. We did have the foresight to get Military Intelligence to check that one. It doesn't fit any of the known freelances.'

Macclesfield gazed bleakly out of the window. He had been Director of the Counter-Subversion Branch of the Security Service for two years, a period dominated by the exploits of Exterminating Angel. The arrest of criminals was properly the province of the police, and therefore failure did not immediately reflect on the Service. Nevertheless, recently there had been noises that M15 was not providing the intelligence and support expected of it. Hence this meeting with the two officers dealing with Exterminating Angel, Jarvis and Halliwell, in charge respectively of sub-sections G9 and G10 in the Department.

'Well, gentlemen?' Macclesfield's tone was crisp. 'At the risk of being tedious, why haven't we got more on them?'

Halliwell picked an imaginary piece of fluff from the sleeve of his suit. 'It's not just us, sir. Special Branch haven't a clue either. In fact, they almost certainly know less than we do.'

'Well, since we steal all their best men it's hardly surprising,' snorted Macclesfield. 'And all those raids they've been carrying out have got them nowhere. So what does that tell us?'

'It tells us that, whoever Exterminating Angel are, they've successfully avoided getting into the address books of well-known lefties,' said Jarvis. 'But actually, sir, I don't agree . . .' He paused, apparently to light a cigar, more probably to annoy Halliwell. 'I think the raids have been most productive. They've yielded a tremendous amount of high grade intelligence. Even terrorism has its silver lining. The public recognize that the security forces must take strong measures to eradicate it. It makes the work of the Department so much easier.'

'Yes, but it still doesn't give us results, does it?' Halliwell's impatience was ill-concealed. 'We may know what each member of the SWP executive had for dinner last night, but it hasn't taken us an inch nearer catching the terrorists.' Jarvis would have replied but Halliwell was not to be silenced. 'That's the logic of buying a giant computer. The task of filling it with data, no matter how trivial and inconsequential, becomes the be-all and end-all of our existence. We lose sight of the real aim of the Service – the protection of the realm against subversion.'

'Hear, hear,' said Jarvis, patronizingly. 'You're absolutely right. The technological tool becoming the mechanical master. But we have made some progress, you know. The lack of hard information is itself significant—'

'Oh, really?'

' – indicating their independence of existing organizations. They're a group that has probably been in existence for a long time, that has perfect cover, with inside knowledge of the media, industry, Whitehall, Westminster. They might even have friends here in Curzon Street.'

'Hummph.' A pained expression crossed his superior's face. 'What about foreign connections? Anything new on that?'

Jarvis glanced across at Halliwell, who replied: 'Not really.

Information given to us by the victims shows some parallels with German and Italian groups, but we haven't got any further than that. The Italian security forces have, as you know, done a lot better in the last year, but there's been surprisingly little spin-off as far as we're concerned.'

'So where are they getting the back-up from?' said Macclesfield. 'Capital, arms, know-how?'

'Capital – they could be on Gaddafi's list of charities,' said Halliwell. 'Or maybe some PLO money found its way to them, possibly via the Red Army Fraction – the Arabs used to be very free with their money. As for know-how, they're too good not to have had some kind of training. Operationally they're consistently impeccable. I don't think they would have been trained in Libya, though. If they had, we'd have heard about it.'

'Can't be certain,' said Macclesfield. 'That particular source is rather unreliable, I'd have said.'

'Quite,' said Jarvis.

Halliwell stared coldly at the side of Jarvis's head. 'Anyway,' said Jarvis, 'connections there may be, but in many respects it seems clear that Exterminating Angel are pretty independent of foreign influence.'

Macclesfield lifted an eyebrow. 'Well, that's refreshing. How can you be so sure?'

Jarvis drew the back of his hand across his upper lip where a thin line of sweat had gathered. As in all government buildings, the heating came out at a constant volume regardless of the occasional mild spell outside. 'Just instinct, sir. It feels homegrown. Its targets and its methods smack of a certain English urbanity. The Europeans never had this edge of humour to their terrorism. It was always hardline teutonic stuff. This is more Kind Hearts and Coronets updated to the political eighties.'

'Oh well, in that case obviously we should just offer them a film contract, and put our men back into trailing aging Russian spies.' Macclesfield grunted in patent irritation. 'Are you seriously suggesting, Jarvis, that they're not dangerous?'

'No, I'm not suggesting that at all. But what I *am* suggesting is that we don't know yet just how dangerous they could be. Think about the early outrages. There was no overt violence, just a kind of educated sarcasm behind them. Like inspired rag stunts, but with political bite. Even when they kidnapped that ultra-right MP . . . what was his name . . .?'

'Hansford,' prompted Macclesfield.

'Yes, Hansford. That was a classic case. No ransom demands, although they could have got them. No bad treatment. Just the injection to cause rapid pigmentation change and then send him back to Parliament black as a piece of coal. The man was a laughing stock for days. Very savage humour, I admit, but hardly terrorist . . . although—'

'Although recently they have been moving into extortion,' interrupted his superior. 'Their demands now have a real threat of violence behind them. And what's more, they've still got the press and public eating out of their hands.'

'Exactly, sir, but what next? If they are as bright as we think they are, then they must be going for something bigger. They understand the fickleness of the press. They know once they stop making the headlines they stop having the muscle. So they've got to escalate.'

'To what?'

Jarvis shrugged. 'Who knows? But possibly outside Britain. I wouldn't be surprised if we were about to witness an attempt at another kind of Euroterrorism.'

William Macclesfield let out a sigh. 'You really would think we had enough to do without having to deal with Common Market brands of anarchy.' He turned to Halliwell. 'Presumably you've communicated these speculations to your counterparts abroad?'

Halliwell nodded. 'Naturally.'

'And now?'

Jarvis shrugged.

'Jarvis.' Macclesfield shook his head, frowning. 'Sometimes I think you talk a great deal of sense to very little purpose. Are you suggesting we just sit back and wait for the third act?'

'On the contrary, sir. I think we should go all out to find them before the third act. The best hope we have at the moment is to keep checking and rechecking with our informants. We know that they are getting impeccable information from a wide range of sources. We need to find out how and from whom . . .'

'Go on. You're not telling me anything new.'

'And some of these areas just might yield international connections. For example, we've noted that at some point or other a lot of the victims have had dealings in the international art market. Private collections, pension fund schemes, speculation. Maybe the European link lies somewhere there. Someone correlating information. Or it could be within the CBI . . . I think there are areas where we should extend our network. Sooner or later we'll make a connection.'

Macclesfield sighed. 'I should appreciate it if you could make it sooner.' He got up from his chair, straightening his tie around the leathery skin of his neck. 'All right, gentlemen, it's all yours. Get on with it. Meanwhile I think I'll dine at the Club. At least everyone there has a clean slate. Or do they?'

He cocked an eye at Halliwell, who smiled and said nothing. It was not a new joke within the Department. In unison Jarvis and Halliwell stood up and began to take their leave. At the door Jarvis turned.

'Oh, Jarvis . . .' said Macclesfield.

'Sir?'

'About tomorrow's committee meeting . . . a few words . . .'

Jarvis returned to his seat. 'Good morning, gentlemen,' said Halliwell, and smartly made his exit.

The silence in the room was broken only by the sound of Halliwell's footsteps receding down the corridor. 'Hasn't it gone on long enough?' said Macclesfield at last.

Jarvis's response was immediate and definite. 'No, it hasn't. We've done very well out of this operation. And there's more to come.'

'But how many more embarrassing incidents can we stand?'

'Embarrassing?' said Jarvis. 'Embarrassing for whom? For Akeroyd, certainly – but so what? We warned them that tankers weren't the only things leaking in their organization. That'll teach them to be a damn sight more careful who they hire. They'll listen to us next time.'

'Yes, I think I can follow your drift,' said Macclesfield, drily. 'But it's quite a risk just to make our point to industry.'

'Yes sir, but I'm sure you'll agree that the risks surrounding subversion are much greater. At least with Exterminating Angel out in the open we can profit from the paranoia and tension they generate. It gives us a free hand. When there's no terrorism people assume there's no subversion, and we have to pussyfoot our way around the guardians of civil liberty. We need them to provide a smokescreen for—'

'Yes, yes, yes, Jarvis,' interrupted his boss. 'I do know this particular line of reasoning as well as you do. It's been said before, and it makes sense, but I don't like it. It's dangerous. An interventionist policy draws attention to us, and that can be disastrous.' He shook his head. 'I'm sorry. I think we've taken it far enough. It's time to start winding it down. If it ever came out . . .'

Jarvis tapped his knee thoughtfully. 'Very well,' he said finally. 'But we can't just yet. Not without risking Luis. If we go in now all roads will lead back to him. That'll make him useless to us, and we'll lose the best source we've had in years. You would agree, wouldn't you, about the importance of Luis?'

Macclesfield sighed. 'Yes, I suppose so. But it's distasteful, and difficult . . . and we can't wait for ever. If you want to keep Luis, you'd better find another way in, and quick.'

'I fully appreciate that.'

'Perhaps by extending our network in some other way . . ?'

'Sir, I think you're absolutely right.'

Chapter Fourteen

Despite the fact that Alex had been called away at short notice to prepare material for the Global video, Anna had decided not to cancel her theatre engagement with Roland and Helen.

She had spent the day up in town at Sotheby's auction house, advising a Dutch industrialist on new purchases. By 6.30 she had refused his offer of dinner and was crossing Waterloo Bridge. A damp March mist was swirling across the city landscape. She braved the cold for a moment and stood watching the view up the river towards Westminster, wondering why London looked more beautiful from this bridge than from any other. Then, passing the grey slab of the Hayward Gallery on her right, she descended into the complex of the National Theatre.

At the main entrance she was searched by the security staff and joined the stream of well-dressed, middle-aged couples clutching their mail order tickets and boxes of chocolates. She took the lift three floors up to the bar and foyer of the Olivier auditorium, where she bought a glass of wine and a programme, and went out onto the terrace to watch the end of the daylight over the river.

She did not bother to read the programme notes. Her interest in theatre had died many years ago, but she still made a point of attending occasionally – what could be more establishment than the odd visit to the National?

She stood watching a barge pulling sluggishly against the tide. She was thinking, as she had many times over the last few days, about the Global operation.

Anna was, in many ways, an unlikely woman to have become a terrorist. Not all illegitimate children grow up wanting to destroy the society that created them, and she had been given more than her fair share of chances to fit in. If her father could not openly accept her existence (it would have ruined his career, her mother always told her), he had certainly been willing to pay to cover it up. The money he had put in trust for her was used to send her to the right schools, so that when she grew up she could move in the right circles, an opportunity he had always denied her mother. But the careful planning backfired. Caught between two worlds she rejected them both. She left her dainty school at sixteen, threw in her acquired accent and headed for London. A year later she had begun an affair with a French film director (a TV hack rather than a New Wave genius) and went to live with him in Paris.

It was there that she began to realise that she had a brain as well as good looks, and, like it or not, it wanted a say in her life also. She started to hang out with a student crowd, listening to what was being said. She discovered that they hated the same things, she from experience, they from ideology. And so when 1968 exploded in her lap she went with it. It was large-scale and romantic, and for her, as for many of her generation, romance could and did go hand in hand with politics. Afterwards, when the smoke had cleared and her companions were beginning to get on with their lives, she realized that she did not have a life to get on with. She came back to London, enrolled at a Technical College, took her A levels, and got a place at the London School of Economics. There, at the end of her first year, she met Alex and later Daniel. It was Daniel who recognized her talents; he had seen her as someone perfectly fitted to move in the world she wanted to destroy, and took her seriously from the beginning. And she had instinctively trusted him. Over the years she, like many of them, had found him occasionally cold and withdrawn, but she still accepted his leadership. His vision was infectious. And she liked the part he had forged for her – up until now, that was.

On the terrace it began to spit with rain. It was almost dusk. The few people who had been enjoying the view headed for the bar. Anna turned up the collar of her coat, but did not move. She was trying to pinpoint what it was about the Global job that disturbed her.

Global's culpability in its marketing of powdered milk in third world countries was beyond doubt. They deliberately suppressed the fact that breast milk was preferable to the artificial substitute, and peasant women, believing the advertizing, bought the product, overdiluted it, and as a result children died of disease and malnutrition. UNICEF attributed a million deaths a year to unnecessary bottle feeding. Obviously, companies like Global should be exposed. It was, however, Daniel's method of exposure that so disturbed Anna. His suggestion was in some ways a stroke of theatrical genius. The milk issue was about women and children. So, to highlight that, they would go, not for the Global executives, but for their families. They would kidnap a woman and child. As a symbolic act it was brilliant. Anna accepted that. But there was something else: something which caught against her soul, which smacked of another kind of terrorism, a kind that Exterminating Angel had always disclaimed. For the first time Anna could not entirely reconcile the means with the end.

She jumped as she felt a hand on her elbow. Looking up, she recognized Roland, his upper lip coated with that fine line of sweat that invariably managed to undercut his otherwise immaculate appearance.

'Anna, my sweet,' he said. 'I thought I'd find you here, away from the crowds. Worst thing about the National I always think, the crush before they open the doors.'

She smiled and kissed him lightly on the cheek. 'Where's Helen?' she asked, looking round.

'Oh dear, she obviously didn't manage to get in touch with you. She said she wasn't sure where you'd be today. I'm afraid little Andrew took rather a tumble in the playground and arrived home all bruised and sorry for himself . . . you know the kind of thing.'

Anna, who had no children, did not know the kind of thing, but nodded sympathetically.

'So, of course, Helen decided to stay home and mother the little blighter. But we didn't want to spoil your entertainment, so I came along anyway.'

Anna smiled to herself. She did not immediately equate Roland with entertainment. 'But aren't you worried?' she said anxiously. 'If you want to go home I'm perfectly happy to miss the play and . . .'

'Miss the play! Good heavens, old girl, I've been looking forward to an evening out for ages. I'm just delighted it's with you rather than some of our more fuddy duddy friends. In fact I wanted to see you in particular. So I hope you won't be offended that I've taken the liberty of booking a table for us after the show at that lovely new little fish restaurant in Covent Garden. You haven't eaten there, have you?'

'Er . . . no, I haven't, but . . .'

'Good, that's settled then. Unless, of course, you've got other plans?'

Anna, used to Roland never listening to a word she said, gave up the battle and nodded. 'Well, thank you. That would be very nice.'

'Splendid. Then we can argue about the director's interpretation over the hors d'oeuvres. Come on, old girl. I think I just heard the first bell.'

The play, which had already had a rough ride from the critics, proved to be a self-conscious little tale about a leftie publisher whose marriage was breaking down after he discovered that his wife was having an affair with a black writer. Anna sat impatiently watching the hero's supposed political ideals disintegrate under a torrent of jealousy and self pity. It was a familiar theatrical formula, especially among writers who believed themselves from the left. Apart from that, it was also a bad play.

She was, therefore, undisguisedly relieved when Roland turned to her during the interval. 'I say, would you consider it very philistine of me to suggest that we miss the rest? It's just that I didn't get any lunch today, and if I have to sit through one more nervous breakdown on an empty stomach I'm liable to have one myself.'

Anna, mildly surprised at a level of wit hitherto unperceived in Roland, laughed and agreed immediately.

Half an hour later they were seated in a secluded corner of a restaurant overpopulated with cane furniture and potted plants, with a bottle of Chablis between them and two generous portions of salmon mousse. For a while they talked trivia – the play, her work, Roland's children, mutual friends, marriage in general. It turned out Roland was a more acute observer of life than Anna had ever given him credit for. Away from Helen there was less bluster in his manner, more quiet intelligence.

'Perhaps it's a little off my pitch to say this, Anna, but I've always had the greatest regard for the way you and Alex handle your marriage. You spend quite long periods apart, you're both independent, but it doesn't seem to cause you any problems.'

Anna raised her glass and her eyebrows at the same time. 'Maybe that's the secret, Roland. We see enough of each other to have a good time, but not enough to get on each other's nerves.'

'But then you're always so pleased to see one another again. That night, for instance, when Alex came back from the north. There was a great excitement in the air between you. I don't mind saying it made me feel rather old and jaded.'

Anna looked up sharply. Without a doubt Roland saw more than he appeared to. 'Oh, it was nothing special.'

'I thought perhaps you'd been worried about him.'

'Why?'

'Well, there was all this Lindop business going on. Rumours of kidnapping in Scotland, you know . . .'

There was just a fraction of a pause, during which Anna's mind moved very fast. 'What kidnapping?'

'Oh surely you must have heard the speculation . . . you know, that Exterminating Angel had maybe taken the chairman of Lindop as a hostage against their demands? Must have happened somewhere in the north.'

She laughed, wide-eyed. 'Well, I never heard that. Anyway, who'd want to kidnap Alex? He's more in danger from rich American widows than he is from any subversive forces.'

'Is he?'

'Is he what?'

'In danger from rich American widows?'

She regarded him for a moment. 'Roland,' she said, this time with genuine surprise, 'are you asking if my husband is unfaithful to me?'

'And if I was, what would you say?'

'I'd tell you to mind your own business. What would you say if I asked you the same thing about Helen?'

He shrugged. 'I'd tell you the truth. That she is occasionally, but that it doesn't do any serious damage. In fact sometimes it even helps.'

Anna shook her head in disbelief. 'Well, I'm damned, Roland. You really are surprising me tonight. Do you usually keep such close tabs on people, or is it just during full moon?'

Roland laughed and wiped his chin with his napkin, leaning over immediately to refill Anna's glass for the second time. 'You still haven't answered my question, Anna.'

She sighed. 'Roland, I'm not sure I know you well enough to answer it. But if you insist, then let me tell you that, yes, I suspect that there may have been odd – very odd – times when Alex has been unfaithful to me, although I'm pretty sure he has better taste than to pick American widows.'

'Splendid!' Roland gurgled. 'And does he know you know?'

'No . . . I mean . . . yes, I think he probably suspects. He's not completely secretive about it. But it doesn't put up any barriers between us. It isn't important.'

Anna had another drink and wondered vaguely if she was getting drunk. She thought about ordering some water.

'And what about you?' said Roland, looking straight at her. 'Have you ever been unfaithful?'

'It's none of your business,' she said automatically, surprising herself by the edge in her voice. She dropped her eyes and looked around for the waiter. Luckily one was hovering quite close. 'Could you bring me some Perrier, please?' she said in a social voice. He nodded assent and disappeared into the background. She broke the silence.

'Look, Roland, I don't mean to be rude, and I know we're friends, but these conversations can often get out of hand. You must know that.'

He shrugged, looking suddenly defeated and playing awkwardly with the stem of his glass. The waiter brought the water and slid away again. She watched Roland carefully, her mind rerunning the dialogue of the last few moments. She looked at his crestfallen face, felt sorry for him and took a chance. She put out a hand and covered his.

'Roland,' she said softly, looking at him directly, 'I'm a happily married woman, and if you're asking me in a roundabout way whether I'd consider playing around . . . then the answer is – no, I'm not unfaithful.'

There was the slightest pause. Then he removed his hand from under hers and looked up. His voice was cold.

'Well, how strange. I've heard rather differently.'

The smile dropped from Anna's face and her heart began to beat faster. 'What are you talking about?'

'Oh, just this and that, my dear. I just happened to meet a friend of a friend who knew Lewis Crammond, and I gather he was waxing rather lyrical about your charms.'

Anna's eyes narrowed. 'Roland, I don't know who the hell your friends are, but they ought to get their facts straight. I am employed by Sir Lewis to give him advice on purchases for his picture collection. I spend time with him. I even have dinner with him. I do not sleep with him.'

Roland lifted up a hand in mock defence. 'My dear, I didn't say you did. I simply implied that you gave the impression you might. I'm sure Sir Lewis is a very attractive older man, and flirtation isn't a crime. As you well know, it doesn't always need an act to besmirch a lady's reputation. Sometimes a mere suggestion can be enough.'

'And just what is it you're suggesting?'

'Ooooh, simply that Alex might be interested to know the

narrow line between your professional persona and your personal life.'

Anna felt a lump of bile rise in her stomach, as if the food had reversed course and was returning to her mouth. Roland seemed to know much more than he was saying. She put down her fork and got up from the table.

'Excuse me,' she said in a slightly coated voice. 'You'll have to finish the meal yourself. I think I may be going to be sick, and then I have to catch the last train home.'

He got up with her, and, before she could move away, put a firm hand around her wrist. 'Sit down, Anna.' The voice was quite hard. 'I'm not trying to blackmail you, or even hurt you unnecessarily. I'm just doing my job.'

They regarded each other. What Roland saw was a bright and attractive woman whose face was flushed with anger. She in turn saw a calm man, without any trace of malice or aggression in his look. There was, in fact, no sign of emotion anywhere in his face. It was that realization, more than his words, which made Anna remove his hand from hers and sit down.

She pulled her wits tightly around her and confronted him with increased caution. People without emotion were infinitely more dangerous than people with. 'O.K.,' she said evenly. 'I don't claim to know what any of this is about, but I think it's time you told me.'

The waiter brought the second course. The serving took an interminably long time. But Anna's nerves had passed. She held Roland's gaze throughout the business and then picked up the fork clear-eyed, and began to skin her fish.

He smiled and there was an edge of admiration in his look. 'You really are a quite remarkable woman, Anna.'

She brushed the remark aside. 'Save it, Roland. Just tell me what you have to say.'

He sighed. Somehow it seemed the glamour of his job always eluded him. Even with the right woman at the right time it was always sordid rather than exciting. The moment passed and he stepped back into his rôle.

'Anna, I need your help. Or rather, the people I work for need it. The unpleasant conversation we've just had is in no way a threat to you. It was simply designed to make you realise how important we think you could be, and how eager we are for your co-operation.'

Anna crinkled up her eyes quizzically. 'Who's "we", Roland?'

'The Government. Or rather, a particular part of the Government, the part that I work for.'

'The Ministry of Defence. Roland, what can I possibly do . . ?'

He shook his head. 'No, Anna, not the Ministry of Defence. That's simply the more public part of my work. A convenient face for dinner parties, if you like.'

He let the words sink in. Suddenly Anna's eyes opened wide. 'My God, Roland, do you mean you're in the Security Service?'

He did not immediately respond, just continued to look at her. In an unexpectedly exuberant gesture she put up a hand to stifle what might have been a nervous laugh.

'I mean,' she said at last, 'are you trying to tell me you work for MI5?'

He raised an eyebrow, evidently taken aback by her reaction. 'Yes, Anna. That's exactly what I'm trying to tell you. That really is one of the more original responses that I've encountered.'

Anna, who was having extreme difficulty controlling the excitement which was coursing around her body, swallowed hard and made a wide-eyed grimace of innocence, her body buying vital time in which her mind could catch up.

'Oh, I'm sorry. I didn't mean to laugh. You must think me dreadfully naive. It's just . . .' Her mind clicked into the right channel and she relaxed. 'It's just that I suddenly felt as if I were a character in one of those stupid spy novels. It's the kind of thing that happens to someone else, not you. I mean . . . I never dreamt . . .'

She stopped, careful not to overplay her hand. At the back of her mind she was visualizing Daniel's face when she told him. She blacked out the image and concentrated on the present, waiting for Roland to speak. He watched her calm herself, and then said:

'Well, now you know. Shall I go on?'

She nodded. She wondered how much of what he was going to say she would already know.

Roland picked at his fish and started to talk. 'As you probably know, Anna, ever since the terrorist group Exterminating Angel started their series of outrages some years ago, both police and the Security Service have been trying to track them down. Part of these investigations are bearing fruit, others are still hazy.'

Anna nodded, her eyes fixed on his face.

'Now, there's one particular area that's of interest to us in the Security Service, and that is where they get their information. And it's that area where we think you might be able to help.'

Anna shook her head. 'I don't understand. How?'

'Well, as far as I can tell from things you've said, and from things I've discovered, your job regularly brings you into contact with some of the more important figures in industry and public life. The same kind of people, in fact, who are obvious targets for extortion when it comes to terrorism.'

Anna raised her eyebrows. 'Yes, I suppose you're right. Funny, I've never really thought about it before.'

Roland smiled reassuringly. 'One never does. But, for instance, you knew David Sloane of Ryder Hawkins Tobacco, didn't you?'

Anna shrugged. 'Not knew him. I met him once, yes. I even did an evaluation for him on his collection. But that was years ago.'

'But you see what I mean. You move in exactly the right circles, and somewhere there may be someone like you, not necessarily a terrorist himself – or herself – who manages to correlate information about the lives and interests and weaknesses of such people, and who passes on that information to Exterminating Angel or their associates. We're talking about a highly sophisticated organization, Anna. Their informants may be quite unaware of their rôle. It may not even be malicious. Someone talks to someone else at a dinner party. That person passes it on . . . information gets transmitted, even from one country to another. The damage is done.'

'How amazing, Roland,' she said quietly. 'But I still don't understand where I come in. What can I do about it?' She smiled a little sourly. 'It may be true that sometimes I do take my job rather more personally than other people, but that certainly doesn't make me less discreet. In fact it makes me more so.'

She dropped her eyes, wondering how successful she was being in her blush. Successful enough, obviously, to convince Roland. He put his hand on hers and squeezed it.

'Anna, believe me, I'm not interested in what you do outside working hours. In fact in some ways that makes you more of a help to us . . . the closer you get to people. That way you can find out who they trust, who they tell their business or private affairs to . . . You can help us find these connections.'

'And then what can I do?'

'You just tell us everything you learn. However trivial or apparently unimportant. We'll do the correlating. That's what we're here for. You just listen to the chatter of the starlings, we'll find the cuckoo.'

'And you can find them? That's amazing. How close are you?'

He smiled. 'Far away enough to still need people like you to help us.' He paused. 'Well, will you do it?'

'Do I have any option?'

He raised an eyebrow. 'Put it this way. We'd hate you to refuse.' He allowed the weight of his words to fall between them. 'And it would be better if Alex didn't know. Any of it, I mean. Wouldn't it?'

She appreciated the subtlety of the ambiguous threat and smiled. 'It's all right, Roland. I understand what you're saying.' She looked up at him. 'O.K. I'll do it.' She suddenly felt very tired. 'Roland, I think if you don't mind I'd like to go now. I'm really not very hungry any more and anything else you have to tell me you can say in the car.'

'Of course, certainly, my dear. I'll get the bill.'

He motioned to the waiter across the room. There was a silence between them. Something fascinated her. 'Can I ask you one thing?' she said.

He nodded.

'Does Helen know?'

He smiled, shaking his head. 'A little. But not enough.'

'How incredible! So you lead a double life?'

'Yes, I suppose I do.'

'Don't you find that amazingly hard?'

The waiter returned and Roland stood up, throwing a wad

of notes onto the plate. 'Oh, one gets used to it,' he said quietly. 'Come on, let's get the car.'

When Anna got home that night (Alex was still away) she stayed up an hour or so, reflecting on the conversation, then slipped out to the phone box down the road. From there she dialled a London number. A man's voice answered.

'Hello, Geoffrey, is that you?'

The voice, initially sleepy, became curt and awake. 'Yes . . Jennifer?'

'Yes, it's me. I'm sorry to call so late. It's just I'm going to have to cancel our appointment tomorrow.' She stressed the last word. 'Something has come up.'

She could almost hear the man thinking. 'Well, of course,' he said at last. 'Can we make an alternative arrangement? What about next week perhaps?'

'Yes, that's fine. What time?'

'Er. . . five o'clock? Usual place? Will that suit you?'

'Oh yes, that's O.K.'

'Are you sure I can't be of any help before then?'

'No . . . no. That will be fine. All right, I'd better go, leave you to sleep. See you then.'

In his flat in Notting Hill Daniel leaned out of bed and made a note on the pad beside him to change the time of the last seminar planned for the next day. Then he lay back in bed staring at the flickering shadows on the wall opposite. Mike was on schedule. There were three days to go to the start of the Bombay job. Whatever Anna had to tell him he did not want to postpone now.

Chapter Fifteen

The manager's office in the Imperial Hotel had seen better days. Its heavy Victorian furniture had worn badly in a century of heat, and the new modern additions looked out of place amongst the mock grandeur. Mike sat by the desk wondering if the British would have achieved a more aesthetic match of styles. He doubted it.

Outside, the heat continued to punish those stupid or poor enough to live directly in its path. Even through the air conditioning the glare of the afternoon sun was frying the atmosphere, making it hard to breathe. Gupta Singh was used to it: Mike was not.

He stood up and the manager rose with him.

'Well, Mr Singh,' he said in an accent some three thousand miles west of his own. 'You've really been most helpful. From what you've told me it's quite obvious that your security arrangements for the sales conference are superb. Frankly I'm surprised by the level of surveillance. Is this a new thing here in India?'

Mr Singh made an involuntary bow. It was a habit he had developed long ago when addressing the British. He'd never been able to lose it, even with Americans.

'Yes indeed, Mr Cooke. Of course in this case the praise is lying entirely with Secor 80, and they are not an Indian company. But there are many such firms in India now also. Since the food riots of last autumn many hotels, or even governments, employ such security forces.'

'Hmmm. Well, I have to admit I was rather amazed when Global decided to come to Bombay after all, after those disturbances. But the chairman decided and that was that.'

The Indian shrugged. He was not privy to the inner workings of large multinational companies and their conferences. His job was to make sure the beds they slept in were clean, and the food they ate was as Western as they wanted it to be – to ensure, in effect, that their stay in Bombay had as little to do with India as possible. Mr Singh was a nationalist. But he saw India's future in her Westernization. He shifted his balance from one foot to the other, not entirely at ease with the young executive.

'So, Mr Cooke, I am pleased that you are satisfied.'

'Oh, yes indeed. In fact I shall be making a report, strictly in confidence, of course, in which I should like to mention you personally. Your help, your attention to detail, your concern . . .'

The manager blushed a darker colour against his white shirt and shook the extended hand vigorously.

Mr Cooke smiled. 'And I'm sure I can rely on you to keep my little visit under wraps, so to speak.' He continued smiling and pumping the Indian's hand. 'If Secor 80 were to know that Global Food felt the need to double check their arrangements . . . well, you know how big companies are . . .'

Mr Singh, who really did not know, nodded vigorously, wondering at the depth of intrigue that surrounded so many Western dealings. In India everybody knew who was deceiving whom and why. In the West it seemed necessary to keep such facts concealed.

'Oh, Mr Cooke, trust me. I shall not let one word slip my lips. Your face is wiped from my mind.'

'Good, good. Oh, and just one thing.'

He dug into his jacket pocket. Mr Singh looked on with horror, suspecting a bribe. It was a delicate line handling the Western preconceptions of India. He knew that most of the staff would have accepted it, but he, like Caesar's wife, felt he should be above suspicion. He had been known to refuse with an outraged self-righteousness. Today, given the importance of his guest, he would simply smile and deflect the note aside.

But to his surprise neither gesture was necessary. From the American's pocket came a letter, typed on an envelope of the hotel's stationery. He could not read the name but underneath he made out the words: Chairman, Global Food International.

'This here is a most important letter for Sir Charles Lanning. Sir Charles himself will be expecting it when he arrives. I had agreed to leave it at the desk for him, but I think perhaps after all your kindness it would be safer and more appropriate to leave it with you. Is that too much of an imposition?'

Mr Singh positively beamed, and for a moment Mike feared

the slight little man might throw his arms around his neck. Instead he took the letter with exaggerated care and there in front of Mike unlocked the wall safe and put it inside. Mike contained his amusement; if only they were running a straight crime racket . . . They could just have lifted a good few thousand dollars at the invitation of the manager. He coughed and averted his eyes.

Again Mr Singh shook hands with his guest, and Mike left the office. Back in his room he packed quickly. A few minutes later a boy came up for his luggage, and Mike followed the struggling little figure down the corridor into the lift. At the main reception desk he checked out, tipped the boy and the desk porter and headed out into the burning world of Bombay. Sliding into the first taxi he gave the driver an address which obviously surprised him. He repeated it firmly, and the man shrugged and drove off.

The car panted its way through the back streets, vying for room with cows, dogs, carts and hundreds of little boys. Finally the taxi drew up beside a ramshackle building which had long since jettisoned any pretensions of civilization. The hotel sign was missing, but most drivers and most freaks knew the place even without the name plate. The doorway, down a few stairs, was a black hole through which Mike caught occasional glimpses of colour. He paid the driver and picked up his luggage. He had taken off his jacket and tie, and his shirt fell open at his chest. His hair, so immaculate a few moments before, was now dishevelled and lying splattered and sweaty across his forehead. He looked smart but in trouble. Inside, the dimness smelled of curry and sweat. The man at the desk regarded him evenly. He had seen everything in his time – big-boned American girls in saris, golden-haired children encrusted with more dirt than beggars, even junkies in suits. It was his job to be unconcerned about these things. He was not interested in the visual eccentricities of Westerners in search of Nirvana. All he was interested in was their money, and that they did not shoot up in the main entrance hall.

The man now standing in front of him looked safe enough. He showed him to the best room in the house, a damp, stifling hovel with a bed, a chair and a broken table. From the cracked ceiling an archaic fan was suspended by a few decaying wires.

The attached bathroom was dirty, and cockroaches scuttled into dark corners as he switched on the light.

Mike nodded and gave him two nights' rent in advance (a sum which would barely have bought him a cup of coffee in the Imperial). He locked the door behind him and looked round. From his suitcase he pulled out a sheet and placed it over the grey blanket. Then he took off all his clothes and lay on the bed, staring upwards at the fanblades churning their danger path above him.

India. India the way the freaks lived it, a long way from the five-star package tours. He felt untimely ripped from the comforts and the cool of the Imperial, but his heart was thumping with relief mingled with jagged excitement. A job well done. He leaned over to his case and pulled out a pen and a piece of paper.

Several hours later, Daniel's P.O. box received this pre-arranged telegram: 'I came I saw I wait to conquer'.

Chapter Sixteen

In England other preparations were being made.

Alex drove slowly along Banbury Road, Oxford. When he found the building he was looking for he turned left and parked in a side street. Before getting out he checked his appearance in the driving mirror. The slightly Afro style suited him, he thought humorously. From the glove compartment he took out a pair of half-tinted spectacles. In the mirror the face of a trendy, well-groomed man stared back at him, square-chinned and sculptured. He smiled, thinking how well he looked the part of a television journalist.

It was 1.50. He was ten minutes early for his appointment at Oxfam.

He approached a large, mid-sixties type, brick office block. In the downstairs Oxfam shop, selling Third World paraphernalia and the leftovers of the affluent, he flashed an ultrabrite grin at a pregnant volunteer worker.

'Hi. I'm Morris Pollard. From the BBC. I called yesterday

to make an appointment with the Field Secretary for Central India. I was told to ask you to direct me.'

The woman smiled back, charmed already. 'Oh yes, Mr Pollard. Mrs Cooper did mention you. She asked me to apologize again that she couldn't be here herself. Only she had to attend a rather important conference in Geneva. If you'll go upstairs to the press office they'll show you what they've got.'

Alex nodded. He knew full well that Mrs Cooper was in Geneva. That was why he had picked this afternoon. After listening politely to the woman's directions he made his way up the grubby staircase familiar to him from his days as a real television journalist. At the end of the ill-lit first-floor corridor covered by posters of present and past famine relief campaigns was the press office. He knocked briskly and entered. Five minutes later he was at work.

The woman's face in the photograph reminded him of the famous Dorothea Lang shot of an American Dust Bowl immigrant. The same impassive look direct into the lens, huge eyes encircled by hollow skin drawn tight across the cheekbones, the hair scraped back into a clenched fist of a bun at the back of her neck, a few stray strands tugging free. Only the sloping eyes and the full mouth gave away her Indian nationality. Black and white pictures levelled out colour, just as poverty levelled out race. He stared at her for a moment, trying to read the eyes, but there were few words. He flicked onward. There were hundreds of similar photographs, many of which he had seen before. He was looking for something different, something particular.

Later there were the pictures of children, some alone, others curled and clinging to their mothers' bodies. After an hour he sat back punchdrunk from the catalogue of sorrow. In front of him there was a pile of selected stills. It was now time to check the film.

Three hours later Alex left the building. Inside the car he stripped off the wig and glasses, checking no one was watching. His cropped hair felt light on his head. He drove into town through the rush-hour jumble of office workers, shoppers and students. His brain still reeled with images of deprivation and he was struck, as he had been before after returning from trips in Asia, by the indifference of the West.

At Balliol College he stopped at the lights. Bicycles thronged the narrow streets, forcing cars and lorries into second place. Alex watched a girl tucking her hair up underneath a scarf, her bike balanced between her legs. Her cheeks were flushed with the cold, her eyes bright. She looked very young. She reminded him of Anna ten years ago. But then so did many women.

The lights changed colour, and Alex moved past the Martyrs' Memorial to those sixteenth-century dissidents Latimer, Cranmer and Ridley. There was a certain feel to Oxford in the winter: he remembered it well. It had a kind of crispness in the air, drier than its sister city in the fens which gave rheumatism to many of its elder dons. Here the wind blew sharp and brisk, the snow stayed hard and crunchy longer, the acerbic atmosphere reflected itself in the leaded windows and grey towers. There was a lot more concrete and glass now than Alex had remembered. But then it was fifteen years since he had lived in Oxford.

He, unlike other students, had made a point of not coming back. He had hated his three years amid the dreaming spires. He had arrived freshfaced from a small northern town, a textile worker's son awed by the crumbling stone-work and the draughty aged rooms. Oxford's casual élitism had frightened and then disgusted him. The condescension for fashionable working-class accents had not taken him in. Later, when his anger was directed into a political context, he became more confident. That was a quality Oxbridge gave to anyone who wanted it, even its opponents. He left with a reasonable degree, which he had not worked for, and went abroad to do Voluntary Service in Indonesia. He came back restless and dislocated, wanting to make public the things he had seen. Armed with a certain arrogance and fast talking he obtained a post with the BBC but, frustrated by the constraints of so-called balance, he had peremptorily quit.

Then, in March 1972, he had met Daniel at a seminar on Third World development. Two days later he had almost run Anna down in the Strand. He got out of the car to shout at her, and had his breath taken away, first by her equal anger, and then by her totally unexpected laughter. Something caught inside him, and had been there ever since. It was the single most eventful week of his life. Everything had followed from those two meetings.

He looked at his watch. Almost time for a drink. He passed a pub he remembered from his student days, but continued without stopping. The air would be freer from memory further on.

Chapter Seventeen

At around the same time Anna was in the main concourse of Waterloo Station, the commuter rush hour in full flood around her. The station, considerably smartened up in the last five years, sported neon hamburger bars and restaurants where there had once been sober Victorian waiting rooms and lost property offices. It was now a world of very conspicuous consumption, bathed in strip lighting and Mantovani music. In the main open square in front of the platforms young boys were tossing down empty hamburger cartons next to Keep Britain Tidy billboards.

In Anna's hand there was a ticket for the train to Exeter St David's.

The first-class section was near to the buffet car, as yet uncrowded. The rest of the train was open plan, but the first class still held its old style privacy of separate compartments. She found the one she was looking for and boarded the train. Opening the door to the compartment with the reserved sign she saw that it already had one passenger, a man in his early forties behind a copy of the *Daily Telegraph.* She smiled at him and he returned the cursory nod which passes for communication amongst the English. She sat down and pulled a book from her briefcase. At just 4.50, a few moments before the train was due to leave, the man pulled out a packet of cigarettes, his hand silhouetted for a moment against the No Smoking sign on the window. He put his head back and blew the smoke out.

Anna looked up and raised an eyebrow, pointing to the sign.

He smiled lazily. Then, as the train pulled away from the platform, he put up his right hand and with a swift gesture unpeeled the Reserved stickers from the window and stuffed them in his pocket.

'All right, Anna,' he said. 'What's the problem?'

As they sped through the London suburbs, past huge billboards which failed to disguise the monotony of endless city slums, Anna started to explain.

Afterwards she sat back in her seat and watched Daniel laugh. It was an unfamiliar experience. He was not a man with whom she regularly exchanged jokes.

'And that was all he said? Are you sure?' he asked, his usual manner re-emerging, questions rather than answers.

She nodded. 'At the time I was too busy thinking on my feet to wonder what it meant. Later I got worried. You don't think perhaps he knows something?'

'On the contrary. I think he almost certainly knows absolutely nothing at all. Traditionally, Roland Jarvis is not known for that kind of depth of perception.'

'Traditionally . . ? What do you mean? Daniel, are you telling me you know him?'

Daniel smiled. This time it was his usual more mirthless variety.

'Roland Jarvis. Forty-two years old. One of William Macclesfield's right-hand men. Recruited nine years ago. Not a good field agent, he was taken out of active service, but an excellent man at the desk. Thorough, careful, remarkably deductive. Not, however, usually a fellow of great instinct. After all, Anna, you would be a perfectly logical contact if they wanted to get their noses into the international art market without causing any great ripples. As we already well know.'

'But Daniel, if you already knew this, why—'

'Why should I have told you?' he cut in evenly. 'Your cover is impeccable, it always has been. Why make you more nervous by telling you the truth? As it is, it's just helped him play into our hands. You're to be congratulated, Anna. It's very unusual for a terrorist to be invited to join MI5. It took me years to infiltrate into such delicate positions of power. And I've never done it so directly.'

Anna shook her head. 'You don't think they're on to us?'

'Definitely not, Anna. I know they are not on to us.'

Anna stared at him. Part of her wanted to pick him up and shake him. She wanted to say: Why? How do you know? How can you be so sure? Is there nothing you don't know? But she couldn't ask those questions. To ask would not merely be irrelevant, it would be in breach of the precautionary rule of need-to-know. But also she did not need to ask. His confidence had, in effect, confirmed what she had always suspected, that Daniel had an informant at the highest level in the Security Service.

She leaned back in her seat and sighed, partly in relief, partly in irritation, reassurances tempered by frustration. 'So what do we do now? What am I supposed to tell him?'

'Tell him what he wants to know. I'm sure you can dig up a little dirt on the dealers' market which will keep him and his friends busy for a while, since they obviously don't have enough to do. Maybe it'll even take their minds off the real problem. Find him the tip of a juicy iceberg which might or might not have reverberations in the real world. Wasn't there something about David Straker's purchase of the Caravaggios that was a little crooked?'

Anna wondered vaguely how Daniel computerized his memory. There were not a great many people who made her feel slow. She had a great respect for the few who did. 'Yes, the Caravaggios would be a good start,' she said. 'There was an international ring operating there, although Straker had no idea what was going on. But Roland won't know that. He'll probably uncover a little fraud, maybe even a few false bank accounts. That would get him excited. And there's nothing in it that could lead to us. Some of it's common gossip, anyway.'

'Splendid. But be careful how you do it. Don't be seen to know too much. And maybe, given the circumstances, you and Alex should stay clear of the Global job after we've got it going. Livia and Wolf can handle it on their own. I suggest that you two put some effort into socializing and being seen in the world at large.'

She raised an eyebrow. 'Alex won't like that very much.'

Daniel's expression did not change. 'He'll get over it.'

The train slowed down into Woking Station. There came the

sound of doors opening and slamming. A flurry of eager, besuited commuters spilled out onto the platform, heading for home and the first martini of the day.

As the train pulled away the edges of the countryside began to appear; the light was dying fast, streaking a dusky, pink line across the horizon. A man passed by their compartment, saw Anna, and hesitated for a moment. She leaned over to Daniel and, smiling, put a hand over his knee. The man registered the familiarity and moved onwards.

Daniel noted the charade, smiled back and said nothing. He knew that Anna had something else to say, that the incident with Roland was not the only thing on her mind. He watched her indecision and decided to help her.

'You're worried about the job, aren't you, Anna?'

She started slightly. 'Why do you say that?'

He shrugged. 'We've worked together for a long time. I just have the impression you are.'

'There's nothing more to say. It's been decided.'

'Why don't you tell me anyway?'

Anna sighed impatiently. 'Oh, Daniel, you know what I'm going to say. I know we have to get tougher. And I'm sure Global is the right target, but I'm just not sure if this is the right way. There's something . . . dishonest about it.'

He sat quite still, following the flow of her words and gestures. She turned away. Through the window she watched the green seeping out of the landscape under the onslaught of twilight. When she spoke again her voice was quieter, more deliberate.

'No, dishonest is the wrong word; maybe immoral is what I really mean. To begin with I think it's cheap to go for the woman and child. It's always the women who get fucked up in our society, they're the classic victims. I thought we were different, up until now we have been. We've always operated with right on our side. That was the whole point about us, we only used terrorism against the guilty.

'But this job changes all that. By using a woman and child it takes us slap bang into the realms of those other groups – Black September and the like – who use terror without morality. And you pay a price for that. What happens to groups like them? They may get what they demand, but they certainly don't take public opinion with them. They've got no broad-based support, that's not what they care about. But we have got public opinion on our side. It's what we've been working towards for years. We risk losing it all with this job. No one's going to take the issues behind Global seriously when they're too busy identifying with the victims rather than the terrorists.'

She stopped talking suddenly, the words spilt and untidy, cluttering up the small space between them. His voice rose above them, firm and unemotional.

'And just how seriously do you think the press and the public are taking us at the moment? We've been integrated into the structure, Anna. Our opposition is manageable. We don't have any real impact any more.'

Anna shook her head angrily. 'I know what you're saying, Daniel. I'm not naive about the problems. I just think we shouldn't deceive ourselves. This is a fundamental change in the way we work. And I'm not sure if it's the right answer. Maybe we haven't talked about it enough. It's too much of a risk.'

He looked at her for a moment, his concentration hitting her like a force field. 'Yes, Anna, it is a risk. But all the talking in the world's not going to alter that. And there is no other answer. Either we deromanticize our image and make the Establishment take us seriously, or we'll be castrated by it. In other words, we change or we stop altogether. The choice is as black and white as that.' He paused for a split second. 'Do you want to stop, Anna?'

She frowned. 'No . . . of course I don't want to stop, it's just . . .'

'It's just that you feel unhappy with it. I understand that. But remember one thing, Anna. The change doesn't mean we've betrayed ourselves. Our aims are still the same. Everything that we do has a symbolic meaning behind it. We're still discriminating in the way we use terror. Nothing is gratuitous.'

There was a long silence. Then she nodded slowly, 'It's all right, Daniel. I understand. I won't cause any trouble.'

He smiled, another cold affair. 'Good,' was all he said. He stood up. The rhythm of the train changed, the brakes beginning to connect in preparation for Basingstoke Station. Reaching up to the luggage rack, he pulled down an overcoat and a small briefcase. Snapping it open, he sifted through some papers, selecting a few pages.

'This is the layout for the Global job for you and Alex. There's also a few extra details that have been added since we talked.' She took the papers but he kept hold of them, looking hard into her eyes. 'There is a point to everything in this operation, Anna, and it's the most important thing we've done. You have to remember that.' He let her take the papers, and turned to the business of putting on his coat. 'We'll be out of contact for a while now. I'd like to do a little work on our mutual friend Roland, see what he's up to. Anything else you need to know?'

Anna shook her head. 'We go ahead as planned presumably. The timing is still the same?'

'I don't see any reason to change it, do you?'

Anna wondered if it was meant as a real question. Basingstoke Station arrived, bright lights and passengers. Sitting back in her seat Anna watched Daniel's long thin form striding off towards the London platform. The atmosphere in the carriage was still charged with his presence.

She waited until the train had pulled out, then began to read the instructions. Halfway down the page she froze. She re-read a paragraph, remembering his words. 'There is a point to everything in this job, Anna.' She felt her anger rise. There was something Daniel had omitted to tell her. She knew now why.

Chapter Eighteen

Alex took the fifty miles from Oxford to Winchester slowly. When he arrived home he wandered round the heavy darkness of the garden. On impulse he took a torch and picked a bunch of early daffodils. Then he went inside, lit a fire, poured a large bourbon and sat down.

He was still thinking of the Oxfam pictures, savouring the element of poetic justice in Daniel's plan, the sense of direct provocation. Alex's radicalism had always been based on direct action, a result of his impatience with the slow procedures of traditional political opposition. During his first year at Oxford he had tried it out as an agitator: an activist in the Union, predictable outbursts in half-empty halls. It had never really worked for him. He lacked the patience. Exterminating Angel had been the perfect answer. There was no humility in their protests, no sense of steady democratization of ideals. It went out to match the manipulation of the State at every step. It played them at their game, and it played to win. In the ten years since he had joined, Alex had become steadily more radical. It had given him a personal as well as a political satisfaction.

He was sitting there, in the semi-darkness of the firelight, when Anna returned an hour later. Without speaking she switched on a discreetly placed table lamp and lay down opposite him on the sofa. After a couple of minutes she turned, resting her head on her right elbow.

'How did it go?'

'Quite well. But apparently War on Want is the expert on this particular subject.'

With an immaculately manicured nail Anna slowly rubbed her cheek. 'And how do you feel about it . . . this particular subject?'

'It makes my blood boil. The pictures of the children especially. It reminds me of a million things I saw in South-East Asia. The same cynical violence justified in the name of profit.'

Anna did not reply. Alex continued to stare at the darkness outside the French windows. 'That's why I think Daniel's idea is brilliant. It's a coup. The punishment so exactly fits the crime.'

'How can you say that? You must know the finer details of the operation by now?' The explosion was sudden. She sat up and swung her legs round so that she faced him accusingly. He looked at her carefully and then nodded. She let out a breath sharply, her eyes screwed shut for a second. 'It's so typical of Daniel to keep the bit about the child to himself until the last minute. I can't believe it, Alex. It's disgusting. The child could die. No one agreed to that.'

Alex sighed. 'Anna, you know nothing like that will happen. It's a piece of theatrics. Daniel knows exactly what he's doing—'

'Does he? You know, sometimes I wonder. Sometimes I think

it's all a game of chess to him. It's not real.'

'That doesn't mean he's not right.'

'You think he *is* right?'

'Well, his logic is impeccable.'

'And is that all there is to it? Come off it, Alex! We're going to kidnap a child, an innocent child – and then deliberately put its life in danger. How can that be right?'

'Innocent?' He gestured impatiently. 'Anna, your emotion is making you naive. Innocence is a relative term. You know that as well as I do. What do you think would have happened if they'd let the children of the Tsar go scampering free in 1917?' His tone became increasingly sarcastic. 'You know what the Good Book says — "the sins of the fathers etc., etc." '

Anna did not respond to the bait. She glared at him and his whole package of love and frustration bounced back. He watched her for a moment, then moved across to sit beside her. 'Annie, I'm sorry, love,' he murmured.

After a moment she slowly sat back on the settee. She was looking at him, but the expression in her eyes was vague.

'There are times when I'm not sure this is working for me any more.'

'What isn't working for you any more?'

She looked away and he gently guided her face back towards him. 'Hey, come on, Annie, this isn't like you. It isn't just about the job, is it? Something else has happened?'

Anna stared back at him but her mind was elsewhere. She got a flash of Roland's face, reptile eyes unblinking, and the thought of further deceit made her suddenly weary.

'Tell me,' he urged.

In the hall the grandfather clock struck nine. 'We don't have time. We're supposed to be going round to Colin and Erica's for a drink tonight, remember?'

'Oh, Christ.'

'I don't know if I can handle it any more,' she said, suddenly angry. 'The next time someone says "one shouldn't criticise South Africa without having been there to see what it's like for oneself", I think I shall stand up, smash one of their precious Ming vases and tell them who we really are.'

He laughed, 'Anna and Alex Weston, turned terrorist by one too many fascist dinner parties.' He mimicked an American TV announcer.

She did not smile. 'You've always been a terrorist, Alex, one way or another.'

He looked down at her curled on the cushions. His eyes followed the line of her calf to the ankles which he had always found so delicate, in curious contrast to the strength of her arms and shoulders. He leaned forward and kissed her. She responded, but her hands remained where they were, clasped in her lap.

'I tell you what,' he said. 'I'll ring them up and say we've got to stay in and clean our guns. Then I'll cook supper and you can tell me what happened.'

His offer of peace lay before her. She nodded and smiled. 'All right,' she said.

Chapter Nineteen

Sir Charles Lanning was not particularly happy to be in Bombay. His memories of India were hot and sweaty ones. He had been here as a young lieutenant eager to make his name in a country where most of the inhabitants were more concerned with Independence than the state of the Empire. He had not liked Indians then, and he had very little desire to renew their acquaintance now. However, as the Board had made plain, if Global were to continue its domination in Third World markets it had to be seen showing solidarity with its trading partners. And what better means of doing that than to hold the conference in one of the Third World's teeming cities?

Of course Sir Charles knew that his own position was gradually being undermined by European and American interests. He was no fool, and had been in business too long not to see the signs. Still, he reckoned there were a few more years to go before the bloodless coups began, and by then he would be only too happy to retire to the golf course and the garden, sit in the shade of his oak tree and watch his grandchildren play in the sun.

Not this sun, he thought irritably, as the taxi drew up in front of the Imperial. He staggered into the air conditioning; the hotel at least was bearable. In the suite he found tea already served and a note of welcome from the manager. He was impressed by the courtesy, and was just beginning to lay out the clean linen suits packed by his wife, when there was a knock at the door.

'Hummn. Come in,' he grunted.

The door opened a fraction and then a little more to reveal the trim figure of the manager, well dressed, hair slicked back across his small head. He made his customary bow and put out a hand.

'Sir Charles Lanning, allow me to introduce myself. I am Gupta Singh, manager of the Imperial Hotel. Delighted to make your acquaintance.'

They shook hands and exchanged pleasantries. Then with a sense of occasion, the manager drew a letter from his left-hand pocket. He proffered it with a gesture of importance.

'It is my great pleasure to deliver this letter into your own hands. It has been in the confines of my personal safe for the last ten days.'

Sir Charles frowned, wondering what particular piece of Indian hospitality the note contained. His name was typed in capitals on the envelope. He opened it and took out two sheets of paper.

As he read them his face darkened. He flicked the page over, then snapped the two pages together.

'Where did you get this?' he demanded, brandishing the note in the manager's face.

The little man took an involuntary step backwards.

'Why, Mr Cooke gave it to me himself. By hand.'

'And who the hell is Mr Cooke?' bawled the executive.

'But . . . but,' spluttered Mr Singh. 'But . . . Mr Cooke from Colorado, from Global's Security Office. He was here only ten days ago to check the conditions for safety and security in the hotel. He was very pleased with what he saw, he said.'

'Never mind what he said,' interrupted Sir Charles, his colour fading now and leaving him chalky white 'Get me the Chief of Police of Bombay. And the Secor 80 man.'

Mr Singh stood there, perplexedly stroking his smooth, brown forehead.

'Well, for God's sake, man, what are you waiting for?' Sir Charles slid easily into the voice that the imperial Englishman had used to his batman through two centuries of finding his boots uncleaned. Down through the years of Independence Gupta Singh recognized the tone of command. He felt anger well in his stomach, but he ran for the door.

Sir Charles sat heavily on his bed. One of his colleagues appeared in the doorway, aroused by the noise.

'Charles, what on earth . . ?'

The man on the bed said nothing but simply handed him the letter.

> Dear Sir Charles,
> This is to welcome you to Bombay, and on behalf of Exterminating Angel inform you that Global Food is the next target on our list for people's punishment. If you wish to avoid embarrassment – both public and private – you are at liberty to comply with the demands stipulated overleaf. If you refuse them we will have no option but to move against you.

He flicked the page. He gave a long, low whistle. 'Oh, my God. This is unbelievable. We can't agree to this.'

'Of course we can't – it would be commercial suicide. I knew something like this would happen. I said we shouldn't have held the conference abroad. This place is full of agitators. We should have stayed in Zurich. At least the police there are the same colour as we are. What kind of protection are we going to get from a load of nig-nogs!'

His colleague, who happened to be head of public relations for Global, did his job. He closed the door, allowing the chairman to express his prejudice in private.

PART THREE

Who has not dreamed of kidnapping Voerster and handing him over to the Blacks of the Johannesburg ghettoes? Who has not contemplated it? I ask you. As far as I'm concerned, precisely the one who hasn't is the true criminal, whereas the one who has thought of it is good, a real human being.

Daniel Cohn-Bendit
(Press Conference to launch
Terror or Love,
the autobiography of Bommi Baumann), 1976.

These are the people who have failed to make the transition from adolescent shock at injustice and falsehood within society to a social commitment.

Gudrun Ensslin's father, 1976.

Chapter Twenty

The following day, when Bombay was in the grip of a blistering heat and the Global delegates were relaxing by the hotel swimming pool, there was a sharp wind blowing on Hampstead Heath in London. It was cold enough for Carolyn Fernley, daughter of Sir Charles Lanning, to put on her boots and winter coat, and make sure her baby was well wrapped up for his morning walk.

Leaning over the bed where her son lay, she crammed the podgy little fists into the woollen mittens and zipped up the playsuit. The baby, with just its face showing, struggled like a miniature mummy restored to life. Carolyn stood back and regarded the fierce, kicking little body with amused affection. Sometimes she still found it hard to believe that it had anything to do with her at all; at other times the bond between them was so strong that the current of love almost took her breath away.

She shrugged, recognizing again the confusions of love and resentments that the child had brought into her life over the last five months. She picked up the constricted little bundle and took it into the conservatory where the pram was ready for the walk. From the rear of the house, outside in the garden, she heard the dog begin to bark wildly. He seemed telepathic in his ability to know when they were going out.

She walked into the sitting room to the large French windows that stretched the length of one wall. But to her surprise he was not waiting to be let in, but bounding across at the end of the garden where the shrubbery merged into the woodland beyond. She smiled. Another squirrel, perhaps, that had strayed inadvertently into alien territory. The dog was very possessive about his world. She began to open the door to call him in when the front door bell rang.

On the steps stood a woman in her mid thirties, well-dressed, wearing a scarf and dark glasses.

'I'm awfully sorry to disturb you, but my car has broken down just along the road.' She motioned to a grey Ford Escort parked about fifty yards away. 'I wondered if I might use your phone to call the AA?'

Carolyn recognized in the voice similar background and education to her own. It allayed any fear she might normally have had about letting a stranger into her house. She stepped back and opened the door, saying: 'Of course, come in. The telephone is in the study.'

As the two women walked across the hall the dog made a sudden loud yelp, and then fell silent. Carolyn stopped in her tracks. That wasn't one of his usual noises. She turned to go outside to look, but as she moved the woman called to her.

She never heard what was said.

A figure came up behind her fast. He slid an arm around her neck and pulled her backwards, bringing his other hand down on her face, covering her nose and mouth with a cloth reeking with chloroform. She struggled for a second, then lay limp in his arms.

Five minutes later the woman left the house with the baby in a carrycot. She put him in the back of the car then drove up the road and into the drive of Carolyn's house. She looked around. No one in sight. She motioned to the man, who ran from the house to the car, carrying the unconscious body of Carolyn Fernley, wrapped in a blanket.

The street was deserted. No curtains moved, no life stirred.

The car took off smoothly up the hill, past Whitestone Pond, and out into the suburbs of London. Beside his sleeping mother in the back, the child lay wide-eyed and gurgling, waving his tiny fists in the air.

Meanwhile, in the city of Geneva, a young, well-dressed woman opened the door of an elegant town house and found herself confronted by two gendarmes.

A few moments later she accompanied them to the car carrying her child in her arms. She was talking hurriedly and anxiously to the woman police officer who was explaining that her husband was not badly hurt, but that the hospital had asked that she be brought as quickly as possible. As the car moved off, a hand reached over from the back and firmly clamped a handkerchief over the young woman's face. She fell back unconscious.

The only real difference between these two operations was that the timing had to be more precise in Geneva. That was due to the imminent return of the au pair girl rather than the Swiss obsession with punctuality.

Chapter Twenty One

The news of the double kidnappings took almost five hours to filter through to the press and authorities in both countries, by which time both of the victims were safely stowed away in their respective confinements.

Daniel had deliberately orchestrated the timing to let the first shock fall outside England, to fall, in fact, straight into the hands of Global executives themselves. Of course, there was a distinct element of risk in this plan. Communication between Bombay and London was unreliable: he had to assume that when the last order was sent through to Mike the rest of the double-edged plans would go smoothly. It was a risk, but a theatrical one, and that was the kind Daniel so enjoyed. It was also the kind that made headlines.

As it happened, this time it paid off, although Mike was not to know that when, at 5.30 p.m. Bombay time, he set off from his dingy hotel room, heading for the seafront close to the Imperial Hotel.

A few minutes later, with a wild sunset painting the sky crimson and the sudden chattering of starlings welcoming the twilight, he strolled through the pompous stone portals of the Gateway of India, that immortal ugly structure built to prove that England had once owned an Empire, and an unfailing sense of architectural bad taste to go with it. A few hundred yards down the seafront he could see the less offensive colonial pillars of the Imperial, its stone basking warm red in the last rays of the sun. Outside, the cordon of police and security men welcomed the arrival of the cooling breeze. Watching from a distance Mike saw them checking every visitor as they went in, even the white ones. Things had got tough since Sir Charles had received Exterminating Angel's calling card.

Mike walked on through the Gateway and sat down near the

water's edge, taking in the sights. Around him gathered the inevitable crowd of children and street people, selling everything from postcards of the Taj to models of stuffed mongooses with cobras in their teeth. And then there were the ones with nothing to sell – nothing, that is, except their poverty or their disfigurement. The contract was substantially the same: what you bought was the right to look, the right to stare at the amputated leg or twisted, emaciated body; and because you had paid you were freed just a little from the guilt that normally accompanied such curiosity. It was a strange contract, distasteful but somehow necessary in a country where deformity and hunger were endemic.

On this particular afternoon, however, Mike was looking for another kind of exchange, one which involved a more active participation for the money given. He glanced at his watch: just after 6.00. It was strange to be so dictated to by time again: the India of the streets had no relationship to clocks and watches, just to the moods of the day.

On the water's edge, where the huge granite monument squared off into the ocean, a few boys were swimming. Their games, which caused huge gales of laughter and squeals of delight, involved pulling themselves out of the water onto the steps, then running back to the top and flinging themselves off again; off the same steps where in 1911 His Majesty King George V had finally set foot, gracing India with his Presence – old Imperial Victoria had never made it. All in all, thought Mike, the children seemed more fitting than the aristocrats.

One of the little boys fascinated him. He first spotted him in the water, bopping up and down, thrashing one arm vigorously and howling with laughter. As the boy reached the stairs to pull himself out Mike realised what was wrong. He had only one arm; the other, truncated just above the elbow, was a thin brown stump which waved slightly in the air as he ran and which unbalanced him as he tried to dive. It was a handicap which the boy was obviously quite used to. He had no sense of any inferiority because of it, neither did it seem to affect the attitude of his playmates. The only people who noticed it were a few foreigners out to drink in the evening atmosphere.

The boys finally exhausted themselves in their rompings and

clambered out. As the sun went down the air lost its baked quality, and the thinness of the little figures made them shiver slightly. The boy with one arm rubbed his shoulder, as if to reconnect the circulation, and started jumping up and down to keep warm. He was about nine years old, thought Mike, the best time to be poor, while childhood still offered its protection of dreams. He went up to the boy, now sitting on the wharf. Mike sat down beside him and smiled. The boy grinned back.

'You want ticket, elephanta caves?' he said automatically. 'See elephanta caves, very good.'

Mike shook his head. 'You don't have any tickets.'

'Yes, yes,' The boy was on his feet. 'Wait, wait mister.'

Mike put up his hand, held the boy's good arm and laughed. 'No, no. I no want ticket. Sit down.'

Disappointment flickered over the boy's face. He sat down. This had been a time for playing. He did not want to have to face the possibility of hustling.

Mike spoke slowly and distinctly. 'Do you speak English?'

The boy nodded.

'Good English?'

'Yes, sahib. My auntie she work in a shop. Many foreign people come, buy. Many tourists. She teach me English.'

'Good.' How many stories of aunties had he listened to since his arrival in India? 'Auntie' was a word that could mean anything. 'Will you do something for me?'

Mike put his hand into his pocket and pulled out a fifty-rupee note. In the West it would have bought him a couple of packets of cigarettes or a round of drinks. Here it was a fortune. The boy's eyes widened in disbelief. He had seen notes like this before, but always in the hands of others, usually foreigners. Mike watched him clench his fingers into a fist as if to keep them from reaching out involuntarily.

'I want you to deliver a letter for me.'

'Yes, sahib.'

'To the Imperial Hotel.'

The boy dropped his head. Mike saw the pinpricks of tears. 'No, sahib. They no let me go in.'

'That doesn't matter. You don't have to go in. All you must do is to go up to one of the policemen, pick an officer, and say:

''I have a letter for Sir Charles Lanning.'' Can you say that?'

'Letter for Sir Charles Lanning,' the boy repeated, flattening the vowels. 'Lanning' lost its English roundness, but it was still recognizable.

'That's fine. Then hand him the letter and go.'

The boy shook his head again. This time he smiled. 'Sahib, trouble at Imperial. They no let me go. They say: ''Who give you letter?'' '

'And what do you say?'

The boy grinned. Then he lifted his shoulder in a shrug, which came out strange and one-sided. He made a wide-eyed face. 'Oh, some tourist, over there.' He waved in the general direction of the Gateway behind them.

'What did he look like?'

The boy smiled. 'Like all tourist. You know.'

Mike raised an eyebrow. 'You're a businessman.'

The boy nodded happily. He put out his hand, unable to be relaxed any more with such a large sum of money so close to him. Mike put the note into his hand, along with the letter, but did not let go of them. 'Where will you hide the money?' he asked. 'If they find it they may take it away from you.'

The boy studied him solemnly, suddenly older than his nine years. 'I have good place, sahib. They no take.'

'Good. So it's a deal then. It's a very important letter. If you do not deliver it many bad things will happen.'

The boy said nothing. He simply took the note and the letter, put them between his knees and brought his one hand up in a formal gesture. They shook hands, and Mike nodded. 'Thank you,' he said.

The boy grinned, jumped up and disappeared behind one of the massive stone pillars. Mike stood up and waited. A few seconds later the boy emerged wearing a pair of ragged trousers and the remnants of an illfitting white shirt, one sleeve falling loose against his body. Without even looking at Mike he started to walk through the Gateway and along the street to the hotel. Mike followed him at a discreet distance, keeping on the other side of the road. Outside the Imperial the policemen were chattering together. The boy stopped a few paces away while Mike continued walking. Then the boy went up to one of the officers, who turned sharply as if to order him off. Out of the corner of his eye Mike saw the flash of the letter; the policeman picked it up and then called to his commanding officer. At the corner Mike turned for a second to see the boy gesturing in the opposite direction, towards the Gateway, talking animatedly. From inside the hotel a man in a suit had emerged. Mike rapidly crossed out of sight into the hinterland of street poverty.

Half an hour later Sir Charles Lanning, sipping his first Irish whiskey of the day, read of his daughter's kidnapping. And in a small tenement building in Chandra Chook a little boy with a beaming face returned home a conquering hero.

Chapter Twenty Two

Somewhere in a tidal estuary on the east coast of England there is an island of about 100 hectares. This island is not so far away from our everyday world: two market towns flourish within a dozen miles, and five minutes' drive brings you to the nearest shop, situated in a caravan site. But this place feels utterly remote. You would think that London was four hundred not one hundred kilometres away. There is something unsettling, even elemental, about the constant sounds which come from the colonies of waders, seabirds and wildfowl on the saltings, or the silhouettes of elm corpses against the flat, grey sky.

This island has a chequered history. For many centuries it was notorious for its smugglers. In the nineteenth century it was bought by a Victorian philanthropist who built on its shores a home for fallen women, plucked off the streets of London. But it did not prove a successful reclamation of souls, and the house fell into disrepair. During the first world war it was a naval base, housing almost a thousand personnel, but in recent years its new owners, one of the older universities, have let it run down, so that now it is virtually uninhabited, save for the farm manager, Frank, and his part-time labourer who keep together a small, unprofitable holding.

It was here, then, to this bleak dot of land in a grey seascape that Anna and her colleague Brian brought Carolyn Fernley and her child.

At a pre-arranged pickup point on the outskirts of London, where the endless suburbia of the A12 begrudgingly turns into countryside, they dumped the Escort and transferred their passengers into a Ford Transit. Carolyn, unconscious, lay on a mattress in the back while Anna held the baby, now quiet after an orgy of crying. And so it was that both mother and child slept through their arrival, missing the moment when the van clambered over the bumpy approach road and perched on the edge of the estuary wall, the island suddenly revealed before them, shimmering like a silver watercolour across the wide expanse of mud exposed by the tide.

Ten minutes later the van pulled up outside a small clapboard cottage where Livia and Wolf were waiting to begin their rôle as jailors.

When Carolyn woke late that afternoon, sick and groggy from the drug, she found herself lying on a bed in a small, white room, with an iron grate in one wall and a boarded window in another. Beside her, illuminated by the dim light from a single light bulb in the ceiling, was a cot with the baby sleeping peacefully. Hazily she noticed a table, a sink, and beside it a portable toilet, and finally an armchair, worn and lumpy, next to the grate. The only decoration in this stark little cell was a mirror set in the wall next to the door and a dusty print of a Vermeer painting.

In those few moments of waking she found herself unable to move, crushed by the weight of fear which had awoken with her, and it took her a while to control her thoughts, to piece together the events which had so abruptly interrupted her life. Then, as her brain cleared, one fear stood out from all the others, and she was on her feet immediately, searching for the child.

With the baby held hard against her she felt her balance falter, and she sat back heavily on the bed. Then she began to cry, the sobs spilling out uncontrollably into the room. She tried to gulp back the flow, but her body would not obey her. Acknowledging defeat she let it come, realizing that she could do nothing, not even think, until the emotion was released.

She cried like this for a long time, and then slowly the blur of tears began to clear and her body gradually relaxed. Even when it was over she did not move, but simply sat with the child in her arms, forcing herself to accept the unacceptable, and begin to adjust to the appalling truth of what had happened to her.

Downstairs Anna and Brian were preparing to leave when the sobbing began. Standing in the small, untidy sitting room they could hear her desperation with perfect clarity. There was an instant of silence as they registered the sound. Anna took an involuntary step towards the door, but Wolf was first, motioning her back and going out, bounding up the narrow stairs to the bedroom.

'There's nothing you can do, Anna,' said Livia quietly from her seat by the fire. 'She'll cry it out and then sleep some more. It's partly a reflex action. And also it's necessary she understand the seriousness of her position. It'll make the next stage easier.'

Anna frowned, pulling on a pair of gloves with exaggerated concentration. 'I'm sure you're right, Livia. But better you than me this time.' She looked up. 'How do we know she won't crack up?'

'We don't,' said Livia simply. 'But that's a risk we'll just have to take.'

Brian put his hand on Anna's shoulder. 'Come on, love. If we don't go now we'll miss the evening tide and that would really screw up the plans good and proper.'

Anna smiled. Good old Brian, always the calm one, always the pacifier. He turned to Livia.

'All going well, you won't see me again until all this is over. Alex will be down first thing in the morning for the video. So better make sure she's scrubbed and co-operative by then.' He smiled. 'And better keep that baby quiet at night. You know how Wolf hates having his sleep disturbed.'

Livia nodded and got up from her chair. They walked together to the front door. Upstairs the sobbing continued unabated. All three ignored it now but their goodbyes were shorter and more formal than usual. Although they would not have admitted it, the sound of such sorrow had affected them all.

Upstairs, outside the room, Wolf was standing staring intently through a window of darkened glass. Through the mirror on the other side of the wall he could see clearly into the room, where the woman sat hunched on the bed. He stood very still, absorbed by what he saw, his face composed, expressionless. It was impossible to tell what he was thinking or feeling, if indeed he was feeling at all. He watched her closely all through her tears, indifferent to the intrusion into her private grief. This was the way he worked: devoid of emotion, always poised to go on the offensive.

He continued to watch her, even after the fit had passed. He noticed the way she composed herself, slowly, thoughtfully. She got up and put the child back into the cot, wiping her face roughly against her sleeve. Then she set her mind to surveying the room. Her attention to detail surprised him.

First she went to the window, checking the wood all round, trying to prise off one of the boards. Without success. That made him smile, watching her slender, manicured fingers fumbling against the heavy grain. Then she passed in front of the fireplace to the door, where she moved out of his line of sight for a moment. He looked away from the window to the outside of the door, and saw the handle move slightly as she gently tried the lock. Finally she left the door and moved around the walls, coming upon the mirror, stopping in front of it, running her fingers along its edges, more absent-mindedly than with any intent.

She was very close to him now, close enough for him to see the sheen on her fair hair, the smoothness of her skin, the soft puffiness around her eyes where the tears had swollen them. He saw the dark spots of her pupils large against the dim light of the room.

She stood for a while without moving, a woman regarding her image in a mirror, performing a ritual usually hidden from men. But this was no exercise of careless vanity. It was about something else, about a kind of reassurance that the woman now facing her could in some way cope. She stared at her image for some moments, and then, suddenly, abruptly, she smiled, a fierce, bright smile that she held for a defiant length of time. Then she turned her back on the mirror and went and lay down on the bed.

It was a gesture that took Wolf completely by surprise. And he realized, in that split second, that it would be dangerous to underestimate her. It was a realization which fascinated him more than he would have cared to admit.

Chapter Twenty Three

It was just after dark when the child first proclaimed his hunger, and when Carolyn learned the meaning of her captivity, and the form it was going to take.

Livia and Wolf had already discussed how they would break the news, and had decided that it would be Livia who told her. It was necessary for Livia to moderate her fear. They needed her composed, at least until they had completed the video.

Carolyn had led a comparatively sheltered life, the kind that her father's money could buy, but her privilege had not closed her eyes entirely to the realities of the world around her. She was not uninformed. Even in Britain kidnapping was an ever-present danger to the rich, and she had heard of the dramatic political extortions of Exterminating Angel, although, if it was them, she did not see why they would have kidnapped her rather than her father.

Livia was well aware of her power as she locked the door behind her, crossed to the upright chair, and sat down. She had seen herself in a mirror, and knew how macabre she looked, her face obscured by a sculptured black cloth mask. She carried a basket covered by a tea towel which she set down beside her.

'Hello,' she said to the woman sitting opposite her in the old armchair. 'I am here to tell you who we are, and why we have brought you here. I'm sorry about this—' she indicated the mask. 'I know it makes me look frightening, but I think you can guess why I have to wear it. We—' she appeared to check herself. 'Would you like a cigarette?'

Carolyn shook her head peremptorily.

Livia replaced the packet of Dunhill in her pocket and continued. 'We are members of Exterminating Angel. You might have heard of us. We are revolutionary socialists. We try to expose certain evils caused by large companies and by governments. Sometimes our methods are unconventional. We want to put pressure on your father's company, Global Food. We shall make certain demands of them, and when these are fulfilled, you will be released. If you co-operate with us, you and your baby will not be harmed.'

Livia paused. She was being deliberately and uncharacteristically verbose. She knew from her experience as a doctor that people could be reassured as much by the sound of your voice as by what you said. Perhaps she was underestimating Carolyn's intelligence; she had not quite got her measure yet.

'Tomorrow morning,' she went on, 'you will read a public statement which we will film, and which will be shown on television. That statement will include the substance of our demands.'

Carolyn nodded. 'I've seen your videos. I know who you are.' Her voice was flat and colourless, but strong. It surprised both women with its force.

'Good, then we understand each other.'

'Now you can fulfill your side of the bargain. I won't cause you any trouble, but my baby is hungry. He needs food.'

Livia saw that Carolyn was not to be patronized; she decided to play it absolutely straight. She reached into the basket beside her and withdrew a bottle three-quarters full of milk. She got up from the chair, walked to the table, and put the bottle down near to Carolyn's hand.

'There is the food you need. That is the ration for tonight.'

Carolyn laughed in disbelief and shook her head. 'You're obviously not used to kidnapping women and children. That isn't enough for a baby of five months. He needs solid, proper baby food now. He'll still be hungry.'

'That is the ration for tonight,' Livia repeated.

'You don't understand. I can't breastfeed.'

'We know that.'

'The milk won't be enough for him.' Carolyn's voice was shaking slightly.

'But that's all he will get.'

The two women looked at each other. Neither moved.

'In that bottle you will find exactly fifty grams of Global Food baby milk powder diluted in one half litre of water, and—'

'That's too much water,' Carolyn interrupted, her voice harsh with fear. 'You've overdiluted it. It won't be rich enough.'

'And you will feed him this ration twice a day.'

'But he needs at least 200 grams a day.'

'Precisely. That, my dear, is the whole point.'

'What do you mean?'

Livia moved back to her chair and sat down, facing her captive. She took a deep breath and began: 'Your son, you see, has his own rather special rôle to play in the kidnapping. As I'm sure you know, Global's dried milk baby food isn't sold only in Britain, it's also sold in huge quantities abroad, especially in underdeveloped countries. In Africa and India Global promotes baby food in various highly imaginative ways. Samples of the stuff are available in hospitals and doctors' surgeries so that mothers get the idea it must be a healthy thing. Global sales reps dress up as nurses and go round telling women in villages that baby food will make their babies big and bouncing.

'What they don't tell them – not even in very small print – is that dried milk is not nearly as good for you as the real thing. It doesn't contain lactose, necessary for the proper development of the nervous system in children. Also, it lacks the antibodies which give breastfed babies much greater resistance against disease.

'In any case, most village women are illiterate. They don't know what quantities they are supposed to give their babies, and anyway they can't afford it. And often they don't sterilize the bottles. So babies die – in their millions.

'Global has spent a great deal of money suppressing these facts. They are now going to have to spend a great deal more to save your son from the same hardships they have inflicted on other children.'

The speech was deliberately long, and deliberately shocking. Livia was well aware of the effect of her words, she had picked them carefully. Carolyn's face was pinched and drawn, her body chilled by the implication of what she had heard. Of course there had been rumours of this before, some talk at home of a boycott on the products of one of Global's competitors, but she had never stopped to consider the facts. She had not wanted to face them.

'Oh my God,' she said, dropping her head and covering her face with both hands. 'Oh my God.'

Livia measured her compassion carefully. She decided to offer a little comfort. 'My dear, there is no reason to suspect that any harm will come to either of you. If Global co-operates – and I'm sure your father has enough influence to secure that co-operation – then you will both be free within a few days. It is not our intention to hurt you.'

'Bullshit!'

The vehemence of her voice, as much as the word, took Livia aback. She remembered Wolf's words of warning. Suddenly the other woman was on her feet, her fear engulfed by a fierce anger.

'Bullshit! What do you care about me and my son? What are you *really* doing this for? You just enjoy having the power to . . . to threaten us. What's it got to do with *us*? If you really want to help these children, why don't you go out there . . . go to India or somewhere? It's got nothing to do with us . . . You're using me . . . . and you're using my son.'

Her voice rose and with her in perfect synchrony came the howls of her baby, screaming his anger – and, more important, his hunger – to whomever would listen.

His crying deflected her rage for an instant, bringing her down again to the immediate reality. Whatever her anger, the baby had to be fed. She turned her back abruptly on Livia, picking up her child and crushing it against her, attempting to soothe him with her physical presence. But the child refused her comfort, demanding a more substantial proof of love. Behind her Livia picked up the bottle and came towards her. She held it out at arm's length, waiting.

Their eyes met for a long moment. Then, without a word, Carolyn took the bottle and put it in the child's mouth. The baby's cries subsided and the room fell into a silence broken only by the sounds of his guzzling. She glared up at Livia.

'He'll cry,' she said. 'He'll keep everybody awake and make neighbours complain. He does that when he's hungry.'

Livia shook her head. 'There are no neighbours, and there are things we can give him to make him sleep. Don't fight us. We are too strong for you. Save your energy for the child.'

She turned and walked to the door. As she opened it Carolyn's voice reached her, clear and with a bitter edge to it.

'And I suppose this is meant to lead to a better world?'

Livia stopped. 'That is the intention. Yes.'

'Funny,' came the fast retort. 'I thought the idea of revolution had something to do with solidarity between women. Obviously I was mistaken.'

Livia did not turn, or even acknowledge the remark. She simply closed the door behind her and locked it. But going downstairs she felt suddenly tired. And when she entered the sitting room, Wolf did not immediately ask her what had happened.

Chapter Twenty Four

Sir Charles Lanning was the only first-class passenger on the British Airways jumbo which left Bombay on the night of March 22nd. Two hours before, he had bid goodbye to his Swiss colleague Heinrich Grossman on his way back to Zurich. The other Global executives were staying on temporarily in Bombay, but the conference had been abandoned, leaving the delegates shocked and tense, holed up in their hotel rooms trying to place urgent calls home to check the safety of their families.

Despite his anxiety, Sir Charles, aided by a few hefty slugs of first-class liquor, slept for part of the fifteen-hour journey. He knew that his exhaustion would not help matters when he reached London, and had trained himself over the years to sleep even when his mind did not want to.

Looking out onto the clear black night he thought about the hullabaloo that would face him on his return. He visualized the meeting with his wife. He was dreading that even more than the meeting with the press. She was a highly strung woman at the best of times, and this would undoubtedly push her over the edge. As a companion Elizabeth had long since ceased to be any comfort to him. Their marriage was a public relations exercise, but she still had the capacity to disturb his life quite considerably when she put her mind to it. In the midst of tragedy she would certainly find a way of needling him. He felt old and tired in anticipation. He closed his eyes. Somewhere across the top of Africa he slept, the stewardess covering him with a blanket as she passed. Dawn arrived over Italy and was momentarily splendid, but by the time they reached London the morning had become a grey, muted affair, weather to fit the times.

As the plane touched down the chief steward approached, and before the economy-class passengers could disembark Sir Charles was whisked off through the front exit and into a police car. Awaiting him there was his son-in-law. As they sped along the M4 into Central London, Derek told him as much as he knew, which was very little, and then they lapsed into silence. Derek sat hunched forward in his seat, nervously fingering his wispy moustache. Sir Charles had always found him irritating, and had never understood what his daughter saw in him. Especially now, he wished for someone with a more robust response to the crisis facing them.

The car plunged into London traffic. The driver put on his siren and the last part of the journey to town was orchestrated by the screech of urgency. Outside the Home Office near St James's Park Sir Charles put a hand on his son-in-law's shoulder.

'Buck up, Derek,' he said. 'I'm sure it's only a matter of time until the two of them are free and back with us.'

'Charles,' began the other, hesitatingly, 'there isn't any question of trouble, is there? I mean I know there may be political implications, but . . .' He trailed off, staring anxiously at the older man.

Sir Charles held his gaze. 'No question. Would I take risks with the life of my daughter at stake?' He waited for this to sink in, then said: 'You go straight home. I know my wife wants you to be with her at this time. I'll be along as soon as I've seen the Minister.' He squeezed the younger man's arm encouragingly and got out of the car.

Ten minutes later Sir Charles was sitting in the office of the Home Secretary. He was no stranger to government offices. His relationship with certain members of the Cabinet and the Department of Trade and Industry was more than equable. His involvement with such a large multinational as Global Food had made him a valuable commercial asset to a government committed to expansion, and he owed his title to a recent honours list. It was, he felt, only fair considering his unfailing political purity over the years.

He had even shared a dinner table with the Home Secretary

on more than one occasion. It made the interview between them less formal than it might have been. However, it did not bridge the gaps between them, as Sir Charles discovered early on.

'I'm sure you appreciate,' Sir Charles was saying, sipping his coffee, 'that I've come home with the full support of Global behind me, backing my actions. Are you seriously implying that the Government is against us capitulating? You do realize the risk to my daughter and my grandson's life?'

The Home Secretary shifted a little in his chair. 'Charles, you know our sympathies are with you. And of course we can't order you to co-operate, and we wouldn't want to. The Prime Minister's well aware of the immense personal strain that you must be under, and he is as concerned as you are, but you must try and see things from our side of the fence. This is not simply a domestic incident.'

Sir Charles made a muted snort. 'And which side of the fence would you see it from if it were your daughter, eh, Maurice?'

The Home Secretary let the remark pass. 'I understand exactly how you feel, but maybe before we discuss this any further there is something you should see. The issue of this kidnapping is more complicated than you realize. Late last night the networks received the video demand we expected. I think you may be surprised. It puts a slightly different complexion on things.'

He put his finger down on the intercom button on his desk. 'I wonder, Miss Phillips, if you could ask Mr Macclesfield and Mr Fernstein to come in, please?'

Sir Charles' eyes narrowed. 'Fernstein? Why do we have to bring in the legal department?'

The Minister nodded. 'Bear with me, Charles. You'll understand why in a moment.'

He stood up as the door opened. The gaunt figure of William Macclesfield, upright and dry, made an amusing contrast with the rotund, fleshy form of Alan Fernstein. The walrus and the carpenter approached the desk. Fernstein put out a hand to Sir Charles. The handshake was cursory; there was obviously no love lost between them. Macclesfield, introduced as the Head of Domestic Security, bowed his head slightly.

After the formalities were complete the Home Secretary sank back thoughtfully into his chair, and Macclesfield turned on a television set specially brought in for the occasion. The four men sat back and watched.

Ten minutes later the screen went blank. The silence in the room was oppressive.

Sir Charles's normally ruddy complexion was ashen. He ran a hand across his forehead, the skin dull and flabby under his touch. Before he could speak the Home Secretary leaned across his desk towards him.

'Sir Charles,' he said in a confidential, sympathetic voice, 'before you say anything I want you to know that we have checked this out with some of the finest paediatricians in the country. It would take a long time for this enforced milk diet to have any effect on your grandson. He's a well-fed fellow . . . he'll withstand the treatment for weeks. There's no immediate danger.'

Sir Charles said nothing and sat completely immobile. Suddenly he whipped his head round to face Fernstein, ignoring the Minister.

'Where the hell did they get their information from? From inside Global?'

Fernstein picked at the arm of his chair, making a feeble, non-committal gesture.

Macclesfield coughed discreetly. 'I gather, Sir Charles, that some of the news footage came from Oxfam – unwittingly, of course – and from other, more extreme pressure groups, not all of which we have traced as yet. As for the details and the facts and figures, well, there are, I understand, a number of agencies – WHO, UNICEF etc. – who have dossiers on Global's milk production—'

'Yes, but not this stuff,' Sir Charles interrupted angrily. 'It makes us look like a bunch of murderers.'

There was an uncomfortable silence.

Sir Charles shook his head despairingly. 'The video is almost more damaging than the ransom. Has anyone else from Global seen it?'

'Only Grossman in Zurich,' said Macclesfield. 'They, of course, received a similar film, except without your daughter.'

Lanning passed his hand across his face again. 'When does it go out?'

Macclesfield exchanged looks with the Minister, who took up his cue. 'Er . . . they have demanded that it be shown on the 5.40 news tonight. But . . . under the circumstances I'm sure all of us would prefer that it didn't go out at all, don't you agree?'

'Don't be mad, man. They've got my daughter. If we don't put it out they'll kill her.'

'I doubt that very much, Sir Charles.' Macclesfield interceded smoothly. 'We have, you see, made an extremely thorough analysis of the methods that Exterminating Angel have used over the last few years. I think I can safely say that it would not be in their interests to harm either your daughter or your grandson at this stage. Their aim now is to get public and press attention. And they cannot do that without the video being shown. That is their prime concern. That must come first.'

'And if it doesn't?'

'If it doesn't, our guess is that they'll wait a little, then probably admit that they have been a little too ambitious this time, and begin negotiations. At that stage Global will be able to make their own arrangements as to terms.'

Sir Charles shook his head, unconvinced. 'Your guess is not enough. My daughter's life is too precious to be dependent on a guess. Did you guess what would happen to Robert Granger?'

'Yes, Sir Charles,' Macclesfield said quietly. 'Actually we did. Metropolitan Properties acted against our advice.'

Lanning looked at him for a moment, then turned to the Home Secretary. 'I gather the Government supports this course of action?'

The Minister raised his eyebrows. 'Charles, I'm sure you realise that what we have here is an incident of unparalleled international terrorism. An attack on a company such as Global, in two countries simultaneously, is obviously tantamount to an attack on the State. That is how the Government is interpreting it. If they get away with this I don't have to tell you what we fear will happen next. In the interests of the civilized—'

'If we were to capitulate,' Lanning interrupted the Minister impatiently, turning to Fernstein, 'how long would it take us to raise the four million demanded?'

Fernstein opened his eyes wide. 'Er . . . some time, Charles. It would depend on various factors. The bank—'

'So even if we let the video out now, we couldn't get Carolyn and the child released until the money came through.'

'Exactly, Sir Charles,' interjected Macclesfield quietly. 'We have, you see, nothing to lose.'

'Correction. You have nothing to lose,' retorted Lanning coldly. 'And you're sure they won't harm her?'

Macclesfield gestured ambiguously. 'As sure as we possibly can be. It's not in their interests,' he repeated.

'And what about the TV channels and the press? They've presumably got the video. They won't just stand back and let you stifle the story, will they? It'll be like manna from heaven for some of them.'

'Ah, well, that's where I come in, Sir Charles,' said Fernstein.

'Yes, I had wondered what you were doing here.' Sir Charles's reputed sarcasm was returning to him: he had not reached the top of Global for nothing.

Fernstein coughed politely, trying to cover up his patent embarrassment. 'From a legal standpoint, I can assure you that the film is highly defamatory towards Global. Some of their accusations are totally unsubstantiated.' He picked his words with characteristic care. 'And your daughter's involvement in what amounts to a confession could not be accepted in a court of law, as she has nothing to do with Global Food.'

'Whereas if I had said it, it would be accepted as proof of guilt. Is that what you mean?'

Fernstein shrugged. 'Not necessarily. It would depend on the circumstances of the confession. What I'm saying is that truth has various legal definitions. Certainly if this was a television documentary we could take them to court and take the shirts off their backs.'

'But the television companies didn't make the video.'

'Yes, but if they show it against the wishes of the authorities, even with a disclaimer, then the law applies to them too.'

Sir Charles sat back in his chair, letting his head fall downwards for a few moments. Then he looked up at the Home Secretary. 'Can you get me Switzerland on the phone, Maurice? I think I'd better talk to Grossmann.'

The Minister beamed through his glasses. 'My dear Charles, no need. I talked to him just before you arrived. He has decided to co-operate with the Swiss Government. The video is not to be shown there either. Obviously that is a big step, but of course to really be effective it must be a joint decision. It would amount to a remarkable stand against international terrorism.'

There was a silence. Lanning had sat on too many board meetings not to know when he had been outmanoeuvred. He addressed his next remark to Macclesfield: 'So what do you do now? Do you tell them we are not co-operating?'

'As yet we have no direct means of communicating with them. But when the video does not go out tonight they'll know soon enough what our attitude is. I think it will be up to them to get in touch with us.'

Lanning got angrily to his feet. 'All right, I agree. But God help you if this goes wrong.'

'Don't worry, Charles,' said the Home Secretary, just a little too quickly. 'I'm sure it won't.'

Seven hours later in his apartment Daniel turned on his television set and video cassette recorder. The mock-heroic music introducing the news blasted out its opening chords. He flipped the phone off the hook and sat back to watch. At six he switched to the cassette recorder to watch the ITV news. Fifteen minutes later he got up and abruptly turned off both machines. He was not surprised at the suppression of the video. It had been framed in deliberately outrageous terms, to invite confrontation. It was a game he had been practising for a long time, for as long as he could remember.

Daniel had been born into an atmosphere of opposition. His earliest memories were hearing stories of the family's escape from Germany in the mid-1930s. His parents had been secular Jews whose millenium was Marxist; they had despised their fellow Jews who toed the line and allowed the Nazis to win power through legalized terrorism. His father had watched the holocaust from a distance with the air of an embittered man whose predictions had gone unheeded – a prophet without honour.

Daniel had inherited his father's passion and his mistrust of open politics. The failures of 1968 had neither surprised him, by then an established university lecturer with a—discreet—support

support for the C.P., nor disillusioned him – he had no illusions to lose. Daniel was not a liberal: for him poltics was life or death, not the price of butter. His answer was underground resistance, Exterminating Angel the vehicle of his aims.

After watching the news he got into the car and headed north-east across the city. The rush-hour traffic had almost dispersed and the journey was easy. London looked drab and decaying. He drove through the urban wasteland of Finsbury Park into Tottenham. Winding through the back streets he parked the car a few roads behind Seven Sisters underground station. Then he walked west a couple of blocks until he reached a small suburban terrace house, divided into two flats. He took out a key and entered the upper one. This was Exterminating Angel's safe house. Rented under a pseudonym, paid for monthly by standing order, it was used for occasional meetings, for storing equipment, and, although this had not yet been necessary, as a bolthole.

At 8.00 p.m. precisely, in the middle of an empty, echoing room, he picked up the phone and dialled Zurich.

Chapter Twenty Five

The room is large and white, with two dark beams running along the ceiling, more for show than for structure. There is a harsh, clean sunlight flooding in through the windows, reflecting off the huge carpet of snow surrounding the house. From the entrance door all one can see is rising slopes of deep white, punctuated by the odd ridge of fir trees. Above the snow a bright, pure, blue sky, so clear that it could have been painted by a child on a piece of paper: two dimensional like the rest of the landscape. Switzerland in winter: clean, angular, beautiful and frigid.

Back inside the room the sun warms the sanded floorboards; rivulets of light run across the wood reaching a double bed in the corner. White sheets to match the snow outside, a cream duvet curving like the foothills of the mountains.

In the bed lies a woman: short fair hair, small features, eyes closed. Next to her a small bundle, a child also asleep. The woman's arm is lying on top of the counterpane, palm upward.

Near the elbow a small tube is taped in place, a slight bump under the surface marking where a needle enters a vein. Moving one's eyes from the arm along the tube one sees a bottle, hung by the side of the bed, half filled with blood. The scene is static. Looking closely one sees the blood level does not rise. Silence. Then the metallic click of a camera, the sound of film being wound on. Another click. The sequence is repeated, again and again. In the corner of the room a man is standing, taking photographs of the woman and the child and the blood. After he has used what must be a whole roll he signals to a girl standing beside him. She approaches the bed and starts dismantling the stand, removing the needle and the tape from the woman's arm.

Downstairs, two hours later, the girl takes a hospital bag of blood from a large gleaming refrigerator. Her companion stands by a table, twenty or so photographs laid out in front of him. In another corner of the room a man is at a typewriter. He looks up. 'You've checked the blood type?'

The girl grins. 'Don't be stupid. Of course I did.'

'O.K.' He gets up, pulling the piece of paper out of the machine, folds it and places it in a large envelope. The photographs follow, five of the clearest tucked inside the brown anonymous covering. And finally the blood, packaged unceremoniously in a black plastic bag. One of the men puts on a large coat and hat, picks up the package and goes outside into the sun and the snow.

A thousand kilometres away, on the tiny island in the estuary, the same scene was being enacted. After the photographs had been taken and Carolyn was lying, sleeping off the drug, Wolf went downstairs to a small converted darkroom to develop the film.

In the kitchen (small and less well-equipped than its continental counterpart) Livia and Brian were sitting at a table drinking coffee. Brian was in a good mood, entertaining Livia with one of his endless stories.

'So then he said, quite seriously, "Take a couple of weeks off. You can afford it." "No, I can't," I said, "I've got a wife and child to support." '

He smiled broadly, enjoying Livia's reaction. He saw it as a challenge, to try to make her laugh.

Brian was not one of the key members of Exterminating Angel. His job as an airline pilot made him unavailable most of the time. Nevertheless his help had been invaluable on occasions. It had been he who had borrowed the helicopter which had transported Akeroyd. He lacked the training in firearms and other guerrilla skills that the others had undergone, but frequently made himself useful in surveillance and, as on this occasion, transport and liaison.

Livia pushed the coffee pot towards him and got up from the table. She opened the fridge, withdrew a bag of blood, then she picked up an empty, washed milk bottle from the draining board and began carefully to pour the blood into it. When it was full she wrapped a piece of tinfoil over the top, moulding the foil to the sides of the glass. As she was doing this, Wolf appeared in the doorway, holding the photographs still wet from the printing. They gathered round to look at them.

'Hey, that's a nice one. She looks suitably drained and white,' said Brian.

'Sadist,' said Livia. She flicked through the photos, picking out four or five of the best ones. 'Is she O.K.?' she asked Wolf.

'Sleeping. She won't remember a thing when she wakes.' He grinned. 'She's lucky we didn't really take the blood.'

'Yes, she'd be too weak to look after the baby. You'd have to take charge,' Livia retorted.

'Now now, comrades,' said Brian. He made the word sound ironic. 'I think I'd best be off if I'm to catch the tide and get this Dracula consignment there in time for the first delivery.'

'Now, you do know which house you're going to?' said Wolf.

'Sure.' Brian gestured extravagantly. 'I know Weybridge like the back of my hand.'

'Esher,' corrected Wolf.

'Oh yes, sorry, Esher.' They all three laughed.

Brian put his coat on, then he embraced them both in turn. In the doorway he stopped for a moment and said: 'Good luck, comrades.' This time he was serious. He strode out into the foggy night.

Chapter Twenty Six

Dawn arrived sluggishly around 7.00 in Esher next morning, leaving a slimy coating of frost on the ground. A mile outside the United Dairies on the edge of town a man lay sprawled behind a tree, wrapped in blankets, unconscious, his milk wagon and his uniform temporarily liberated in the name of terrorism.

Outside The Grange, home of the Lanning family, a police car was parked, the windows misted over. In the front seats were two policemen, dreaming of breakfast and struggling to keep their eyes open until their reliefs arrived at eight. From down the road came the comforting sound of a milk float, rattling its slow progress from door to door. Stopping outside the front gates the milkman, in a white cap and striped apron covered by a sheepskin overcoat, walked up the drive, his body obscuring the crate of milk that he held in his right hand, his breath blowing steam in the early morning cold.

The policemen took no notice as he approached the front door, and in the alcove deposited the ordered four pints. They took no notice as he slipped a plain buff envelope next to the wall by the bottles. They had orders to apprehend anyone suspicious. The milkman did not come into that category. He walked away carelessly whistling, evidently enjoying his job, back to the float and off again down the road and out of sight.

Two hours and two policemen later, the door of the house opened, and a middle-aged woman in a blue housecoat came out and stood on the step, blinking in the daylight. Her face was tired and strained, her eyes glazed from the after effects of tranquillizers.

She bent down to pick up the bottle and her figure suddenly froze, her hand suspended over the crate. A few inches from her grasp, like a black sheep in a herd of pedigree white lambs, a bottle of fresh blood sat among the pasteurised cow's milk. She picked up the envelope and opened it, her hand shaking. At her feet fell four photographs of her daughter, arm strapped up to a blood drip. The note inside read:

THIS IS A PINT OF YOUR DAUGHTER'S BLOOD. THERE WILL BE ANOTHER PINT IN TWO DAYS' TIME IF OUR VIDEO IS NOT SHOWN ON THE 5.40 NEWS TONIGHT. AND THEN ANOTHER, AND ANOTHER. WITHIN TEN DAYS YOUR DAUGHTER WILL BE DEAD.

The policemen in the car saw the woman open her mouth, heard the cry almost before it hit the air, and watched her crumple onto the doorstep. As if on cue, from down the road a few straggling weary newsmen equipped with cameras began to approach the house, pulled from their beds by emergency phone calls from their news editors.

There was only one hour's difference between this scene and the one that took place on the rich outskirts of Zurich.

Later that same morning William Macclesfield arrived back at his offices after a somewhat stormy second meeting with the Home Secretary and Sir Charles Lanning. The video was now scheduled to be shown that evening on British TV, though the Swiss had still refused. Macclesfield's suggestion, that the blood might possibly not belong to the hostages, had fallen on very deaf ears. He was hardly surprised. Lady Lanning, it appeared, was a somewhat hysterical woman, and her reaction had determined her husband's decision.

Macclesfield folded his long body into his chair and sat for a while staring at the brass inkstand on his desk, a melancholic look on his face. On the surface he was a remarkably modest man, discreet to a fault, and not usually wrong in his judgement. He was, he had to admit, a little depressed by this latest turn of events.

A sharp knock on the door broke him from his trance. 'Ah, Jarvis,' he said, 'come in. I've just seen the Home Secretary . . .' He quickly related the morning's events. 'Well, any observations?'

'So, they've got them to show the video . . .' Jarvis mused. 'Hmmm, smart move, the blood. They knew, didn't they, how Lady Lanning would react. They predicted it and exploited. Very clever. Who would have known that?'

'A number of people.'

'Not such a number. It shows once again their level of penetration. We expected pressure, but not so soon, nor so accurate.'

'Pressure from other directions, too.'

'You mean the Government, sir?'

'Of course the Government. And the police. They know there's something going on.'

'We're not bound to share all our information with them. It's well understood.'

'Well, in a case of this magnitude, Jarvis, you're playing it very close to the line. It's leading the Department into trouble. Results are expected. We have to give them something. Do you understand?'

'Yes, I see.'

'We'll have to sacrifice Luis. I don't see any alternative. Do you?'

Roland sat for a moment, deep in thought. Then he leaned forward to rest his elbows on the tip of Macclesfield's desk. Finally he spoke. 'There may be another way, sir.'

'What?'

'India.'

'India? Their man in Bombay? Won't he have left?'

'Perhaps . . . perhaps not. Maybe that's just what they expect us to think.'

'The Indians have been looking and they haven't found anything.'

Jarvis gave a sympathetic shrug. 'I don't think that surprises either of us, really. Why don't you let me send a man out?'

Macclesfield nodded. 'All right, Jarvis. I'll give you till Monday. No more.'

'Done.'

Chapter Twenty Seven

The video was finally shown to the public on the third evening of Carolyn's captivity. On the island Livia and Wolf watched it in silence, while Carolyn lay dozing upstairs. Dusk was falling, and with it came the rain, sweeping across the island from the North Sea, flattening the grass and stirring up the mud along the paths. The sky crept low over the treetops and the clapboard cottage echoed with the dense, incessant rhythm of the downpour.

Later in the evening Wolf and Livia were sitting by the fire when the phone rang. Wolf took the call. It was Daniel. Global had made no further moves to meet the ransom demands. In Switzerland the video had still not been shown despite a second consignment of blood. The Swiss Government, firmly committed to law and order and the backing of Swiss companies, declared it to be a bluff. The Swiss press, although giving wide coverage to events in England and the contents of Exterminating Angel's video, supported this stand.

The British Government and Global UK, reluctant to be seen as weaker than their Swiss counterparts, were hardening in their attitude. According to Daniel's contacts there would be no further concessions, at least for the moment. It would depend on what happened in Switzerland, on the response in Britain to the video, and finally on the reaction of Exterminating Angel. It would be a long wait, but they had expected that.

Wolf returned to the room and relayed the news to Livia. As he finished talking the ghost of a smile crossed her face.

'So, the worm finally turns,' she said softly. 'And we stay put for a while?'

'Yep. Then if nothing has happened after five days or so, another video of the child being fed, or another pint of blood. Daniel sounded almost pleased . . . like he'd been waiting for this to happen.'

'He had,' she said, staring into the fire.

'What?'

'Nothing. Just replaying old conversations.'

Neither spoke for a few moments. The fire hissed its way through a moist apple log, like a breath released through clenched teeth. The wood gave off a fragrant, almost sweet smell. Wolf stretched out in his chair, pushing his long legs towards the grate, and let his head fall back with a noisy sigh.

'You know, sometimes I wonder what I'm doing here,' he said, shaking his head. 'Looking after a woman and a kid.'

'You know exactly what you're doing here,' retorted Livia. 'You always do.'

He reached out to grasp a log from a box next to his chair, and with casual accuracy tossed it into the fire.

'It reminds me of when I was a kid and we used to go to the movies,' he continued. 'I always liked the Westerns best. I remember I used to identify with the Indians.' He grinned. 'Very confusing . . . Anyway, what really used to piss me off were the pictures with women and children in. They cluttered things up. What I liked was the action.'

'The mark of a true revolutionary.' Livia shook her head, amused. 'Preferring Indians to cowboys and action to talk. If they ever catch you, Wolf, the psychiatrists will have a field day.'

He snorted a laugh and got up from the chair to pour himself a thick fingerful of Scotch. She watched him move; big shoulders, slender hips, wiry, tough. His face was aging faster than his body. The lines etched along his forehead and down from his mouth gave him a kind of permanent scowl. It was the pattern of a face in action, concentrating. When he was younger, operating with one of the German groups, she remembered hearing tales about his womanizing. He had been prettier then, a little like Jagger, with full arrogant lips, smooth skin, a pout rather than a scowl.

She had never met him during that period, only seen a photograph once of him in a group. That had been taken in the mid sixties soon after he arrived in Berlin, leaving a respectable home in North Germany and a widowed mother who had mortgaged her life for the dreams of post-war New Germany. Her husband had died when Wolf was a child, and since then she had worked herself into the ground to get her colour television and her washing machine, even finally to get another husband, but in the process she had lost her son. By seventeen, Wolf had already rejected her answers and was heading for the big city.

'Where are you? You look miles away.' He had been watching her thinking.

She smiled. 'I was thinking of old times. Or rather, of your old times. What was Berlin like in those early days?'

'Berlin?' He shrugged. 'Just like you'd imagine it . . . the centre of the universe, at the very least the centre of post-war Europe. Or that was how it felt. It was always the place in the headlines when I was growing up. It seemed like it was where it was all happening, that's all.'

'And was it?'

'Oh sure. Sex and drugs and rock 'n roll. For an eighteen-year-old kid what else is there?'

'And how did that lead to politics?'

'Oh come on, Livia, in those days that *was* politics. You didn't think it was, but *they* did. Christ, the burghers of Berlin. Any guy with long hair, it was hardly safe to go out on the streets. We used to sit around in cellars smoking dope, singing Dylan and preaching revolution. It was crazy.'

'And you loved it.'

'Sure I loved it.' Wolf stretched his arms upwards and clasped his hands together on top of his head. 'I was a working-class kid who'd got out of home and was going to change the world. I remember the first job we ever did.' He grinned suddenly at the memory. 'We were going to leave a bomb outside the American Express office. Everything was fine, we left it there and then went and sat in a café half a kilometre away and waited for it to go off.' He paused, sipping his Scotch, obviously enjoying the retelling. 'We waited and waited, then Klaus said, "God, I forgot to set the detonator." ' Wolf waved his arms in the air dramatically. 'So we went back to the alley at the side of the American Express where we had left the bomb. We were approaching it, about fifteen metres off, when BOOM . . . great explosion, the fucking thing went off, blasted us to the ground, scorched our faces.' He sighed, shaking his head slowly, his voice quiet again. 'God, we were so untogether then.'

'Then how did you manage to get a bomb in the first place?'

'Are you kidding? We never could have done it ourselves. The police gave it to us. Through an agent provocateur. Never underestimate the fuzz, Livia.' He waved a finger at her in fake seriousness. 'We were such idiots then, all of us. We didn't know a thing about politics. It was only when I spent a year in the nick later on that I began to read, even to think properly. That's when I stopped listening to Dylan.' He grinned. 'Too personal, not political enough. I knew he'd finally turn to God. Saw it coming. Didn't trust him.'

'Anti-semite,' said Livia mockingly.

'Who, me or Dylan?'

She watched him, intrigued by the depths of his mirth. There was a quality of extremism to him, even now, which somewhere she had lost in herself.

'Did you ever think you'd still be doing this, Wolf?' she asked on impulse. 'Years back, if someone had prophesied this scene, would you have believed them?'

'Sure.' He grinned good naturedly. 'What other trade do I have? What about you? Didn't you ever have the urge to "settle down".' He used the term with an exaggerated mockery. 'To have children, begin a new race of revolutionaries?'

She smiled with her mouth, although the expression in her eyes was more ambiguous. 'No,' she said.

'Ever think of going back to Italy?'

'I could ask you the same question.' Livia did not like the questions turned on herself.

Wolf did not reply, but continued to look at her.

'O.K.,' she conceded, smiling. 'No, I don't think of it.' She looked at him, her face serious again. 'That was another era.'

'After Paulo's death . . .'

She broke him off. 'You know how it is. It's the risk we all take. Yes, of course it changed me. Before then it was a game. I didn't think it was a game, but of course it was. I was like you, living out movie images. "Les Chinoises", remember?'

She stopped speaking, staring into the fire. He waited for her to continue and when she didn't he said: 'And then?'

'I decided to live my life more deliberately.'

'You're strong, Livia.' There was no admiration in his voice, just the blandness of the fact.

'No, I'm just realistic.' She smiled, deliberately turning the subject from the past. 'Makes me a dull companion, yes? It jumps a lot more when Alex is here.'

He shrugged. 'Maybe. On the other hand no one's going to be jumping around here for a while.' He paused. 'What are we going to do about her?' He jabbed his finger upwards. 'Are we going to tell her that Daddy has decided to stall?'

'No, not yet. Let her settle. Get used to us a little. When we can't hide it any longer then we'll tell her. No point in causing more trouble now.'

Upstairs, as if on cue, the sound of crying began. The baby, reawakened by hunger and indignation at his treatment, began his noisy protest. For the last two days it had been like this, spasmodic howling throughout the night. Carolyn had refused Livia's offer of help to make the baby sleep. Instead she started the ritual of her footsteps, pacing the room with the child in her arms, trying to soothe him.

They listened in silence for a few minutes. A log fell out of the fire, spitting sparks. Wolf kicked it back into the grate. The kick was harder than necessary.

'Can't you stop it crying?'

'It gives her something to do. She needs the distraction.'

'Why don't you let me talk to her?'

'And say what?'

He shrugged. 'I don't know. Maybe if she's going to be here for a while we should tell her a few of the facts of life. Politically educate her.'

Livia snorted. 'You've been reading too many novels about Pattie Hearst. I doubt whether anything you could say would change her particular viewpoint on the world. Her life is built on privilege, remember.'

'I could try.'

Something in his tone caught Livia's attention.

'Does she interest you, Wolf?'

He looked at her for a moment, then laughed loudly, another gale of sound. 'If you mean would I like to fuck her, the answer is I've already done so. Fucked a hundred women just like her. It always left me with the same bad taste in my mouth.'

They were interrupted by a sudden crash from above them: a crash and a scream of pain. They were both on their feet immediately, Wolf before Livia, bounding up the stairs. Outside the door he stopped and looked through the mirror.

Inside the room everything was still. In front of him Carolyn was sitting in the armchair, her arms folded calmly in her lap. The baby was in the cot, stunned into silence by the noise. Strewn over the floor were remnants of the Vermeer print, the glass shattered, the frame buckled.

Brusquely Wolf shoved his mask over his head. Livia reached out to restrain him, to say something, but she was too late. He had already turned the key and was striding into the room.

There was a second's silence as the two of them faced each other. There was a sharpness in the eyes, a tension. Then from the chair she said quietly: 'I want something to stop my baby crying.' Another split second's pause. 'And I want it now.'

Wolf took two steps across the room and stood above her. Then he slapped her across the face. He caught hold of her upper arm and pulled her out of the chair, flinging her to the other side of the room where she fell clumsily onto the bed. He went after her. Sitting down close, his hand on the front of her dress, he pulled her upright to face him. Then he pointed the index finger of his other hand between her eyes, jabbing it into her forehead. He heard the sharp intake of her breath as she registered the pain, and felt Livia's shadow behind him.

'All right, now *you* listen to *me*,' he said between his teeth. 'Just remember who you are and why you're here. You have no rights. We hold the power of life and death over you and your precious baby. If you want something, you ask. You ask nicely, and maybe . . . maybe we give it.'

She said nothing.

'In other words, you don't demand, you grovel. Understood?'

Again no reply. She was looking straight into his eyes, unblinking. He shook her head slightly. She opened her mouth a little, as if to speak, but no words came. Instead she ran her tongue round her lips, slowly and, it seemed, intentionally. She let out a long breath, her eyes glazing. He became aware of the warmth of her leg next to his. Her body seemed to relax.

'Yes,' she said evenly. 'I understand.'

From behind him he heard Livia's voice saying something. From where she stood in the doorway she could not have seen Carolyn's gesture, only noted the change in the physical language of Wolf's body.

It was enough to alert her. 'Let's go now,' she said, making her voice deliberately rough. 'I'll bring her something to make her baby sleep.'

Chapter Twenty Eight

In India Mike was acting exactly according to plan. Daniel's vision was one of poetic unity. Bombay had been the first place to hear news of the Global kidnappings. So it would also be the first to know of its successful outcome. Until that time Mike's instructions were to lie low.

Since checking into the nameless hotel he had gone to considerable trouble to make himself inconspicuous. He had, it was true, spent a lot of time alone in his room reading, or watching the fan go round. But then, Bombay was hot, it was quite common for foreigners to be lazy, especially the kind of foreigners who frequented the dingier parts of town. He had not, however, become a total recluse, realizing that this also would draw attention to himself, and would make the hotel owner worry about the possibility of coming across another body OD'd on junk. Such accidents did not help relations with the police.

So he had taken a middle course, blending in with the company offered just enough to be considered normal. It was not hard to do. The freaks of Bombay had their own easily identifiable patch in the city. Many of the cheap hotels shared the same streets, an area clustered on the edge of the more expensive, touristy haunts. There were a certain number of restaurants and cafés where you were sure to encounter fellow travellers eating toast and eggs for breakfast, or sipping juices in the late afternoon heat (there was a lucrative business to be made out of supplying Western exiles with home comforts).

Installing himself daily in Leopold's café, he became part of the scene. He learnt to recognise the regular junkies, the two Western prostitutes whose beat passed by the open doors of the café. The third night he had even been approached by one of them, her lank, fair hair falling over emaciated shoulders, sallow, pitted skin and vacant eyes. Junk was cheap in Bombay, but then so were bodies.

It was one of the horrors of the city, that its poverty was not restricted to Indians. There was a particular obscenity in Western destitution. Kids had come East with the smell of incense and flowers in their hair, mouthing tales of peace and love and spiritual regeneration. Or maybe for some of them it had always been the lure of dope and cheap living. Whatever the reasons, the dreams had soured as the travellers' cheques had been spent. Even the consulates had grown tired of extending funds and compassion to the flotsam which had begun to arrive on their doorsteps. For some nationalities it had been harder than for others. In most Indian cities the majority of foreign junkies were French, and Bombay was no exception. The French Government was not interested in repatriating their misfits. Better that they should stay washed up on the streets. Eventually presumably they would take one dose too many and die. Another death in a country of so many. It would hardly notice.

Mike pondered these things as he lay for long hours in the midday heat. He wondered also about the progress of the kidnappings back in Europe. Unless or until Daniel contacted him he was a spectator again. Here in India the reaction had been tremendous. The newspapers had led with nothing else for days. Two separate kidnappings in two Western countries: it was the clearest example for years of the capacity of terrorist groups to organize and operate in unison. Not since the heyday of Munich, Vienna and Tel Aviv had the world seen such boldness and co-ordination.

And it had all started here in Bombay. The *Bombay Times* was secretly – in fact, not so secretly – delighted. Of course, they claimed, security arrangements in Bombay had been too tough for the terrorists to crack, so they had been obliged to act elsewhere, but nevertheless the city basked in the glory of the fact that the conference of Global Food here had inspired the idea. Now they and the rest of the world sat back and waited for the reaction. Would Global pay up or take a stand? The Indian papers had been divided on that one. The *Times of India*, as might have been expected, had taken a moral line pontificating on the terrorizing of innocent victims. But the more sensational papers had gone to town on the horrors of Global's exploitation, paying special attention to the point at issue – the question of baby food, many tonnes of which was consumed in India. It was fair game now: the cats were among the pigeons.

The first hint of a change of atmosphere did not come until two days later. It was then that the *Times of India* reprinted an editorial from one of the serious British Sunday papers.

> **The tactics of the notorious Exterminating Angel have, for five long years, deceived a large number of the British people into believing that, if the ends are right, the means can always be justified. That is certainly no longer the case. However much Global Food is culpable of exploiting the Third World, their crimes have been eclipsed by this latest blatant act of terrorism.**
>
> **With the kidnapping of the two mothers and their young children we can finally see Exterminating Angel for what they are. Terrorism, whatever rules it is played by, is an unacceptable game. And terrorism, whatever its ends, is a dangerous and anti-democratic means. Exterminating Angel have shown us that if violence is the only way to achieve results, then the innocent will always be the final victims. That they have turned to violence is no surprise: it is the logical outcome and one they have defined for themselves. The tragedy of the two mothers now in captivity is only overshadowed by the tragedy of a nation whose institutions of Government and Industry have lacked the moral courage to stand firm against intimidation, and whose resolve has been softened by the mask of public benefactor assumed by these self-appointed bullies. They have been at liberty too long. It is time we saw them brought to justice.**

That night Mike made a point of spending the evening with one of the more affluent travellers in a nearby hotel. Late that night, when they were both too stoned to talk any more, he suggested listening to the news on his companion's radio, to hear 'what's going on back home'.

The World Service did not mince its words. It was then that Mike realized the weight of Government pressure and the shift in press opinion. He decided it was time to go home. The next day he spent three hours in a queue in Bombay's Victoria Rail

Terminal. By midday – and with a little help from a few crisp bank notes – he had secured a first-class sleeper for Delhi leaving that evening. From there he could get a flight home, using his other passport. No one would check. He arrived back at the hotel just after one, his body drenched in sweat, and took up his familiar position underneath the fan. There was nothing in his actions that was careless. All he had to do now was wait.

Chapter Twenty Nine

Carolyn had a lot of time to reflect over her behaviour on the night that Wolf had hit her. Since then they had left her almost totally alone. The only time she saw them was when they brought her meals and the baby's milk. It was the woman who came, sitting by her side watching her eat each mouthful, checking that she did not hide anything to give to the baby later. The meals passed in silence. Carolyn had long since lost her appetite, but fear of weakness forced her to eat. As she ate, Thomas stayed hungry. She held her anger inside her.

She knew by now that something must have gone wrong with their plans. Apparently her father had not been able to raise the money immediately and she would have to wait. She decided, in so far as it was possible to decide anything in her present state, that there was no point in worrying. It could not help things. All through her childhood she had watched her mother worry. Worry that her father's business, then in its infancy, would fail; worry that he did not love her enough, that she was growing old, worry finally that there was perhaps too much money. It had eaten her away and left her jagged and cold. In contrast, her father had been exactly the opposite, running his life, his business, even his marriage on ruthless, pragmatic lines. His opposition had destroyed their marriage, but he had stayed younger than her for longer, and there had always been the odd woman to share his bed. Carolyn had loved her mother more than her father; as a child she had been very close to her, had shared her pain. But she had also recognised early that her mother was a victim, and that her father handled the world better.

And she had determined that she herself would not be crushed.

So when it came to her own marriage she had picked a man who would never threaten her in the way her father had her mother. It had been easy. She was attractive, rich, and had wanted a home and children. Derek had been less stupid than the others, with a position of his own in the world. He, too, came from wealth, although it was aristocratic rather than commercial. She had picked him, although she let him think it was the other way round. Their marriage was not a great success, but then neither was it a failure. She felt in control of her world. And she enjoyed that feeling. It reminded her of her father.

It had been her father's side of her nature that made her rub her leg against Wolf's that night. There had been no plan in her smashing of the picture, except to release her frustration and perhaps to provoke a reaction from her jailors. But when, after his blow, she was sitting next to him, her mouth caked dry with the threat of further violence, and she had moistened her lips to speak, she knew instantly that he had read it as something else, something that he was looking for. She had played to it automatically, and for a second had been caught up in its power. The moment had taken her totally by surprise. She was not a woman who usually responded instinctively to sex, especially when she was not in control of the situation.

Later, when she was alone, she had been furious with herself, and felt soiled by her action. But alongside that came the realization that if she could throw them off their guard, even for a moment, there might be a way to escape. If that happened, she wondered what she would do.

That question was answered for her the night they told her about her father's decision not to pay.

It was late in the evening. Her watch read 9.00 p.m. The woman came in, followed by the man. She had not seen him since that night and she felt a slight sickness in her throat. It was a sensation she recognized as fear.

'We thought you might like some fresh air, Carolyn,' the woman said. It was the first time she had ever used her name. 'You've been here for five days now. It would make you feel better.'

Carolyn's mind raced. She remembered stories of how captives are promised freedom before they are killed. A confused memory of a kidnapping in Italy where the terrorist had waved goodbye to the captive and then shot him. She felt her heart thumping.

From across the other side of the room Livia felt it too.

'It's all right. This isn't any kind of trap. There is something we want to tell you, but we won't harm either you or the child. I give you my word.'

Carolyn began to open her mouth to dismiss the bond of a terrorist, but she closed it again. She believed the woman.

'What about Thomas?' she said.

'He's asleep. We'll leave him here. He'll be quite safe. It's not for long. Wouldn't you like some fresh air?'

Carolyn nodded dumbly, alarmed by the effect kind words were having on her. She felt suddenly like crying. This is all part of their plan to make me weak, she thought fiercely. I must stay aloof.

Outside, the evening air was wild with the prospect of freedom. She gulped down huge breaths, unaware up until that moment how stale and unhealthy the room had been. It was cold outside, a March wind shivering the trees; she felt the rush of it on her cheek. She walked unsteadily, blindfolded, depending on the woman's arm to guide her. How unfair, she thought, to have to trust a jailor. After a few moments the blindfold was removed. Looking around her, Carolyn thought it had probably not been necessary. She was standing in the middle of a path, with thick, moonless darkness all around. Through the line of trees which fringed the track she could see nothing. No sign of lights, no sound. It was unearthly. Then, in the distance a small recurring noise broke the silence. Small and mechanical. Carolyn recognised the dim buzz of a telephone. The woman looked back into the darkness from where they had come. The man's voice behind her said:

'You go. I'll walk her.'

The woman hesitated for a second, and then walked quickly back into the darkness. Carolyn felt there had been some silent communication between them that she had not understood. It was clear in that moment that they probably knew each other very well.

She stood still, the masked man close to her. She once again had to beat down a rising fear. She took a deep breath and turned away.

'Is it all right if we walk a little?'

'Sure.' His voice held an edge of mockery.

They walked another hundred yards or so. On all sides the darkness lapped at their feet. On the left the line of trees broke, revealing an expanse of fields with another beyond it. She stopped and looked into the distance. She just had to try.

'Why don't you take your mask off?' She heard her own voice, dark like the air.

'Because you would be able to recognise me again.'

She caught again the trace of an accent. The same as the woman's? Not exactly, she thought.

'You're not English are you?'

'No, I'm not English.'

'Where do you come from?'

His answer was a laugh. Taking a step closer to her, he put out a hand, cupped it around her neck and drew her towards him. She froze at his touch, then deliberately relaxed, and moved her head against his chest. Through the jacket she felt the warmth of his skin. Her head turned to the side and she looked out into the darkness of the field. I could run now, she thought. I could run and maybe he wouldn't catch me. The image of her son came flooding back into her mind and the smell of freedom drifted away on the wind.

He put his other hand on her back, sliding it down to the base of her spine. The air was still. He spoke very quietly.

'If you tried it, I'd kill you.'

The pressure of his hand increased, pushing her groin against his.

She felt the fear inside her turn hard. She knew quite clearly that she hated this man more than she had ever hated anyone. She put out one of her hands and stroked the surface of his jacket. With the other she pushed him away from her playfully. When there was a little distance between them she looked into his eyes through the slit in the black material.

'And if you tried it, I'd kill you.'

He laughed loudly, but said nothing and released her. In the distance they both heard the woman's footsteps coming towards them. Together they walked back to the house, she blindfolded again. As they entered and the woman guided her up the stairs she heard his voice behind them.

'Why don't you tell her what's happened? I think she's under some illusion that she may be free soon.'

She lay in bed that night in furious speculation about the reasons for Global's refusal to meet the ransom demands. Gradually, around 3.00 a.m., as her turmoil hardened into resolve, she stopped hating her father, stopped the river of self pity. She began instead to put her mind to ways of escaping.

Chapter Thirty

It was mid afternoon in Bombay, the hottest time of the day. Those who did not have to work were sitting still. Mike was lying on his bed. There was a soft knock at the door. He got up slowly, feeling the stale heat as soon as he moved from under the path of the fan. At the door stood two policemen, one uniformed, the other in plain clothes.

Without a word they pushed him aside and entered the room. 'Hey,' he started to complain. 'What's the meaning of this?'

The uniformed officer replied with scant courtesy: 'Passport.'

Mike rummaged through his suitcase and produced it. The officer passed it to his colleague, who looked at the picture, checked the entrance dates and handed it back. It was a gesture that unnerved Mike more than he expected. The uniformed policeman looked at him.

'And tell me now what is the purpose of your visit to India?'

Mike adopted a tone that he hoped his interrogators would interpret as a hippy drawl. 'Listen, man, I don't know what this is about. I'm travelling around Asia, O.K.? Just looking at the sights, that kind of thing – '

'This is your first hotel in Bombay?'

A tricky one. These guys were not your regular fuzz, Mike could see that. His entrance date into India would not tie in with the date of his arrival at the hotel. He wondered if they were following a specific lead, or if it was simply that the security forces were spreading their net a little wider. He had not expected this level of surveillance.

He played it vague. 'Er . . . no . . . there was another . place . . .— the Eldorado, some such name. I don't really remember.' He frowned, trying to look spaced out.

The man in plain clothes was wandering round the room, poking under the mattress, looking inside the drawers. He went into the bathroom. Mike followed him in and stood at the door. The officer ran his hand around the top of the high window.

'Ah ha,' he exclaimed, bringing his hand down with his fist clenched. He opened it and in the palm of his hand was a dark lump, wrapped in plastic. Smiling ironically at Mike he passed the lump to his colleague who unwrapped it and held it to his nose. Mike did not need to smell it. It was obvious what it was.

'Well,' said the policeman, still smiling, 'hashish, my friend. Did you think perhaps you were in Goa? Here in Bombay we have different standards. Would you like to tell us about it, where you got it from, where perhaps you are taking it?'

Mike expostulated, at length and with great fervour. As he talked his brain was working quickly. The dope was not his, he had been careful not to be in possession at any time during the last few weeks. He was furious with himself for not checking the room when he took it. It was not unusual for freaks to stash their dope in hotel rooms and pick it up later. On the other hand, it was hardly enough, by Indian standards, to bother to stash. And if it did not belong to a freak, and it did not belong to him, there was only one other answer as to how it got there.

As he was led out into the steamy daylight to the battered police car Mike began to wonder whether this was just a simple drugs bust. He realized that for the first time in many years he was afraid.

The fear was just beginning. For the next eighteen hours, withstanding the filth, smells, overcrowding and the unremitting heat took most of his energy. At the police headquarters he was contained in an area which allowed each person about one square metre. It was literally a pen, a place the size of a tennis court in the open air under a burning corrugated iron roof, bounded by heavy duty wire netting.

Mike found himself a spot in the corner and squatted in the

dust trying to regain his self-possession. He looked around him. Many of his companions were familiar to him; he had seen them in his hotel, in the surrounding restaurants, in the streets. There was something curious about them as a group, but he could not quite locate what it was. Drug busts, especially on this scale, were not an everyday occurrence in India – in fact, normally the authorities were completely indifferent to the ways Westerners chose to explore their private hells. This raid was obviously connected to the events surrounding the Global Food conference. But how? Perhaps it was a case of being seen to be efficient, a big feature to get into the *Herald Tribune* and show the world that India too was doing her bit to try and round up international terrorists. But that did not quite ring true.

A man Mike recognised from the hotel came up and squatted down beside him. He was tall, dark-haired, with a Northern accent.

'Hi, Terry.' Terry was the name on the passport Mike was using. 'Man, this is a crazy thing to happen. I just don't get it. Not in India. Maybe in Thailand, man, but not here.'

Mike shook his head. 'Did they find anything on you?'

'They planted some smack. Man, I don't even use smack, for God's sake,' he exclaimed indignantly. 'It's weird. Why bother? They're not even out for money. And another thing. They only picked up the guys. There were two Aussie girls next door to me with a chunk of O bigger than your fist. They didn't even touch 'em. Did you notice?'

Mike started. No, he had not noticed, but now he did. Instantly alert, he took in his companions. All men, all about his age, his build. Some with shorter hair than his, but no longhairs. This was what had been at the back of his consciousness. In the fierce Bombay heat there came over him a chill of apprehension. They knew who they were looking for.

At that moment there was a commotion outside the pen. Mike turned his head to see what was happening. A group of Indians – jailors, police and others – were approaching, walking around the enclosure, examining the prisoners. As always with such gatherings the noise was continuous. A couple of the men inside the pen were shouting abuse. For an outsider it had the makings of farce rather than tragedy. The group passed round the corner of the enclosure and stopped five metres away from Mike. He stayed squatting, his head down, his face partially obscured by one hand.

'Hey you.' One of the policemen dug him in the ribs with his baton. 'Up.' Mike stood and raised his eyes. He looked from one face to another, from the large bearded Sikh holding the baton, to the dapper figure of the plain-clothes man who had arrested him, coming finally to rest on the small, sweating, round face of his old acquaintance at the Imperial, Mr Gupta Singh.

For an eternal ten seconds the two gazed into each other's eyes. Then Singh turned excitedly to the policeman.

'Yes indeed, officer. This is Mr Cooke. I am seeing him in front of my eyes.'

PART FOUR

Compared to the wholesale violence of capital and government, political acts of violence are but a drop in the ocean . . . High strung like a violin string, [the anarchists] weep and moan for life, so relentless, so cruel, so terribly inhuman. In a desperate moment the string breaks.

Emma Goldman, 1910.

Unless the moral fibre of the régime is in a state of advanced decay, and the political will paralysed, the urban terrorist will fail to make headway beyond the stage of provocation in which, according to plan, public opinion should have been won over to their cause, but is in fact antagonised.

Walter Laqueur, 1977.

Chapter Thirty One

The next day Carolyn made an important discovery. Lying on the bed that afternoon with a sharp wind blowing outside she felt a draught coming through the wall by her head. Pulling aside the bedclothes she found a small patch of wallpaper peeling off from the surface. She poked it and her finger went right through the plaster, into a space between two loose bricks. A spot of daylight danced into the room. Over the next hour, working with the ends of two hair grips, she managed to enlarge the gap. Thus she caught her first glimpse, in daylight, of the outside world.

Peering through the hole she could see a small, scrubby garden with a deserted flowerpatch and a low, white fence. Beyond that there was a gravel road and a large, brick barn containing an old plough, and a few bales of hay strewn in the entrance. A spindly hedgerow ran away from the house towards a low, flat skyline. It was there that she caught sight of the strangest thing.

The rig of a large sailing boat, its red sails full in the wind, was breezing along across the top of a field. She withdrew her head, her eye smarting in the cold air from the hole. She looked again. No, it was not an apparition, it was indeed a sailing boat.

At that moment she heard a step on the stairs. She sprang back from where she was crouching, hurriedly rearranged the bed in its original position and sat down on it, trying to look nonchalant. Without looking up she could sense their scrutiny through the mirror which she had learnt to expect several times a day. She had steeled herself against the intrusion, making sure that her moments of weakness were hidden from her jailors.

A minute later the creak of the steps came again. She lay back on the bed and thought about what she had seen. Red sails . . red sails. It rang a bell somewhere. A child's jigsaw puzzle, a television programme. Sailing barges. A river perhaps, or a coastline?

The information was useless. Even if she could find out where she was, who would she tell? Outside the boarded window she heard a noise. A door below opening. She leaped off the bed and pushed it away from the wall to get a better look. She saw a man – the man, she knew him from his build and his walk – at the gate, going out, closing it behind him and heading to the left out of view. Despite herself she was interested in the face, which only passed in front of her briefly. Mid thirties, maybe older, she thought. Untidy hair, dirty, corn-coloured; chiselled nose, full mouth. He might have been good-looking, she couldn't tell.

Then she heard the noise of a vehicle. It was a sound she had heard before, but her knowledge of cars was too slim for her to identify it. Now she saw a blue Ford Transit pass the house, driving out of sight to the right. She tried to piece it together with the other information she had: the barn, once or twice the noise of a tractor in the distance. It was a farm, obviously. But why should they risk having other people so near? It seemed careless. She felt puzzled. Nothing seemed to fit: too many pieces and no structure.

She got up and went over to the cot. Thomas was awake but quiet, gurgling softly. She was not sure what they were putting into the milk, but even his waking hours now were more subdued than usual. She missed the exuberance of his bursting little personality, although she was grateful for the respite from his hungry tears.

For the ten thousandth time she spoke internally to him. 'Thomas, how do we get out of here?' Idly she fiddled with the cot. Kneeling beside him she put her fingers through the bars to play with him, her other hand trailing along underneath the wooden slats. Her fingers encircled the leg, and moved downwards to the cool, hard, metal castor at its base. She picked at the brittle iron surface. How unnecessarily heavy it seemed for such a small piece of furniture as a cot.

In that second she froze, rerunning the last thought through in her mind. That was it. What she had in her hand was a weapon. If she could find a way to work the leg off from the cot and use it, then she might be free.

She stood up abruptly and began pacing the room. She felt sick from the excitement surging up inside her. One thought kept recurring. It forced her suddenly into the armchair, her fingers picking at the material fraying on the arms. Could she do it? Could she really physically attack someone? Carolyn had never used physical violence in her life. As an only child she had been spared the scraps and squabbles that come with brothers and sisters. She had even been known to walk out of films where the violence was too unrelenting. What she was contemplating now was no idle push or shove. It was substantial injury. Because unless she wielded the weapon with all her strength, unless she could be sure to bring it down on someone's head very hard indeed, then it would not be hard enough. She would lose and there would be no second chance. They would kill her and Thomas. It was that thought that lifted her up out of the chair and made her slap the wall in fury. Thomas, startled by the gesture, exploded into cries. Carolyn snatched him up from the cot and continued her pacing. She pulled him close to her and whispered hard into his neck.

'We'll do it. We'll do it. We'll do it and then we'll get out of here.'

Chapter Thirty Two

In the bare, windowless room into which Mike was ushered he was faced by two men. He recognized one as the uniformed policemen. The other was a European, clean-shaven, wearing a crisply laundered white shirt, seated at a desk in front of a small, directional electric fan.

'Now then, Mr Merchant,' he began, revealing a Birmingham accent beneath a cultured drawl. 'Or should we call you Mr Cooke? Or even by some other name?'

Mike offered no reply.

His interrogator sat on a plain wooden chair, his elbows resting on a desk, fingers pressed together in front of him. 'Let me explain the powers open to us,' he said. 'You have been found in possession of 300 grams of cannabis resin. Although the Indian authorities are sometimes lackadaisical in these matters, in your case it is probable they will choose to proceed. Are you familiar with the hospitality of Indian prisons, Mr Merchant?'

In the silence that followed Mike noticed the large, immobile ceiling fan. He could not resist raising his arm to wipe the sweat from his brow.

The other continued: 'Or alternatively they can concentrate on the exploits of Mr Cooke. Threatening behaviour. Malicious impersonation. Conspiracy to kidnap, to murder. National prestige is at stake, Mr Cooke. No country wishes to be seen as less than uncompromising in the struggle against international terrorism. Under the circumstances the British High Commission would not seek to moderate the rigours of Indian justice.'

Mike felt his concentration oozing out through his sweating pores. He had to control the urge to ask for the fan to be switched on.

'But if you choose to co-operate we can arrange for your return to the . . . the mother country. There will, of course, be serious charges there, too, but the scope of these may be . . .' he savoured the word, 'negotiable.'

Silence again. Mike slouched in his chair, his head drooping. The other two sat, alert, still, gazing at him. Minutes passed. Then the interrogator abruptly broke into his stupor.

'So what is it to be, Mr Cooke? Speak up.'

Mike focussed on a spot on the floor a few inches from his left foot.

'Or perhaps you would like some time to yourself without distraction, to think about this?'

He nodded to his colleague, who briskly jumped to his feet and approached the prisoner. In a trice Mike found himself off the chair, sprawled on the hard wooden floor, handcuffed. The policeman whipped out a hood, black, made of a heavy woollen fabric, and deftly pulled it over Mike's head, tying it with a string around his neck.

Within moments Mike's head felt like a hot, sticky lake. It was too heavy to support, yet when he fell to the floor the blood ran to his brain and seemed to split him open. In this delirium he fancied his head had actually been damaged and blood was pouring down his body. It was unbearable.

Hours passed. Or minutes, he couldn't tell. Then hands seized him roughly, voices barked.

'Hands on the wall. Higher!' A blow to his arm. 'Feet back. Feet apart. Further!' A vicious kick at his ankle.

He felt his own scream, reverberating round the bag. But the pain roused him. He recognized himself again. He had been here before. Several years previously, in County Armagh, he had joined a course, supervized by a former internee. All the trainees had been subjected to this and other forms of torture to prepare themselves for possible interrogation by the Army. He had discovered then his own technique of resistance. For some it had been mental arithmetic, for others the ritual repetition of revolutionary slogans. Now he began his own internal chant, the old childhood comforter, 'Our Father, Which art in Heaven, Hallowed be . . .'

He did not know how many times he fell, how many kicks to the kidneys he sustained. At one point his clothes were ripped from his body. The relative coolness more than made up for the humiliation. It began to seem he had spent the whole of his life like this, spreadeagled, aching and burning.

Suddenly light pierced his stinging eyelids. He gulped and gasped at air. Life began again.

Water splattered into his face. A hand grasped him by the hair and hauled him into the chair. The same hand struck out, viciously slapping him back and forth across the face. The interrogator's face loomed, grotesquely huge, six inches in front of his.

'Right, Mr Cooke,' it said, 'let's start again.'

Chapter Thirty Three

It was ten thirty in the evening in the apartment block which was Daniel's home. He had, of course, been watching the news. The kidnapping had been relegated to a mention in the second half of the programme. Daniel could smell the changes in attitude that were manifesting themselves in the press. He was not pleased. But it was a waiting game.

The phone rang. Daniel picked it up. The call came from a

phone box. Daniel automatically switched on his answering machine.

'Hello? Dr Elks?'

'Speaking.'

'This is Wastepipe Cleaning Services here. A message was left on our machine earlier today that you wanted to contact us. What can we do for you?'

'Oh, that's very kind of you to call. I thought my drain was blocked, but it seems to have cleared itself.'

'Very well. I'll wish you a good night then.'

'And good night to you too.'

Both replaced their receivers. On a piece of paper Daniel jotted down the word 'wastepipe'; next to it he wrote these numbers: 23, 1, 19, 20. W is the twenty-third letter of the alphabet, A the first, and so on. This meant he must go to a phone box and call the number 231 1920. It was a simple method, but there was no reason for anyone tapping the phone to suppose the code indicated a phone number. Daniel doubted his phone was tapped – the quality of reception was much too poor for that – but he left nothing to chance, even at the cost of a certain inconvenience.

Memorizing the number he erased the tape and burnt the piece of paper in an ashtray. Then he picked up an overcoat and hat and headed outside. The nearest public telephone box was in Ladbroke Grove tube station, but old habits of caution directed him towards a more obscure one in the Crescent near the entrance to Holland Park.

Walking through the litter-strewn streets he passed walls covered by torn old posters for rock concerts and political meetings, and graffiti. His choice of this part of London for a home was deliberate: it was the contrast between the pampered, chic, Georgian terraces and the run-down, garishly painted houses where lived the alienated, radicalized black young. This vivid contrast, and the atmosphere of latent violence that it engendered, excited him. He had always been impressed by the story of the socialist politician who used to read the *Daily Express* every morning in order to maintain the level of his anger. Daniel's anger was of a colder, more measured variety. But any fuel that he needed to sustain it was provided by the streets of Notting Hill.

He reached the phone box and dialled the number. The same voice answered. 'Trevor?'

'Yes, this is Trevor. What have you got for me, Robert?' Neither of them had met, since the first time some years before. They probably never would again.

'There's a message through from Bombay. It came in an hour ago. Bad news, I'm afraid. Your man's been picked up.'

'Damnation. How did it happen?'

'No information on that. But photographs and prints have been received. Can he be identified?'

'Almost certainly.' Daniel paused to think. Although Mike, as far as he could be sure, had no record on the files for terrorist activities, he would probably show up with MI5 for his earlier days of hippy activism. At worst that would give them one member of the group. Could that lead them back to the others? He didn't think so. Mike's connections were tenuous. They had always made a point of avoiding being 'known associates'.

'Will he talk?' Daniel's informant asked.

'No, I don't think so. He's pretty tough. And even if he did he doesn't know enough. He might confuse rather than help. What will they do? Continue to interrogate him there or bring him back?'

'He'll be brought back.'

'O.K. Anything else?'

'No, not at the moment. But if you ring me on the same number samc time tomorrow, I may have more for you.'

'Will do. And Robert . . . thank you.'

'For nothing, Trevor. Keep up the good work.'

Daniel put down the phone and opened the door to the box, escaping from the smell of urine. He walked slowly home. Had it been overconfident to leave Mike in Bombay instead of withdrawing him? Perhaps so, but who was to know the Indian police would be so efficient? He thought no further of Mike, except to assess the chances of his talking.

The Bombay chapter was over. The operation now hinged on events in Switzerland. There delegates and journalists had started arriving for the World Health Assembly which as usual would debate a resolution restricting the marketing of baby food products in underdeveloped countries. Pressed for a view on the kidnappings, some African delegates were frank in their criticism of certain Swiss food and drug companies. One highly placed government minister from the Caribbean publicly questioned whether Switzerland was an appropriate country for the headquarters of a UN agency devoted to health. Murmurs began in the Swiss press, and even in Cabinet, about the effect of all this bad publicity on export markets for Switzerland's crucial food and pharmaceuticals industries. It seemed, according to Daniel's contacts the Swiss might choose to settle the matter before any more damage was done to their international reputation.

It was vital, Daniel thought, to keep going. If the Swiss cracked, then Global UK would give in too. He weighed up the risks against the increasingly optimistic prospects. By the time he turned the key in the lock of his front door he had decided that the job would continue. Daniel was not in the habit of making the wrong decision.

Chapter Thirty Four

In her jail on the island Carolyn watched her son grow weaker. That morning with breakfast came the news that they wanted her to record another video and she should be ready next day. After the woman went out Carolyn told herself there would be no tomorrow. No more posturing for the cameras. It had to be today. The urgency gave her the push she needed.

Everything depended on their sticking to their established pattern. Carolyn had observed that every other day, usually – not always – during the afternoon, the man went out for one hour, leaving the woman alone in the house. She never entered Carolyn's room: there was obviously an understanding between them not to approach her when only one was in the house. The man had not come near her since their walk. She was sure the woman had insisted on this. It was this insistence that made the woman the target.

On this particular afternoon she saw the man leave the house and heard his car drive away. It was 2.30. Time to get the weapon ready. For several days she had been planning what to do about the cot leg. She took Thomas out of the cot and laid him gently on the bed. He was sleeping peacefully. Then she put the cot on its side and wrenched at the leg. It did not budge. Carolyn felt the first tickle of panic. What was this cot made of anyway? It was built like a sideboard. She raised the cot off the floor and brought it down hard.

There was a crash and an unholy splintering sound as the leg broke off. Breathless, she pushed it under the bed and propped up the cot against the wall. It held steady. Then she moved to the table and gently pushed it over, letting the objects on top fall to the floor. As she went down on her knees and started to pick things up she thought she heard the stairs creak. She felt herself being watched through the mirror but she didn't dare look up. Then she returned to her armchair and waited. Nothing happened. The woman was not coming in. Carolyn took a deep breath. She picked up Thomas and placed him in the cot, making sure it was steady.

Then, standing with her back to the mirror, she pulled the weapon out from under the bed and weighed it in her hand. It was quite light but the iron castor was solid enough. She made a few passes with it in the air. It was unwieldy, but it felt as if it could be quite nasty. She tried hitting the bed once to gauge the force of its impact. She looked down at the dent left in the bedclothes and felt her heart start to pound. She must do better than that. Harder.

Luckily there was no time for reflection now. The man was seldom away for more than an hour. She looked at her watch. Twenty minutes gone.

One thing remained. The baby. For the plan to work, Thomas must be crying. She shook the cot. The child, dopey from its last feed (and sedation), blinked up at her wide-eyed and unconcerned. She became frantic. There wasn't time for this. He had to cry. She took a breath, picked him up and began to shake him, shake him brutally until the little body was flopping uncontrollably in all directions, and to her utter relief she heard the sobs of pain and indignation explode into the air. She put him back in the cot, and went over to the door. She banged on the panel, hard and insistent, shouting: 'Please, please come. There's something wrong with Thomas. He's having some kind of fit.'

No need to pretend with that voice. The edge of hysteria was real enough. She paced the room, checking one last time that the leg was hidden down the side of the armchair. Then she leaned over the side of the cot. At that moment came the footsteps, the pause to glance through the mirror, the sound of the key in the lock. She closed her eyes tight and got ready.

'What's the matter?' The woman's voice sounded concerned.

'I don't know. He's . . . he's not breathing right. He can't seem to . . . OH GOD, WHAT'S WRONG?'

She started shaking, sobbing. The woman came up behind her, placed her hands on Carolyn's shoulder and moved her firmly but gently to one side, so that Carolyn was standing next to the armchair.

'Don't worry. He'll be all right. I'll look at him.'

Livia bent over the cot, her hands reaching out for the infant.

It's now. It has to be now, thought Carolyn. In a few seconds she'll see Thomas is all right. She stepped back towards the chair, bent slightly and put out her hand to grasp the weapon behind her back. For a split second she stood rooted, paralysed, staring at Livia's curved back. Then, as if she were watching someone else act, she raised the leg up over her head and brought it down slowly, ever so slowly, onto the woman's skull.

As the blow connected, Livia had been straightening up, turning to speak. She could hardly have registered anything before the castor hit her, smashing against the side of the black hood, ripping through into the ear and deeper. She screamed and put her hand up as the force of the blow whirled her backwards. The cot was sent crashing, hurling the baby onto the floor.

Carolyn, also caught off balance by the blow not connecting, sprawled onto the floor. All was chaos: the child, impotent, furious, roaring his complaint: the mother flat on her face, separated from her weapon; the kidnapper, propped up against the bed, shrieking, demented.

It was the professional who recovered first. Still holding her hand to the side of her head she moved instinctively for the weapon. Her right hand closed over it and she crawled across the floor towards Carolyn. Carolyn regained possession in time to see the sawn-off cot leg start the slow, graceful parabola designed to complete itself in contact with her skull. In an instant she changed, her faculties sharp, in command again. Beyond thought, her hand shot out, clasping the castor in mid air. Now the two women were on their knees, facing each other, the weapon held between then. The child silenced, terrorized by the rage around him, the only sound their panting, the other woman's breathing punctuated by the pain.

Unexpectedly, Carolyn dropped her end of the weapon. With a sudden, clear intent she brought the flat of her right hand round and with a vicious thwack caught the woman on the side of her head where the blood was already seeping through the cloth. Livia screamed. She dropped the cot leg, her grasp loosened by the agony, and fell to the floor. Connecting only with her fear, Carolyn seized the weapon and brought it down on her adversary's skull, the weight of her desperation impelling the blow.

There was a sudden release of breath, like a balloon deflating, not even a scream. And then it was over. Livia slay still.

Carolyn froze, the weapon still in her hand, poised for another blow. She looked down at the crumpled body and suddenly everything went blank: the rage, the fear, even the desperation that had propelled her, all drained away. She watched in total transfixed horror as a small stream of blood began to ooze onto the floorboards and flow towards her. She dropped the cot leg dully onto the floor and got up, all power of thought disintegrating.

Just in time, she realized she was losing control, sliding towards a gulf of hysteria from which she might not emerge. She pulled herself back.

She had to get out. And get out fast. Before the man got back. The thought of him returning sharpened her will. She grabbed the baby, bundling him into his coat, and headed for the door.

As she got to the head of the stairs she looked back, just for an instant. There was nothing to see. The room was silent, the body just a blur of clothes against the wood grain of the floorboards. She took a deep breath and fled downstairs.

Chapter Thirty Five

At the bottom of the staircase she found herself confronted by two closed doors. Entering the one on the left she found a dining table with signs of the meal that her captors had recently eaten. She stuffed some bread, cheese and a handful of ham slices into the large pockets of her coat. Through the next door was a hall full of coats and wellingtons. Knowing that she could not survive in her flimsy town shoes she hurriedly searched until she found a pair that looked her size. They were a little big but there was nothing else to be done. Beyond the room was a sitting room. Her eye picked out a record player, books, a whisky bottle. There was a chart on the wall headed 'High Water Times at London Bridge'. That puzzled her but she did not have time to think about it. There was something else she was looking for, a mental note she had made during the planning, but in her frantic passage she could not recollect what it was. Next she came to the kitchen, where she grabbed some bananas and a bar of chocolate and stuck them into a plastic bag. Then she was out through the door, out into the yard, and the free cold air.

She had already decided on an initial plan of action. Straight ahead of the house, where she had seen the sailing ship, was a river or something: whatever it was, it could not be an escape route. She also discounted the gravel road that ran by the house. It was much too exposed, the man might drive up it at any minute. So it had to be the other direction, behind the house into open country. She moved through the back garden and climbed over a low, bramble-covered fence at the side into a ploughed field. A hedgerow stretched beside her. She followed it, passing another scruffy, overgrown garden to her right, and beyond that another small house, built in the same clapboard style, its back door hanging listlessly off its hinges, the whole atmosphere one of waste and abandonment.

From far away came the sound of a car engine. Her heart pounded furiously. Involuntarily she broke into a trot. In the distance a dog barked. She began to run. At the end of the field she crashed into a copse of optimistic young elms, stumbled over a root and almost fell, catching her balance against a tree. This is not the way, she thought. I must collect myself. I have an advantage, and if I stay calm I can hold on to it. I have to think before I act. Don't hurry: he doesn't know which way I've gone.

She looked down at Thomas, who seemed unshaken by the near fall. She hoisted him further up her body, noting the slight ache in her upper arms. He looked all right, but he was suspiciously quiet. She could not remember what had happened to him during the fight. She knew there had been some kind of fall, but already the scene was a blur in her memory. She shook her head. It was pointless to worry about that now. Best to be thankful for his silence and hope that he instinctively understood something of what was going on.

The sound of the car had stopped. It must have arrived at the house. By now the man must be climbing the stairs, coming upon the rag-doll form sprawled across the floor. What would he do? He'd get help, reinforcements. Telephone somebody. In a flash Carolyn remembered what it was she had been looking for in the house. She could have used the phone. She hadn't seen it as she dashed through the rooms. It must have been there somewhere. How stupid! She put the thought to the back of her mind. Whatever she had not done, it was too late now. There were other things to face, like the possibility of him coming after her. That thought got her to her feet again. She started to walk, still keeping close to edge of the field, hiding herself as best she could in the cover provided. Eventually it must lead somewhere, to a road, or another house. At the end of a long field she broke through a gap in the hedge. She found herself on a dirt track, wide enough to take a vehicle.

Something didn't feel right. If this was the farm boundary it was too scrubby, too inconclusive. Ahead there was nothing but a bank of grass, rising up out of nowhere, it seemed, and flanking her to the left and right as far as she could see. She wondered about taking the path, but the bank tantalized. Maybe over its horizon there was a farmhouse, smoke curling from its chimney, and a woman baking bread in the kitchen. She smiled bleakly at her romanticism. Looking carefully around for signs of life, she headed across the path and up the bank.

It was a short but sharp climb, and it left her winded by the sudden exertion. She pulled herself over the skyline, out of sight of the place she'd come from, and flopped to the ground. Wearily she looked up.

What she saw astonished her. Stretching before her was a vast panorama of mud, broken maybe two hundred metres away by the snaking line of an encroaching river. The greyness was total: grey sky, grey water, grey mud. A long way to her right what looked like an estuary opened out into the sea, and against the distant horizon was the blurred outline of a bleak concrete edifice. A nuclear power plant, perhaps. But her immediate view, stretching out into the flatness, was of saltings, corrugated heaps of salty mud, broken by channels and rivulets of water, topped by a pale green slimy weed.

It was a scene of incredible power. Wild and yet so silent and calm, a kind of beauty wrung from its intense desolation. It was uncompromising, it was unearthly. Carolyn was struck with wonder.

She tried to digest the importance of what she was seeing. Before her was a vast expanse of water, a channel of some kind with land a mile away on the other side. Yet behind her, where she had seen the red sailing boat, there was also water. So what was this, a spur of land jutting into the sea, a peninsula? Or an island? She felt suddenly trapped. But wait, her kidnappers had a car, so there must be some kind of land connection or causeway. If she could find that, she was halfway to freedom. She looked to both sides. To her right there seemed nothing but sea, so she chose left, struggling down the bank to the edge of the saltings. Half walking, half running, she set off.

Chapter Thirty Six

Anna parked her car in the drive, surprised to find Alex's Peugeot already in the garage. She pulled off her coat as she went in through the back door, throwing it onto a chair and calling out: 'Hi, I'm home. You're early.'

There was no reply, but from upstairs she thought she could hear voices from the bedroom. She flung her bags down on the table and looked at her watch. 4.30: three hours before they were due to meet Roland and Helen for dinner. Sometime during the evening she would have to find a quiet moment with Roland to feed him more of the stories she had worked out with Daniel. For the rest of the time she would have to act as if there were no conspiracy between her and Roland, and Alex would have to act as if he were not aware of any such conspiracy. But they had been putting on acts like this for years. It should be no problem.

It shouldn't have been a problem, but it was. She was finding her whole life a series of studied hyprocrisies. The excitement of the game was beginning to wear a little thin. Maybe it's the tension of this operation, she thought as she went up the stairs. This one had been getting to everyone.

On the landing she opened the bedroom door. Alex was standing by the bed, stuffing clothes into a holdall. In his hand was a Walther P38. He was checking the magazine, loading it.

'What on earth . .?'

'Trouble,' he said brusquely, not looking up. 'Get some things together. We're going to the island.'

'Why? What's happened?'

'The girl's escaped with the baby. Smashed Livia's skull in with an iron castor. Wolf's out there looking for her.'

'Oh my God.' Anna sat heavily on the bed, the breath suddenly knocked out of her body.

'Come on, Anna. Get ready. We have to go.'

'Is she . .?'

'I don't know. Wolf says she's alive, but unconscious.'

'Where is she? Has he got her to a hospital?'

Alex looked up at her sharply, frowning. 'Don't be stupid, Anna.' He paused, letting the words sink in. 'And start moving, we're late.'

Anna felt stupid. She felt as if someone had just pulled the stuffing out of her brain, leaving her empty inside. She put her head down into one hand, suddenly very tired. She felt a hand on her shoulder, shaking her slightly.

'Annie.' Her husband's voice was kind but impatient. 'Not now. You can do this later, in the car. Now you have to get ready. We should have left already. I couldn't get hold of you.'

'I was out buying some . . . Oh my God.' Her hand shot up to her mouth. 'Roland and Helen . . . we're supposed to be having dinner with them tonight.'

Alex swung away angrily. 'Jesus . . . well, you'd better cancel it.'

'What should I tell them?'

'Christ, Annie, I don't know. Tell them anything. Tell them you've got a headache, or the curse . . . whatever you like.'

'Don't be ridiculous, Alex. I have to have a proper excuse. I'm supposed to be talking to Roland tonight. I can't just duck out.'

He looked up at her again, coldly. 'Well, think of something. But think of it fast. We have to get out of here.'

She got up wearily from the bed. 'O.K. Pack a bag for me. I'll meet you downstairs.'

On the landing she stood for a second collecting her thoughts. All this time I've been waiting for something like this to happen, she thought. Waiting to know how we'd cope when it got rough, how we'd react to each other. We mustn't row. We have to hold it together. She shook her head as if to release the anxiety inside her. Then, reconnecting with her energy, she ran downstairs to the telephone.

On the other end of the line Roland was urbane and sympathetic.

'No, no, no. Don't worry. Things like this happen all the time.'

'Well, not to us they don't. It's not my fault, I swear. I know

I told him, he obviously just wasn't listening. It's even written on the kitchen calendar, as large as life . . . dinner with Helen and Roland. I'm sorry, Roland, it's a ridiculous cock-up, but I really do have to go with him, I gather this client is rather important.'

'Anna, my dear, don't fret, we quite understand.' His voice was light and social, Helen was probably in the room. 'We'll see you both another time. Oh, but yes, there is one thing. One of my colleagues at work has a painting he'd like you to run an expert eye over. Found it in an attic or something. If he brings it into work over the next few days, maybe, say tomorrow or Friday, we can meet for a drink in town and I'll show it to you.'

At the other end of the line Anna drew a sharp breath, thinking on her feet fast.

'Er . . . yes, yes of course. I'd be delighted. But . . . I'm not sure if I can be of any help really, you know. It doesn't sound like my period.'

Roland laughed. 'Oh, my dear, I'm sure you're being modest. No . . . if you do have a moment I know he'd appreciate it, and so would I. I'll give you a call.'

'Um . . . no. I mean I'm going to be doing an awful lot of running around these next few days, Roland. Exhibitions to see, that kind of thing. I tell you what, I'll call you, and we'll fix something up.'

'Fine . . . Good. All right, well give my regards to that scatterbrained husband of yours. Tell him he'll forget his wife one day and that will really serve him right.'

Outside in the car Alex smashed a gloved hand against the dashboard. 'Christ, Anna, how can you possibly have agreed to meet him? We don't know what we're going to find there. We may be on the island for days. Why didn't you make some excuse?'

'Because sometimes, just sometimes, Alex, I can't think ten jumps ahead. How was I to know that he wanted to see me?' She replayed the phone conversation in her head. 'In fact, why does he want to see me? I don't have anything to tell him, so why was he so insistent? Maybe that's the question we should be asking ourselves.'

Alex threw her a dark look. 'We have enough questions without that one. It's all right, Anna. Daniel is sure Roland doesn't suspect anything.'

'I wish, I really wish I could believe that, Alex.'

'Come on, Annie. Don't be ridiculous. He's probably got nothing better to do.'

He turned his attention to the ignition, and they pulled out from the drive. They drove for a while in silence. Alex put his foot down on the accelerator, moving swiftly through the traffic, making good time. When they reached the motorway he turned to her.

'You'd better tell Daniel.'

'Sure. Maybe he could meet Roland instead.'

'What's that supposed to mean?'

'Just what I said. We're all running around like chickens with our heads off and what's he doing? Sitting in his precious study marking exam papers and controlling operations. It didn't occur to him to go down to the island, I suppose?'

Alex looked at her coldly for a second. 'Daniel's on his way there now, if you really want to know.'

'What?'

'He has known Livia for longer than the rest of us, remember?'

Anna dropped her head. 'Oh, my God,' she said through clenched teeth. 'Oh, what an idiot I am.'

She looked ahead at the road disappearing under the tyres. 'Alex, we never should have done this job. It felt wrong, right from the beginning, I said—'

'Cut it out, Annie. Whatever you said is irrelevant now. We did it and now we've got to get on with it. We should have expected problems.'

'Problems!' She heard her own voice rising. 'Livia's lying there with her skull smashed in and you say problems—'

There was a screech of brakes as Alex brought the car to an abrupt halt by the side of the road. He turned to her, his face black.

'Anna, we're in touble. And that means we've all got to keep our wits about us. There isn't any time for recriminations or for a lot of uncontrolled emotion. Do you understand?'

She looked at him without replying. She knew he was right

but she couldn't bring herself to speak. The silence between them grew cold and tangible. She turned her face back to the road and focussed on a line of trees in the distance.

'Why don't we just get back on the road? We've still got a long way to go.'

He looked at her for a few seconds longer, then slammed the car into first gear and took off fast from the grass verge. The rest of the two-hour drive was completed in silence.

Chapter Thirty Seven

On the island the evening came down early, dank and low. Carolyn felt the light draining away from her, mixing into a soft mist over the water's edge. On the right the saltings had given way to a narrow fringe of gravelly beach. The sea was much closer here, only a hundred metres off. The bank continued, giving her a kind of security, but one which she knew to be spurious. It would be easy for her pursuer to climb onto it and so command an excellent view of the route she was following.

But there was no alternative, and after what seemed like hours of freedom she felt as if she had thrown off at least the immediate danger. She was beginning to feel light-headed. This was partly exhaustion – her captivity had left her low on energy – but she understood it was also a reaction to the excitement of the day. The intensity of the emotion was still high inside her. She was acutely aware as she jogged through the silent landscape that she was living through some of the most important hours of her life, and that sense of the extraordinary filled her with a feeling close to euphoria. It was a euphoria that was equally close to madness. The world around her was spinning. Either she span with it, or tried to fight the momentum. Instinctively she joined it.

Dusk was already upon her when she decided to stop and rest. The baby had suddenly become an intolerable burden, his weight exaggerated and heavy in sleep. She came to a small cluster of blackthorn bushes and crawled within its cover. She sat with her back propped against the trunk of a bush, the grey evening creeping across the water towards her, her body sweetly aching with tiredness. Everything was very still.

As she sat looking out to the water Thomas awoke, stirring against her and opening eyes wide with trust. The sight of his little body in motion after so many hours of unholy quiet filled her with a sudden intense happiness. She began the comforting ritual of feeding. She gave him banana, which he liked, and which he had not tasted for two weeks. She broke it up in her hand and put it into his mouth with her fingers. He loved it. She did not give him too much as she realised that his stomach had shrunk and he would only bring it up again. Then she gave him the bottle of baby milk she had brought. He began sucking greedily, but was dozy by the time the bottle was only half empty. She took it away from his mouth and rocked him gently. He lay quietly, watching her solemnly through flickering eyelids which closed and then opened again to check she was still there. She held his gaze, marvelling at his lack of anxiety, at the total trust. He fell asleep again.

She looked out towards the rising river. A bird flew across the water, cutting through the swirling mists, coming to rest only ten feet away. It was black with a long red beak. She found herself entranced by its shape, its movements, its alert, neat appraisal of the world around it. A splash of red against the grey sky, at home in its environment. She sat immobile, also part of the landscape, and she felt content. She felt a unity between her and the rest of the world, a sense of peace in the midst of danger.

She resisted the temptation, suddenly acute, to lie down and go to sleep, to let it all wash over her. That would be insane. She made herself get up, alert again, clutching the baby, walking fast, at once aware of the impending darkness.

A few moments later the bank and the path beside it curved round to the left. She followed it and then, as a new horizon formed itself, she stopped, her heart beating fast.

Away in the distance of the blue-black twilight her eyes registered two pinpricks of light, like the eyes of some monstrous cat lying submerged in the river mud. She watched for a while. The dots flickered, becoming a little sharper, and revealed themselves to be headlights. From their position in what seemed like the middle of the mudflats she realized she must have found the causeway, and that it was still passable.

She also realized that if she could see them, there was just a possibility they could see her, and that, whoever was in the car, they were not her friends. She ducked down, moving back against the bank, covering the red sheen of Thomas's coat with her arms. But as she began to climb the bank, looking for better cover, something made her cautious. Later she would wonder if there had been any sound, or if it was just her soul in tune in that moment with the world around her. Whatever it was, it put her immediately on guard. She wormed her way to the top, to where a gorse bush offered her camouflage. It was through its spiky, stubby shoots that she first saw the two men.

They were standing not twenty metres away from her. One was dressed in a boiler suit and boots, while the other, with his back to her, had the unmistakeable build of her enemy: the solid, square shoulders, the hair still a lighter colour than the rest of the world despite the approaching darkness. Carolyn froze, horrified by their proximity.

But they were not interested in the countryside; they were arguing. The voices were buffeted by the wind which swept the crest of the island.

'Hell, man. Firearms now. What is this?' A heavy East Anglian accent, not the voice of her pursuer. 'I don't like this at all. A bit of honest contraband, that's O.K. But guns, that's another thing altogether.'

'Oh, come on, Frank,' said the other man. The voice made her shiver. 'You know how it is. They're just a little extra protection. We just have to show we mean business. It's not serious.'

'Well, it looks serious to me, stalking across the fields carrying that blunderbuss. Look at it. You could shoot an elephant with it. What kind of gun is it, anyway?'

The man laughed, the laugh lost in the wind. 'It's an AK47. Russian. Don't worry, Frank.There isn't an elephant in sight.'

The other man spoke again, angry, but the words unclear. The wind was turning, sweeping all the sounds before it inland. She heard the word 'no' a couple of times, forcefully spoken by the man in the boiler suit. She began to wonder if she had at last found an ally, but was disturbed to hear laughter, crude and sudden, between them. Then there was a silence. A voice came again, clearer, as if someone had turned in her direction.

'O.K. But I don't want to know any more than I do. Are you expecting people on this evening's tide? Someone's crossing the causeway. It'll be the last vehicle across tonight.'

The other man replied, but this voice was completely lost. She heard them moving off, the grass breaking under their boots, and she lay with heart pounding, waiting for their footsteps to die away. Even when she was sure they were gone she forced herself to wait a little longer. Then she gingerly lifted her head. The farmer had gone. But not her enemy: there he stood, fifty metres to her left, staring out to sea, his assault rifle held loosely in his right hand.

The air was suddenly chilled. With a horrified fascination she watched his head begin to turn to face the spot where she was lying. Desperately she wriggled into the ground, pressing her cheek into the sodden grass. She felt the itch of a small insect clambering up her neck. Thomas, enclosed in her arms, made a small movement which she recognized as the prelude to awakening. She directed all her energy into tranquillizing him through her touch. An agonizingly long minute passed. Then he subsided, gradually resuming his slumber.

The next thing Carolyn heard was the scrape of boots on the gravel road. The man approached, and without pausing passed her hiding place. It was a couple of minutes before she dared risk a look. When she did so she saw him, two hundred metres away, striding purposefully along the path in the direction of the causeway.

Carolyn put her head down onto the wet grass and closed her eyes. She did not open them again for some time. Twilight turned to darkness and folded softly over her.

Chapter Thirty Eight

Anna had made herself very calm by the time the car pulled its way off the mud of the causeway and onto the stony bank that became the island path. Behind them darkness was fast engulfing the river, in front a line of cypresses stood in bleak silhouette on the horizon, caught by a top wind.

Anna loved the island. She had first seen it as a child, when she had been taken sailing in the estuary. Then it had been her romantic dream, the kind of untamed place that every child needs in its make-believe world. Later she had exploited the romance. She had brought Alex here when they were first beginning. They had made love on the beaches of her childhood fantasies, and spent a blustery English summer watching the birds on the mudflats. There had been a lot of love between them then. Later, when the group had been looking for locations, Alex had mentioned it; she had not, and the fact that he was willing to risk the memories had made her angry and sad. Such magic is fragile, and although the island had at first proved strong against intruders, she knew now, as they drove along the path, that the magic was gone, crushed by their corporate realities. And she knew it would never come back.

Across the field they caught sight of Wolf coming towards them. Alex brought the car to an abrupt halt, rolled down the window and put out a hand in greeting. Wolf clasped the hand in a hard wrist-grasp, nodding to Anna. She nodded back.

'No luck?' Alex's voice had already crossed the divide into action. Anna knew that she would not be able to touch him now until something had been exorcized.

'Nothing,' replied Wolf curtly. 'I've searched the buildings and the orchard. She's out somewhere in the open.'

'What about the beach?'

'I've covered half of it. No sign.'

'And the causeway?'

'I've checked it regularly. She wouldn't have found it yet. Anyway, it's closing now, isn't it?'

The wind had sprung up around them, scattering their words as they hit the air.

'Almost. Daniel will just make it. If she tries anything now he'll see her. After that, it'll be too late.'

Across the car Anna spoke. 'What about Livia?'

'I don't know.' Wolf shook his head. 'She's still unconscious.'

'And Frank?'

'Don't worry about Frank. He won't cause any trouble.'

Wolf took a step back from the car. 'I'm going to stay here and wait for Daniel, then try the other side of the copse.'

'O.K. I'll meet you at the house, or follow you out.'

Alex rolled the window back up. Anna felt the chill in the night air. She was in a heated car: what could the woman and child be feeling now? That was not her problem, she told herself, roughly stamping out the images in her mind. A few hundred yards along, the path became completely obscured, trees on either side reaching over to blot out the sky. No, she thought, there is no magic left here now.

When Alex stopped the car outside the little clapboard house she got out immediately, leaving him to park the car and bring in the bags. There would be no talking between them now either.

Upstairs, the room where Carolyn and her child had spilled so much emotional energy was empty, the door hanging carelessly wide. The door opposite was closed. It now held another prisoner. Anna went in quietly, her feelings numbed against what she might find.

It was a small room, monklike in its starkness. No doubt a century ago it would have slept four or five children, whilst their parents conceived more in the next bedroom. But now there was just a single bed by the window, its sheets and blankets hardly disturbed by the narrow shape of the body beneath. Livia's head was heavily bandaged. Wolf had done a good job. Anna was grateful for the coverings. It meant she did not have to look at what was beneath them. Not yet anyway.

She moved closer. Livia was lying utterly still, stiller than Anna could ever remember seeing her. The sight touched a memory inside her of a night when they had slept next to each other in a barn, during one of the early jobs. She remembered then looking at the same face caught in sleep. But this time it looked different. The stillness was more powerful, and that frightened Anna even more than the white face and drawn lips.

She studied her for a few minutes. In the early years of the cell, before the operations had started, Anna had been sent on a field medical course. She had learnt to set and splint broken limbs, to clean and dress wounds, even learnt when it was better to leave the injury completely alone. But she had been lucky, they had all been lucky. There had been few opportunities to put that knowledge into practice, and when there had been, it was, of course, Livia as the trained medic who had taken control. It was the final irony now that the physician could not heal herself.

'Livia?' She spoke softly but distinctly, her mouth close to her comrade's ear, the good ear.

In the silence that followed, Livia's eyes flicked open, staring straight ahead of her. The pupil of her left eye was enlarged. Anna understood immediately that she could not or would not move her head. She bent her own body over the bed so that she could look down directly into her friend's face.

'Hello,' she said.

Livia moistened her lips. 'Hello.' A ghost of a smile. 'Have they?'

Anna shook her head. 'No, not yet. But they will.'

Livia moved her lips. The voice was faint. 'Is Daniel . . . here?'

'He's on his way. Are you in pain?'

'No.'

'Can I get you anything?'

Livia closed her eyes, then just as slowly opened them again. 'No,' she whispered softly. There was a pause. Both women knew the question that was in the air.

'Livia?'

The woman on the bed took in a breath slowly, collecting her energy; every word was expensive. 'Don't know,' she finally managed to say.

Anna put her hand on her friend's arm, and said nothing, not trusting her voice to stay steady. She straightened up. Livia closed her eyes immediately, as if relieved that the audience was over.

Downstairs Alex was standing in the kitchen, pulling on a pair of boots, the side of his coat bulging where the automatic lay next to his hip. Daniel appeared in the doorway, Wolf right behind him.

Anna was looking at her husband. She shook her head and swallowed hard. 'I don't know . . . I don't know.'

Daniel moved past Alex, putting a hand on his shoulder. He did the same to Anna, and then went up the stairs. Anna did not move, or respond in any way.

'Anna!' She heard the note of metal, the warning in Alex's tone. She blinked once or twice fiercely. Wolf clapped his hands together, as if impatient to start. He looked at her sharply. 'She'll be O.K. If it was a serious fracture she'd never have regained consciousness.'

Anna started. 'You know that's not true. We've no way of knowing how much internal damage there is.'

'I tell you, she's all right,' said Wolf sharply. He turned away from her, picking up the gun propped up against the wall. 'O.K.?' he said to Alex.

Anna realized that, as always, they each had their own method of dealing with horror. Wolf's was just different from hers. Alex nodded, buttoning up his jacket, Wolf tossed him a hood. 'Put this on if you spot her. We don't want to fuck it up any more by having her recognise us.'

They turned. 'We'll be back when we've got her.' Alex's voice reached back from the doorway. Then they were gone, the door banging dully on the catch behind them. Anna stood for a moment watching them move off into the cold dusk, then turned inside.

The sitting room was cold, with last night's fire still in the grate. She wished it was warm, wished that she could simply curl up in front of it until the day was over. Once again the thought of the woman out there somewhere in the darkness came back to her. What could she be experiencing now, with night around her and a fist of fear in her stomach?

In general Anna was much tougher than her sleek appearance led people to believe. Since she was a child people had consistently underestimated Anna to their cost, until Alex, that is, and Daniel. She was not worried about cracking up. Despite the pressure she knew she could do her job. But there was something in the plight of this girl which had penetrated her barriers and reminded her of herself. They shared something, she and this woman. Not just a privilege of birth, or the confidence that money buys. It was something else, something in this woman's character that had made them underestimate her – to their cost.

Above her she heard the floorboards creak. Daniel was moving about the room. The noise broke through her thoughts, and she turned purposefully back into the kitchen. She took a torch off a hook on the wall and went out into the yard to collect some logs. Since it was not her job to do the hunting, she might as well get on with the cooking. Later, whatever happened, people would be hungry.

Chapter Thirty Nine

Outside it was cold. The wind had swept a chill in from the water, a damp which clung to the gorse bushes and the grass, even coated the pebbles on the beach.

The sweat of fear on her body had turned cold also. The coat she was wearing no longer brought any comfort, and the only source of warmth was the small, pulsating body which was now pressed close to her skin, with her coat buttoned up over him.

She was standing with her back against the edge of the sea-wall, looking out onto the rising tide. A little in front of her the causeway ran like a ribbon out into the channel of water. About a hundred yards out she could see a film of water over the path, then further on it re-emerged onto dry land. Beyond that there was just darkness swallowing everything. She could not see where the path met the land on the other side, although she knew it must be at least half a mile across. But what she did see was enough to make her afraid.

Carolyn knew now that her only chance of freedom lay on that narrow strip of gravel. She understood that the island was not very big, that it held little shelter, and that with reinforcements it would be only a matter of time before they found her – if not tonight then tomorrow morning, and if the night got colder she might not make it through to morning anyway. Certainly by the time the tide had drained again, exposing the path, it would be light, and the causeway would be under constant surveillance.

From a hiding place in the bushes she had seen both cars cross from the mainland and disappear out of sight inland. The fact that they had left the causeway unguarded – and there was no sign of it being watched – worried her. Did that mean it was no longer safe to cross? Certainly if she waited she would be sure to fail. There was only one thing to be done: she had to take the risk of crossing now. She also knew that with each second's delay the risk grew greater. But still she stood there, her mind numbed by the fear of the darkness ahead. The baby wriggled against her skin. It was a small, sleepy movement, a rearrangment of cramped limbs, a statement of his faith in her protection, and in that instant it made her fear for him larger than her fear for herself. She began to walk.

Out in the open on the edge of the causeway she paused to look around her: nothing, no sound, no shadows. No one was waiting for her. Night was upon them, a sliver of a moon poking through fast clouds, shedding little light on the black, swirling waters ahead. She took the first few steps along the path. The gravel crunched under her feet. The noise smashing through the silence seemed so intrusive and echoing that she stopped, half thinking the footsteps had come from behind her. But no: she was alone and no one could hear her. The rising waters blurred the edges of the sound; only a bird would distinguish it as human rather than natural. She began to walk fast, or as fast as the uneven ground would allow her. In front the path was still dry, save for a few puddles in the hollows.

At first the causeway led downwards. Ahead of her, over the stones and boulders which marked the edges of the track, water was trickling inwards in tiny but constant rivulets. She had no idea what that implied, no way of telling how fast the path was closing. Anyway it was too late now. She quickened her stride. As she moved forwards the water began to lap gently at the edges of her boots, the cold seeping through into the ends of her toes and the soles of her feet.

After four or five minutes the water seemed to lessen, and ahead she could see the path dry again. She relaxed, becoming gently mesmerized by the rhythm of the silence and the lack of human souls. This piece of the earth was not used to human footsteps. She had often wondered what atmosphere nature created for itself when left entirely alone. Now each footstep took her further into that void. She was awed by the darkness, oppressed by a sudden, cold loneliness. The silence was not peaceful – it was dense and alive with sensations she could not identify. She realized that whatever atmosphere had been created here it could not be shared by humans; it was too powerful for any single person to handle. Her trespassing made her an intruder.

Abruptly, without warning, the mud close to her erupted, and a thrashing of wings and a screeching above her head made her catch her breath. She ducked and cringed. The baby slipped downwards in her grasp, and she let out a cry as she struggled to keep hold of the little form. Over her head to the left the bird replied with a perfect single note, wheeling off into the darkness leaving her alone again. She regained her balance and stood, trembling, waiting for the thudding in her chest to stop and for the silence to return.

Ahead of her the moon slipped out from behind the clouds into a stretch of clear sky, and illuminated the world around her. What was revealed in that moment's vision told her that she had failed. All around her the river was pouring in across the causeway, taking over the land. Hundreds of little streams were gushing greedily over the stones and flooding onto the path. Moving her eyes from the swirls of water in front, she looked at the sides. There that takeover was almost complete. A shaft of moonlight ran across a long, shining sheet of water. No rocks, no mudflats disturbed its even surface. The land was covered and it was getting deeper and deeper by the minute. Ahead of her the path was under water for as far as she could see, and then there was only darkness inky and impenetrable, filled with the rising sound of the sea.

In that instant she knew that escape was no longer the issue, that there were other kinds of death closer to her. Instinctively she turned and began to go back, her feet sucking in and out of the water with each step. It was getting higher now, rising up near the top of her boots. Progress was harder, it was impossible to run. The baby was a dead weight against her, pulling her down. In her haste she stumbled and almost fell. The decision to return had come too late. She could feel the panic mounting inside her, the sound of her pulse in her ears blocking out thought.

It was then that there flashed into her mind how it had been when, as a child, she had swum too far out to sea, away from her father's arms. In those few seconds when she had believed that she was going to die she had crossed from childhood into an adult world. She had the same sensation now: a sudden, clear knowledge that she was very close to death. The ferocity of that revelation broke through the panic for a moment, giving her a clarity of vision that allowed her to regain control, if only for an instant. She forced her eyes from the black liquid engulfing her legs, and focussed instead on the edge of the island, silhouetted in the distance, but nearer than it had been. If she kept her wits about her she should be able to make it back and cheat death a second time. That knowledge gave her sudden courage. She made herself slow down, bracing her body against the force of the incoming tide, feeling for a firm foothold before she committed herself, making each step sure instead of frantic.

The painful pace continued, the water still rising, up over her knees by now, surging against her, almost bowling her over. Her boots were waterlogged, making her legs intolerably heavy and numbing her feet. The tide was flowing in at an angle, its current pulling her towards the edge of the causeway, where the mudflats would envelop her. She gritted her teeth, willing herself to keep a straight course. The new-found courage ebbed away, leaving her alone and frightened, unable to silence the drumbeat of the blood thudding behind her eyes.

Then slowly, as if nature had capriciously granted her a last minute reprieve, the water level began to drop, the ground rising to meet the edge of the shelf of land. She moved faster, leaving the fear behind her, and suddenly she was on dry land, the water already just a dark memory behind her. Directly ahead she could see the path again and beyond it the black shape of the land filling the horizon. She closed her eyes for a moment, her throat blocked by the sobs of relief, tears pouring down her cheeks. She had made it, she was safe.

When she opened them again she saw, through the gloom, fifteen yards in front of her, the figure of the man, waiting silently for her on the edge of the island.

She looked at him for a long time. Neither of them moved. Then she dropped her head and began walking towards him. She knew then that she had lost, and that the price of her failure could mean death, for both her and her child.

Chapter Forty

It was 11.30 p.m. when Roland Jarvis came out of Green Park underground station. He headed north into the labyrinth of Mayfair, through traffic jams and late night crowds pouring out of theatres and restaurants, until he reached Curzon Street. Crossing between two silver Rolls Royces parked near the Christian Scientist Church, he approached a large, brick building which in some ways resembled a conventional department store. Its appearance was so bland as almost to draw attention to itself. The ground-floor windows, like those of the Bank of England – and for similar reasons – had been bricked up and plastered over, and no plaque or sign could be seen on any of the doors. The upper windows were obscured by Civil Service off-white curtains. The only eccentric detail which might have betrayed the nature of the building to any passers-by curious enough to crane their necks was the collection of large radio aerials on the roof.

Jarvis showed his pass to the security men and took the lift up to the fourth floor. As the lift doors opened he was confronted by his colleague Halliwell, briefcase in hand and ready to leave.

'Evening, Gerald. Working late?'

'I could say the same about you.' Even outside Macclesfield's office they treated each other with scant courtesy.

'Any news on Skidelski?'

'I gather he's arrived. I don't know what progress has been made, if any. By the way—'

'Good,' said Jarvis, terminating the conversation. They parted company and Jarvis entered his office, locking the door behind him.

On his desk there was a pile of mail, which he ignored, moving straight for the computer terminal in the corner. The computer itself, a Dual ICL 2980, was housed in a nearby building in Mount Row; it was linked to the computers of the Inland Revenue, the Department of Health and Social Security, the Department of Employment, the Police, as well as many other of the two hundred computers used by central government. Jarvis sat in front of the VDU and punched in his own code, a combination of letters and numbers which unlocked the machine and enabled him to obtain information on most of the individuals whose data was stored there.

Michael Skidelski, he learned (d.o.b. 21/2/1948. N.I. No. YK 69 97 61 D) was also known as Lawrence Burnley, Terry Merchant. Born Hereford. Polish father, refugee 1939, fought in the RAF. Irish mother. Educated Hereford Grammar School, London School of Economics. Active in various pressure groups, particularly Vietnam Solidarity Campaign. Not known to have been a member of any political party. Known agitator during student unrest at LSE 1966–68. Arrested and convicted twice: 1968, obstruction (during Grosvenor Square demonstration); 1971, possession of cannabis.

Jarvis skimmed through this with only marginal interest. There were thousands of files like this one. Most of the subjects had two kids and a mortgage by now. It was what had happened since that interested him. He read on.

There was a follow-up from an officer who had reviewed the case in 1979. It said, in part: 'After his career as a student activist, Skidelski travelled for long periods in Asia and South America. He is believed to have supported himself through drugs trafficking. After 1975 he settled in Plymouth and worked casually in the building trade. No evidence to suggest recent political or criminal activity.'

So much for that surveillance. Jarvis made a mental note of the reviewing officer's name.

Medical, social security, bank, police and other records followed. There was a photograph, a copy of a passport snap dated 1974. A man with a dark, curly beard and long hair stared at him from the VDU. Jarvis looked at him long and thoughtfully. Then he picked up the telephone and dialled. After some difficulty he got through to the man he wanted.

'Inspector Carr? Jarvis here. Security Service. How's Skidelski?'

'Nothing yet, and to be frank I'm not sure he's going to give. Care to join us?'

'Later maybe. If you do get anything, give me a ring, will you? Time's getting short.'

'O.K. But I don't promise miracles. I'm not really sure he knows that much.'

Jarvis put his finger on the receiver button, released it and then dialled an outside number. Twyford 35592. He let it ring. There was no answer. Alex and Anna were still out. There was nothing particularly suspicious about that, it was early yet. Jarvis sat back in his chair and blew out his cheeks. This assignment was the most crucial of his career. Not only was it the biggest operation he had controlled, but he had chosen to handle it in a rather unconventional way. Macclesfield had made it clear that his approval was only tacit. A success would make his reputation, but if things went wrong Jarvis was in no doubt whose head would be first to roll. He wondered, not for the first time, if he had been wise to adopt such a softly-softly approach.

He unlocked the bottom drawer of his desk and took out an orange file. It contained typed reports, photocopies of documents and a number of photographs, as well as notes made in his own neat handwriting. He had kept it in his drawer for some six months, referring to it almost daily. It was the dossier on Alex and Anna Weston.

In the beginning their names were just two of scores obtained through the source known as 'Luis'. The yield was so rich that the Service could hardly manage to follow all of them up – particularly given the special constraints of caution and security necessary in this operation. At first the Westons had been thought unpromising. It seemed unlikely that people leading such impeccably bourgeois lives could be involved in terrorism. Cover of some kind was expected, but this seemed just too elaborate to be false. Nevertheless, a routine investigation was carried out, and this had thrown up some intriguing facts.

'Alexander Graham Weston', read this first report, 'born 1944, educated Magdalen College, Oxford; VSO in Indonesia 1965–67; BBC researcher 1968–69, director 1969–71; company director Challenge Travel Ltd. since 1973 . . .' An unremarkable biography, but not to MI5. Exterminating Angel's videos demanded technical expertise, and for years they had been looking for a suspect with just such a television background. Nowadays all TV producers and directors and most journalists were automatically entered in the Registry, but this policy had only been introduced in 1972, lack of funds having prevented it before then.

The survey on Anna provided further cause for suspicion. Her attendance at LSE at a particularly stormy phase of student politics . . . the surprising change of direction to postgraduate courses at the Royal College of Art and posts at Sotheby's . . and, most damning of all, the revelation that many of her clientele were colleagues and acquaintances of victims of Exterminating Angel.

So it was decided to find out more about Mr and Mrs Weston. The kind of surveillance was discussed at some length. To have the suspects followed would be risky. Even someone of only average tradecraft could spot a tail, and the Westons, it had to be assumed, were more than average. The use of bugging devices in their home was ruled out on similar grounds. It was Jarvis who came up with the unusual suggestion that he himself would work under cover; he would strike up an acquaintance and thus observe them. The reason he gave was quite simple. The Jarvises lived in Basingstoke, only ten miles from the Westons' home near Winchester. The two couples inhabited the same social world; they probably already had friends in common. Jarvis was ideally placed to carry out this task.

The real reason was more complex. Jarvis's career as a street man had not been entirely auspicious. This had dogged his later reputation as an operations officer. He was regarded, somewhat unfairly, as sound but not brilliant. At forty-two it was possible his career had already peaked. He needed a coup to ensure promotion to a position consistent with his high self-regard.

Infiltration had proved unexpectedly easy. A mutual friend (a member of Alex's squash club) was found and an introduction arranged. In no time Jarvis and his wife became part of the Westons' circle. The work was engrossing, but fruitless: the evidence remained circumstantial. Anna parried Jarvis's probes with consummate skill; or perhaps she was, after all, just innocent. As a matter of course their phone was being tapped and their mail intercepted, but that had proved singularly uninteresting. Nevertheless something niggled. They played their parts superbly, yet something rang hollow. Anna's politics degree, for instance; she was undoubtedly bright, but came over blasé and surprisingly uninformed about current affairs. Alex's past was equally opaque. Any curiosity about his pre-travel business career led to a subtle but definite change of subject. Jarvis felt frustrated. Perhaps they had seen through him and were maintaining their cover whilst preparing to flee. He did not think so, though. If something were amiss, Luis would have reacted. And Luis remained blissfully ignorant, apparently, of MI5's interest.

Then came the Lindop affair. Alex's suspicious absence in the North (and his cool return in the middle of the dinner party) reassured Jarvis and gave him a growing confirmation of their guilt. Jarvis was delighted. It was the vindication of his skill as an agent and of his faith in the project. Evidence against the Westons was building up. Akeroyd had not seen his kidnappers, except for a brief moment, and one bearded policeman with his cap down can look much like another. But he had heard them, and the voice of a masked man with a gun pointed at you is not something you forget in a hurry. Jarvis was confident Akeroyd would be able to pick him out. The next step, clearly, was for MI5 to pass on this information to the police.

It was not, however, what Jarvis had in mind. He knew what an arrest would bring. The Anti-Terrorist Branch would interrogate them, and probably learn very little, but they would secure a conviction, and maybe one or two other members of the gang would go down too. It would be the end of Exterminating Angel, at least for a while, and everybody would congratulate one another. But in time the organization would reform, outrages would start all over again, and this time the Security Service would have no means of observing them. In the long run it was better, surely, to leave things as they were, at least until there was some clear strategic or political advantage to taking action.

To arrest them would be against all Jarvis's principles. It would defeat his object. He was not just interested in the terrorists. By themselves they were nothing. Successful subversion depended on the support of well-placed civil servants, lawyers, journalists – the liberal intelligentsia. These covert radicals had to be identified, isolated and discredited. Very discreetly, of course: M15 was supposed to be a 'secret' service. Secrecy always implied deviousness, and to conceal things from your enemy it was sometimes necessary to deceive your friends. Jarvis saw nothing wrong in that. Subversion existed autonomously, acting according to its own rules. It was only logical that its opponents do likewise.

Macclesfield was less convinced about Jarvis's views. He had not succeeded to department head by being foolhardy, and he saw more clearly than Jarvis the risks to public order and good relations with the police. In the end Luis was the crucial factor. Arrest of the Westons would certainly have been traced back to him. And it was considered absolute priority that Luis not be compromised.

Outside the Curzon Street office Jarvis could hear the call of a tawny owl which visited from nearby Hyde Park. He lit a small cigar and put his feet up on the desk. He went back to the file, turning over the pages until he found the item on Anna that had inspired him. It was the photocopy of her medical record. Complaints of backache . . . termination of pregnancy in 1980 . . . recent prescriptions for Mogadon.

Jarvis had been surprised. Hadn't Anna once mentioned to Helen that she and Alex were unable to have children? Jarvis had tried to fit these facts into the picture he had formed of her, the bright, controlled social front she had presented. The signs of stress were interesting. Could it be that the life of a revolutionary was beginning to pall? Middle age approaching, opportunities missed? Something, obviously, was wrong: how could he exploit it?

He would recruit her. She could hardly refuse, if she was who she said she was. To do otherwise would be out of the character of her cover. What's more, Jarvis could be confident that, because of Luis, his offer would be taken exactly on face value. So Anna Weston was made to sign the Official Secrets Act. She told him nothing useful, but that was not the point. He had made a wedge, and later, when the time was right, he would drive it in.

Jarvis put down the file and took another puff at his cigar, blowing the smoke into the stale air. They had caught Skidelski. He was being interrogated and as far as Anna and her friends were concerned, he might be saying all kinds of incriminating things. Jarvis now had the pretext and the pressure point he had been waiting for. Would the time ever be more right? He reached out for the phone and dialled an internal number.

'Hello, Duty Officer? This is Jarvis, G9. I'll need a man in the morning, at six . . . Who? Boyd? Fine. And a car . . . Good. . . And one more thing. Send him along to the stores . . . Yes, I want him armed . . . Right. Good night.'

Chapter Forty One

Anna was sitting in front of the fire when they brought Carolyn home. She heard Wolf's voice, rough and loud, calling out orders, and she knew from his tone that the search was over. She listened as steps echoed up the stairs and the door above opened. She sat still, thinking about the room they were entering, the cold air and the scrubbed bloodstain in the middle of the floor. She should be doing something, involving herself in the drama above, and she realised that her reticence had to do with the woman. She did not want to know what was going on upstairs. So she sat immobile staring hard into the flames.

Behind her the door opened and Alex came in, pulling off his hood and gloves and tossing them into the chair opposite her. He came up behind her and leaned his head over, searching for her lips. It was a familiar gesture, but this time she did not respond.

He straightened up, aware of her rejection but choosing to ignore it. He slumped down in the chair opposite, letting out a long breath, blowing it through his cheeks.

She watched him from what seemed a long way away. 'Where was she?' she said at last.

'In the middle of the causeway. Incredible. She nearly killed herself.'

'Who found her?'

'Wolf. He was looking very hard. He obviously knew she might try something like this. He almost went after her, but then she turned back of her own accord.'

'Did he hurt her?'

Alex shrugged. 'I don't think so. She was too scared. She walked straight into his arms. I think she'd had enough.'

Anna said nothing, thinking about the island at night. Then she asked: 'And the baby?'

Again a careless gesture, as if it were an effort to speak. 'Seems O.K. I think they're both of them knocked sideways by the cold. Maybe even in shock a little.'

'Does she want some food?'

'Perhaps later. Wolf's up there now. Leave them for a while.'

From the room above she heard voices, muffled but loud. The woman's voice said 'no', an edge of fear in it. She stood up involuntarily. Alex looked up at her and shook his head.

'Leave it, Anna. He knows what he's doing.'

'And just what is he doing?'

'I expect he's showing her the damage she's caused.'

The remark penetrated and Anna sat down.

Upstairs in the smaller bedroom Carolyn was standing against the wall, Wolf's hand tight around her wrist. A few yards away Livia lay sleeping, her face drained of all colour. Carolyn had turned from the sight, but it was clear she had registered it. Her shoulders began to heave slightly, and she dropped her head and began to cry, a soft rhythmic sorrow, releasing the tension and washing away the shame of her weakness. By her side Wolf shook her, turned her to face him, pinning her arms to her sides, his fingers digging into her flesh.

'Do you see her? Do you see what you've done? I could kill you, you know. I could kill you now. An eye for an eye.'

But despite the violence of the words there was no anger in his voice, no real threat. What they were going through was ritual, nothing else. She shook her head slowly in a deliberate movement, keeping her eyes down. There was no more spirit in her, no more defiance. She wished he would leave her alone to let out the pain in private. But she understood that part of her punishment was this public admission of weakness, of defeat. She didn't care. She was beyond the need to preserve any form of appearance.

He pulled her head upwards, impatient for a response. She let him do it, let her eyes come up to meet his through the slits of his mask.

'Well?' He was demanding something. She gave it instinctively.

'I'm sorry,' she said simply.

The victory was so easily won that she knew he was disappointed, that her weakness had somehow not satisfied him. She had held her own, even in defeat. He let his arms drop and stood looking at her. She knew he would not hit her, as she had at first feared, would not threaten her or demand anything more. It was over. The tension between them was dissipated. All that remained was the taste of stale hatred. He pushed her slightly away from him and she walked of her own accord out of the room, across the hall and into her cell. She moved like a zombie, without thought, and went straight in and lay on the bed, face down into the pillow.

Downstairs Wolf strode into the sitting room. Disregarding the atmosphere he found there he said to Alex: 'Watch her, will you? I'm going for a walk.' He turned, throwing a remark back over his shoulder to Anna. 'Maybe you'd better give her something to eat. She's exhausted.'

Anna looked up. 'What are we going to do with her?'

Standing in the doorway he shrugged. 'Who knows? Kill her, let her go. Daniel will know, why don't you ask him? We only do the work, he has all the thoughts.' He left, slamming the kitchen door behind him.

They sat in silence. Then Anna got up and went into the kitchen. She cut some bread and cheese and put them on a tray with a glass of orange juice. Outside the locked door upstairs she hesitated. She put down the tray, pulled on a mask, unlocked the door and went in. The room was still. The baby in the cot was sleeping. His mother lay face down, crying. Anna walked over to the table, setting the tray down with a clatter. She stood looking at the figure on the bed.

'I've brought you some food,' she said, making her own voice lighter, more nondescript than usual.

No response. Anna knew that she should leave, should turn around and walk out, locking the door behind her, but instead she sat down on the bed, watching the prostrate figure, following the rhythm of her rib cage as it clutched out for breath and then exhaled sharply with a sob. It looked like a painful process. She put out a hand and touched the girl's back. She felt her skin hot and sweaty through the wool of the sweater. She let her hand slide across the woman's back, let it linger for a second, then lifted it off. She repeated the action slowly. Again. And again. Time passed. Anna sat there caressing the sorrow out of the woman she had helped to kidnap. She said nothing: there was nothing to say. Gradually the sobs began to quieten. The contractions of her body began to level out. Then there was a silence, a long, powerful silence when the meaning of the gesture became apparent to them both. Anna was shaken by the exactness of the communication. She shook her head deliberately although the girl could not see the movement.

'I'm sorry. I can't help you. But I won't let them hurt you.'

The girl moved her head slightly, turning her face out of the pillow to stare at the wall, her eyes close to the dirty, smudged paintwork. 'You're too late. You're too late. It's all been done.'

Anna withdrew her arm, suddenly afraid of contact. She stood up.

'Eat something. You'll need your strength if you're going to get through. Eat, please.'

The woman on the bed flipped over suddenly, looking up at her, her face puffy and scarred from the tears. Anna stared back, mesmerized by the look. Yes, she recognized the face. It was a face she had seen many times before, at school, at tennis parties, at cocktail evenings. She knew this woman. She had grown up with so many like her.

The woman rubbed her cheek bones with her knuckles. 'You can't change anything this way, you know,' she whispered. Her voice was muffled and hoarse. 'All you do is cause more pain.'

Anna stiffened, saying nothing but unable to move. Carolyn

continued to look at her. Then, with a gesture of infinite sadness, she turned on her stomach again, buried her face into the pillow, and said: 'Leave me alone.'

Anna turned on her heels and went straight out of the room, not looking back for an instant. She locked the door and stood on the landing outside, trembling. Then she laughed, a sudden, brittle laugh, and moved across to the other door, behind which her friend was lying, one part of her skull bleeding slowly into another. She couldn't change anything. All she did was cause more pain. There was nothing more to say.

Later, downstairs by the fire, she and Alex began to quarrel. They both knew it would happen, were both edgy and ready. He hid his anger better, though; on the surface he appeared more rational.

'It's getting to you,' he said softly.

She shrugged, keeping herself clamped tight inside. 'No, I'm fine. Just tired, that's all.'

He came round, handed her the coffee and sat down opposite her. She dropped her eyes from his gaze.

'Anna, you'd better let it out.'

She pursed her lips, saying nothing.

'Anna,' he repeated. 'You can't lay this thing on other people, not now. Everyone has to handle their own tension. We can't work against one another like this. You've been whirling out in space ever since we got into the car this afternoon. We need you on the ground. I need you on the ground. Here.'

Need, she thought. Men always 'need' women. Need them, want them, desire them. They seemed barren emotions. She looked up.

'You don't need me, Alex. You're doing quite well alone.' He did not reply. 'You're still enjoying it, aren't you, in some way?'

He sighed impatiently. 'We've had this conversation before. This is what we do. This is our life. If you want to say "enjoy" – O.K., in some way I enjoy it.'

'Even now?'

He shrugged. 'It doesn't always run smooth. That's part of it.'

'And that makes you withdrawn sometimes, tense?'

'Sometimes, yes.'

'Then it's the same with me. I just want to be left alone, O.K.?'

He frowned at her for a moment, then nodded slowly. 'O.K., Annie, O.K. But there are things you're not telling me. Now if you can handle them, fine. But if you can't . . . then you risk the whole operation by—'

'The whole operation!' Something inside her snapped. She felt it go. 'Fuck the operation, Alex. What about us? What about the risk to us, you and me?'

He did not flinch. 'All right, what about us, you and me? What's wrong with us?'

She shook her head. 'Nothing,' she said flatly.

'No, Annie, not nothing. Something. Something big. You're so far away from me. I can feel you out there, hating me. Everyone can feel it. You may think you're hiding it, keeping it together, but you're not. Your vibrations are bouncing off the walls in all directions. I'm not even sure whose side you're on any more.'

They stared at each other, the chasm opening up wider between them.

'Maybe Daniel was right,' he said tautly.

'What do you mean?' she snapped.

He sighed. 'Before it began. He said it might freak you. Said maybe we should keep you out of it altogether. I told him he was wrong. Obviously he wasn't.'

'Oh yes,' she said, her mouth thin with anger. 'And just what else did Daniel say to you that he didn't dare say to me?'

He watched her carefully, picking his words. 'He said that it was going to be tough for you because she was like you. That she might remind you of yourself. That her innocence might turn you soft, confuse you. Fairly accurate as it turns out, don't you think?'

Anna looked away, towards the fire. A log split in two, sending sparks spitting out into the hearth.

'Regular little psychoanalyst, isn't he? Is that why we joined the cell, Alex? To get our therapy free?'

He ignored her. 'Is he right, Anna?'

'Oh Christ, how should I know?' She got up, restless suddenly. 'Yes, her innocence freaks me out. Yes, I wonder what we've become. She's so ordinary, Alex. There's no evil in her, not even any violence except the violence we've caused.'

Alex opened his mouth, but she stopped him. 'Yes, I know what you're going to say. That it was necessary. That we discussed it. It had to be done. I know all the answers, all the incontestable ideological truths, I understand them all. But what I don't understand are the feelings. The feelings that I have and you don't share. The confusions, the sentimentality, call it what you will. Because you don't share them, do you? You don't really understand what I'm talking about. Do you? . . . Do you?' She repeated the question softly.

The silence sat heavy between them.

'I don't know what to say, Anna. Of course I wish it hadn't happened like this . . . but . . .' He trailed off, not wanting to find the right words because he knew they would hurt her.

'But the excitement is still the same.' She finished the thought for him. 'That knot is still inside you?'

He shrugged. He seemed about to reply, then changed his mind.

'And it would be the same if I were upstairs and she were down here.'

'Oh, for Christ's sake, Anna.' His voice was suddenly very angry. 'Don't be ridiculous.'

'I'm not being ridiculous, Alex. She is me. I could be that guilty.'

Alex knew inside that he should be responding to her pain. She needed his love a great deal at that moment. He put out a hand inside himself to locate that part of him that was Anna, to draw on the spring of love to comfort her. He put out the hand, but he could not find what he was looking for. He stared at her with a kind of horror and wished that she would stop, and become the old Anna again. She shouldn't ask this of him, not here, not now.

He smiled and took hold of her hand. 'Annie,' he said tenderly.

She sensed the lie, and withdrew her fingers as if his touch had burnt her.

'It's been a long day. We're both tired,' he said, the smile fainter on his lips now the physical contact was lost. 'I do understand everything you say, Annie. We'll talk about it. But not tonight. Why don't you go to bed? You'll feel better in the morning. There'll be less strain then, I promise you.'

She turned away from him immediately and walked towards the door, her movements numb.

He grabbed her hand again. 'Annie, I love you,' he said firmly, wanting the words to take away his inadequacy, to bridge the gap between them.

She smiled vaguely, as if her thoughts were somewhere else. 'I'm sure you do, Alex. The question is, is it enough any more?'

Without waiting for an answer she walked past him, out of the door and upstairs.

He sat staring into the fire for a long time. Before he met Anna, Alex had had a series of affairs with women; women whom he had liked and got on well with, but whom he hadn't loved. These affairs had always ended up the same way – with him cooling off, finding no excitement any more, feeling trapped and leaving them. It wasn't their fault. There was so much energy and idealism in Alex and no way to express it. Then came Exterminating Angel and for the first time in his life Alex knew what he was here for. What incredible fortune, he often thought, to have all that and Anna as well. But it was always a delicate balance. For Wolf and Livia and Daniel it would have been out of the question; they knew their way of life could not be shared. Perhaps now he, too, would have to make that choice.

He raised the whisky bottle and squinted through the amber liquid at the still-red ashes in the grate. Or perhaps he was slightly drunk and more than slightly maudlin. After the operation was over they'd go away, he and Anna, maybe take a holiday in the sun somewhere, and they'd talk, really talk, they'd sort it all out and then things would be all right again.

Chapter Forty Two

Anna slept for three hours after she left Alex. Wolf returned later and also went to bed, throwing his fully-clothed body onto a mattress in the dining room and falling asleep immediately. Downstairs Alex stayed watching the fire burn low, while Daniel kept vigil over Livia. In the room upstairs Carolyn also slept, too exhausted to do anything else. Outside, a frost came down, coating the island with ice crystals and painting lace-pattern cracks on the windows of the cottage.

At around 3 a.m., when the night was at its blackest, Livia's condition became measurably worse. She had lost consciousness again soon after Daniel arrived, but her breathing and her pulse remained steady. Now came further signs that her coma was deepening. Her breathing became shallower, and Daniel could feel her pulse weakening. Then there came the periods when she seemed to have stopped breathing altogether, when her stillness felt unearthly. And then, just after dawn, imperceptibly she died. Daniel sat silently by her side, as he had sat for the last five hours, watching her. He called no one, even when he knew she was dying. She would have approved. It was the end of a long, private affair.

After a while he went downstairs and told Alex. Together they woke the other two and, as dawn began to break on another leaden grey sky, the three men carried her body out into the thickest part of the wood and buried her. The cold on the edge of the day was ferocious. Standing by the sitting room window watching them walk into the distance, Anna could see their breath turning to smoke as it left their mouths. She stood at the window all the time they were away, thinking nothing, her mind numb with sleep and sorrow. It was the same for all of them. Sleeplessness and the continued level of tension heightened the surrealism of the death. They had known it was likely to happen, but the fact of it released no emotion. It was as if they each strangely took their cue from Daniel whose extreme calm was at the same time both reassuring and terrifying. Anna had no idea what he was feeling, if indeed he was feeling at all.

She waited, looking out into the half light. A layer of mist hovered above the ground. In the distance she saw the three of them returning across the fields. Wolf was walking in front carrying the shovel, Daniel and Alex behind, talking. As she stood with her arms wrapped around herself watching them approach, she knew they were talking about her. She felt very separated from them all by Livia's death, as if part of herself had been removed. They, the men, would go their own way, responding to the needs of the moment. But she and Livia had always operated on a different level. They had shared that difference even though in many other ways they were quite opposite characters. Now she was alone. She turned away from the window and went into the kitchen to make coffee. The day had begun.

Later she and Daniel returned to London, leaving the island as soon as the causeway opened, long before the rest of the world was awake, and before the commuter traffic could clog up their progress into the city. As she left the cottage Alex followed her, his face grey with tiredness. He took her in his arms and held her for a long time. She leaned her head against his shoulder and stared out across the fields, feeling nothing.

'I'll be home this evening,' he said. 'Brian's coming down to take over.'

She didn't reply, simply broke away from him and got into the car.

She understood that her leaving was a statement of disapproval from Daniel, that she was being removed from the job. He had not said as much – in fact he had said almost nothing, simply noting that Roland would be waiting for her to make contact, and that it was best for her to be on home territory, away from suspicion. But what she should tell Roland was not discussed: Daniel did not seem interested.

As the Rover swung out onto the causeway it seemed to Anna that she had never seen the river looking so desolate and so beautiful. Daniel drove slowly, salt water spraying up into the suspension as they ploughed through the pools left by the tide. They passed a flock of ducks with their long tails up, feeding in the mud. She looked to the right, down the estuary out to sea where a weak sun was rising behind the gaunt concrete nuclear power station. Everything looked bleak, but peaceful. She wondered again what kind of world it had been that Carolyn had found there last night.

They reached the end of the crossing and Daniel guided the car up the short steep incline and over the ridge that marked the beginning of the rest of the world. Behind them the hermetic atmosphere of the island: in front a sprawling, scruffy caravan site deserted for the winter, its large tin boxes a jumble of colour after the long lines of the grey mud landscape. Anna shivered at the shock. She pulled her coat more tightly around herself and lit a cigarette.

They drove in silence. Daniel's profile was impenetrable. When they had left the countryside behind and the monotonous brick and concrete of suburbia was building up around them, she turned to him and tried again.

'When Roland calls, what should I say?'

'Say whatever you want. Whatever comes into your head.'

'You don't want me to deliberately lead them away from us, lay some false clues?'

'I don't see much point, do you?'

'But are you sure we're safe, Daniel? Are you sure they can't trace Mike back to us?'

'Anna, no one can ever be sure of everything. You must just play it as it comes.'

A set of traffic lights turned red. Daniel brought the car to a slow halt.

'Daniel, why don't we finish the job? It's got out of hand. Why don't we pull out?'

'Because it's not finished yet.'

'But they're never going to pay. You know that.'

He smiled softly and she caught the edge of it in the driving mirror. 'I'm not talking about the money, Anna. Anyway . . .' His manner was patient. 'The Swiss have opened negotiations. They've shown the video. They'll settle, and when that happens Global UK will follow suit. We're going to win, Anna.'

'No, we're not, Daniel. It's a delusion.'

'Anna, you're not listening.'

The lights turned green and he let in the clutch. She said

nothing. It was useless. She couldn't talk to him, she couldn't stand the silence. She turned on the radio, to the noisiest station she could find. The slow journey to the city was completed to the jarring sounds of Radio One.

When they reached London, Daniel drove her straight to Waterloo Station. The streets were crowded with a flood of commuters pouring out into another city day. At the entrance to the station Anna continued to sit, half turned in her seat, wondering if there was anything left to say. She gazed at the man sitting beside her. She had known him for nearly ten years: she did not know him at all. She stared at him, at the thin stubble across his cheek, at the sleep caught in the corner of his eye. She noted the white tips of his knuckles on the steering wheel, the calm in his bearing, the control in his eyes. Whatever there was still to say, she could not say it. Not to him. She had no idea of how to begin to get through. Maybe Livia's death had gone deeper than even he realised.

A taxi hooted at them, breaking the spell. Wordlessly Daniel leaned across her and opened the door. Automatically she got out, gave him one last look and closed the door. He drove off immediately, without looking back.

An hour and a half later, at 9.30, Anna was back home, the frost still hard on the lawn, and the milk and the papers newly delivered. In Winchester everything was supremely normal, but then everything always was. She sat at the kitchen table, sipping a cup of coffee, wondering whether to go back to bed, refusing to think beyond the practical. She jumped slightly as the phone rang. But whoever it was rang off as soon as she lifted the receiver.

Ten minutes later Roland arrived. She heard the doorbell and saw him through the corner of a curtain, smart, dressed for work. She wondered whether to answer the door, but somehow she was sure he knew she was there. Anyway, if she did not see him now he would only come back later.

His pinstripe suit was cut in a fashionable style, contrasting oddly with his umbrella and briefcase. He looked rather funny, she thought. He nodded a greeting and walked past her into the sitting room.

'Yes, I think I will. I know it's early, but it feels to me like an occasion for Scotch. A dash of soda.'

She felt his eyes on her as she poured the drinks. It was not exactly unpleasant; she felt no obligation to speak. He was going to control the conversation, that was obvious. She felt bowed down by lassitude and indifference.

For a few moments neither of them spoke. She sat curled in her chair, her legs tucked under her, holding her cup of coffee and looking around the room. Even in the harshest light of morning it was beautiful, made with care, and with love. But that had been a long time ago. She looked over at Roland. He was watching her, smiling brightly. He knew something of what she was feeling, Anna was sure of that. He timed his re-entry into the conversation.

'I'm so sorry to disturb you this early, Anna. I called a couple of times earlier, but you must have been asleep. I hope I didn't get you up?'

She smiled distantly, shaking her head.

'How was the evening? Dinner go all right?'

'Fine, Roland, thank you.'

'And Alex?'

She returned his gaze evenly. 'He's at work, Roland. We're alone.'

'Good, good. Well, Anna, I've come with some remarkable news. Since you've been such a help I thought it was only right that you should be one of the first to know.'

She waited. She could think of nothing to say. It suddenly did not seem very important. She felt sleepy.

'A few days ago we found the man working with Exterminating Angel in Bombay. We cracked the Indian connection.' He used the word self-consciously, like a connoisseur savouring a good wine in front of friends. 'And as a result of that connection, I think I can safely say that we now know who we are looking for.'

She stared at him heavy-eyed, and she waited. She knew instinctively that she should wait, that he wanted her to.

'Yes.' His body, like his words, was oblique to her, like a psychoanalyst's. 'We know finally who Exterminating Angel are.' He raised his glass and slowly sipped the Scotch. 'But, alas, what we don't know yet is where they are keeping the hostages.'

Still she did not speak. But their eyes continued to meet. She smiled again, from a long way away.

'You look tired, Anna,' he said abruptly. 'You must have had a late night.'

She nodded faintly, not replying.

'To return to what I was saying. So, you see, we still have rather a problem. We could round up two, maybe three, of the group just like that.' He clicked his fingers. 'But of course that wouldn't help us find the woman and the child.'

Another pause.

'However, I think there's a chance that we could do some kind of deal with them. Would you like to hear about it, Anna?'

She was counting the stripes running diagonally across his tie. She had got to nine. 'Yes,' she said softly. 'Please tell me.'

'Good. What I've suggested to my immediate superiors is that we get in touch with one of the group whose identity has been confirmed beyond any doubt, and offer him – or her, in this case – the chance of immunity, along with her partner. In return for this considerable clemency all we would need is the name of the hideout. It's a remarkably attractive bargain, don't you think, Anna?'

Anna looked down into the bottom of her coffee cup, then across the room to a print on the wall above Roland's head. She had very little idea of what she was going to say when she opened her mouth to reply.

'And what would happen if she didn't agree to help you? What then?'

'That of course would be up to her.' His manner became brisker. 'Entirely up to her. For us the end result would be exactly the same. It would, after all, be only a matter of time. We would find them, now that we know who they are. But if we find them on our own then there can be no special arrangement. So you see it really makes no difference to us.'

Roland stretched his legs in front of him. He was very relaxed.

'Naturally, we'd appreciate that she'd need a little time to think it over. Although, given the urgency of the situation, we couldn't give her long, and she would of course be under constant surveillance while she made up her mind. But I would hope that she would come to quite a speedy decision, wouldn't you?'

He finished his drink and stood up with a lightness surprising for one with such a heavy frame. For the first time the two of them looked directly into each other's eyes. Had Anna been more alert she might have detected a touch of admiration in his gaze. For a moment neither moved, then Anna said quietly: 'Tell me, Roland, were you surprised when you found out who they were?'

He smiled, a distant private smile. 'Yes, I suppose I was. But then after I gave it some thought I realized that I'd probably known all along. Strange, isn't it?'

He did not move. She looked away from him out of the window.

'You'd better sit down, Roland. Sit down.'

Chapter Forty Three

At the back of Anna's home there is a stretch of open country called Shawford Down. This occupies a small hill, ideal for anyone wishing to observe the house. Shortly before Anna's arrival by taxi from Winchester Station that morning, a man came to the top of this hill. He picked an unobtrusive spot against an oak tree and sat down to wait with his binoculars and his Nikon fitted with a 1000 mm. lens. This was Anna's comrade, Brian.

When Roland arrived in his Morris Marina Brian was able to take a clear picture of him. He also noted the presence of a second man who remained seated in the car while Roland was inside the house, but the only details he could pick out were his moustache – trim and dark – and a flashy gold ring on his wedding finger. He wore a dark blue polo neck jumper and smoked, Brian thought from the colour of the filters and the packet, French cigarettes. The two of them left seventy-five minutes later. It was by then almost midday. Brian noticed the short wave aerial, of the kind used by the police, and the number plates, London Central.

This information seemed to warrant a telephone call to Daniel.

Brian walked briskly to the other side of the Down to the phone box outside Shawford Station.

He put his call through, using the customary code, then crossed the road and sat on a bench outside The Bridge pub for the ten-minute wait for Daniel to ring back. He had spent the last week flying a charter to and from Nairobi, so he was not fully informed on the progress of the operation. Daniel had woken him early that morning with a cryptic phone message that told him something was wrong. He then brusquely ordered him down to 'the West Country' to watch the house. Brian was more than worried. Was Anna in trouble? If so, that was bad news for all of them.

The phone rang. Brian gave Daniel the information. Then he asked: 'What's going on?'

'Listen carefully. We're going to have to close down the operation.' Daniel paused to think; Brian knew better than to interrupt. 'I'll get in touch with Wolf and Alex and tell them to wrap it up immediately. You get over to the Tottenham house and wait for them to arrive. They'll have to dump the woman and child, get rid of the van, then drive to London in Alex's car. They ought to be with you by nine. I'll phone at ten.'

'Daniel—'

'I'm sorry, Brian. There's a lot more, but I can't go into it now. Just do it, will you?'

'Are we in danger?'

The answer was so long coming that Brian thought for a moment they had been disconnected. 'No, Brian. Not if we keep our heads.'

Six hours later two cars stood at the beginning of the causeway, poised, waiting to cross to the mainland. Wolf sat in the driving seat of the Transit, with Carolyn and the baby lying drugged in the back. Alex was to follow in his own car, a Peugeot 604.

The day had been spent in preparation for this moment. In an incinerator in the garden they had burnt every object in the house which pointed to them as individuals: every book, every piece of paper and article of clothing, even the contents of the vacuum cleaner. The house had been thoroughly cleaned to remove fingerprints. The bloodstain in the upstairs room had been scrubbed white. While Alex was doing this Wolf patrolled the perimeter, looking at the boats in the estuary to see if any might have the island under surveillance. He saw nothing suspicious, but then the river was always busy, so it was difficult to tell.

Both men carried out their tasks in a systematic, unhurried way; it was something they had done many times before, at the end of each operation. Had they moved faster they might just have been able to leave the island by launch at full tide, but that would have left the cars behind, as well as other incriminating evidence, and neither of them was willing to be so careless.

Daniel had emphasized how important it was to leave no trace. He had also been circumspect in what he had told them. He had spoken to Alex first and, not wishing to alarm him, simply said they were to pull out, the risks had become too great. To Wolf he had told a more complete version of the truth. And remembering Livia's words, he had entrusted to Wolf one particular task, more dramatic than the others, that had to be done. If there was any chance that the security forces were on their track, then they had to be sure that there was no one left behind who could identify them. And the island had one inhabitant who had regularly seen them without their masks.

So it was that half an hour before the causeway was due to open, Wolf had left Alex packing up the cars and had crossed the fields to the farm manager's house. Frank was in the office doing the accounts. Bent over the pages of figures he could not have noticed Wolf enter from behind, not until he felt the arm encircle his neck and the knife enter his right side below the rib cage and slide upwards until his body stopped twitching. Wolf had a horror of ballistics evidence.

When he had wiped the blade clean he pulled out the drawers of the desk, flung some papers about and lifted a cash box onto the table. It was not hard to open. It contained about £80 in cash. Wolf folded the notes carefully and stuffed them into his breast pocket. From the door he looked back. A farmer on a remote island killed for a few pounds petty cash. It might make the headlines in the more popular press, though hardly on page one.

* * *

In his office above Curzon Street, Jarvis put down the telephone. In the doorway appeared the gaunt figure of William Macclesfield.

'Well, any news?'

It was unusual for his superior to leave the confines of his oak-panelled room. Jarvis shook his head. 'Not yet, sir. They haven't left. The police say everything looks quiet, although they've been lighting fires. There's still an hour left of the tide.'

'And does the woman have any idea?'

'No, sir. She still thinks we'll wait until morning, after her husband has left. That was the bargain. But even if she knew there's nothing she could do now. It's too late.'

'And you're sure this is it? You're sure she told you the truth?'

'Yes, I'm sure. She's got nothing to lose. She thinks she's just bought her freedom. She's at home now, waiting for him to come back, and then together they'd leave tonight for Ireland.'

Macclesfield raised an eyebrow. 'Your suggestion?'

Jarvis smiled. 'Well, it's close enough to look like a holiday. And it would have got them out of the way.'

Macclesfield looked past him out through the permanent lace curtain to the grey sky beyond. 'But it's cold.'

'I don't expect she was thinking of the weather, sir.'

'No, I don't expect she was. And what about Luis?'

'Luis believes the woman is responsible.'

'Well, she is, isn't she?'

'Not really. She was just there.'

'And Luis will still be clean, after all this is over?'

'I believe so, sir. Then we can dangle him again.'

'And who's to know the line has a noose on the end?'

'Precisely.'

'You did well, Jarvis. Strong nerves. I'd have been inclined to give up before now.'

'Thank you, sir.'

'By the way, the Swiss terrorists have released their hostages.'

'Yes, I heard.'

'Poor show, the Swiss giving in like that. Panicked by the effect of the UN Conference, I suppose. Still, their security forces don't have the experience we have.'

'No, sir.'

'We will make a clean job of it, won't we?'

'Yes, sir. They've got explicit instructions.'

'Good, good,' his superior muttered softly, and turned towards the door. He, unlike many of his colleagues, did not enjoy the ending of assignments. It was in those moments that the smell of the chase was replaced by the rather sad, seamy aftertaste. When it came down to it there was always some kind of betrayal involved. He would on the whole prefer not to know the details.

'Don't worry, sir,' said Jarvis's voice after him. 'I'll take care of the details.'

Now they stood together, Alex and Wolf, binoculars focussed on the mainland almost a mile away. Nothing moved. Wolf's grey anorak shone slightly, the fading light catching the drizzle on its surface. The sky pressed down low onto the evening horizon. In front of them the thin ribbon of land wriggled its way into the darkness and over to the other side. It was time to go.

The two vehicles moved off in slow convoy across the estuary. Wolf in the first, his Kalashnikov assault rifle on the seat beside him; Alex in the second, twenty metres behind. The crossing took almost ten minutes, a slow, plodding progress, tyres sucking in and out of mud puddles. Around them gulls wheeled and screamed, crashing into the shallow water in search of food.

They approached the mainland, mud giving way to solid ground, and began the last slow climb up the promontory out of the basin. In the distance a church clock struck 7.00 as the Transit topped the ridge and pointed down towards the caravan site. Wolf looked out on a deserted landscape, everything normal, in its place – apart from one thing.

The road ahead was totally blocked by three well-placed tree trunks.

Wolf slammed on the brakes and reached for his gun. As his fingers folded round the butt there was an explosion of automatic rifle fire. The two front tyres of the Transit were instantly reduced to shreds. A single bullet from a marksman shattered the windscreen, passing through the space occupied a split second before by Wolf's head, and ricocheted round the back of the van.

Wolf pulled down the door handle and threw himself out, his gun already firing.

He never reached the ground alive. Bullets swept the area around him, tearing up the turf and slicing through the mud. In the half second it took him to hit the earth his head and chest were already split open, spurting blood. He lay still, his body splayed out in the dirt.

Alex saw nothing of this, heard everything. Thirty metres behind, the Peugeot was an open target, caught in the basin of the estuary. Instinct and training impelled him out of the car, flat, elbows on the ground, aiming at the skyline behind which he could hear the firing. He was baying at the moon. The answer came from another direction entirely, from that part of the sea wall one hundred metres to his right. A blaze of gunfire. The petrol tank caught. A second later the Peugeot exploded, engulfing his body. He was dead before the flames took hold.

Evening continued to fall, the light bleeding away over the estuary. The gunfire petered out. There was still the sound of flames hissing their way through the metal shell. Across the sea wall gulls screeched in outrage. From behind their cover, figures began to stand up, clambering over the logs, moving towards the carnage, guns at the ready. But they were not the first out from behind the barricades. As soon as the firing ceased two men leaped out and ran towards the scene, carrying a video camera and sound equipment. They circled the vehicles, recording, with emotionless efficiency, the death of two of the world's most superstar terrorists. It was a little too late for the early evening news bulletins. But it would be the perfect lead item at 10.p.m.

Inside the damaged Transit Carolyn Fernley lay sprawled on the floor, a small pool of blood seeping out from a single neat hole in her chest. Next to her the baby slept, unharmed.

Chapter Forty Four

It was just after nine when Daniel turned off the Winchester by-pass towards the village of Compton. He drove slowly, taking each corner with exaggerated care. The night was clear and sharp, a thick wedge of a moon picking up the contours of the hills in the distance. The air had lost that bitter edge of last night's cold. March was turning to April. Winter was losing the battle, soon there would be a smell of spring in the air. On the outskirts of the village Daniel turned left up an unadopted road lined with horse chestnuts just beginning to bud. A little further on he swung into a gravel drive leading to a detached nineteenth-century house set back from the road. A single light glowed from a downstairs room blending into the moonlight along the path.

Anna heard the car pull up and was at the door before Daniel had time to ring the bell. As she saw him the shiver of a shadow passed across her face and she dropped her eyes. He was not the person she was expecting. Without a word she turned and walked back into the sitting room. He followed her and sat in the armchair next to the fire. She sprawled on a settee, avoiding his eyes, her head resting on her elbow. Her hair, unusually for her, looked dishevelled, and there was an odd vacant look in her eyes. He watched her, peeling off his gloves and tossing them on the floor beside him.

'What a lovely house you have, Anna,' he said. 'It's a creative side of you we don't normally see. How do you ever find the energy?'

She looked round vaguely. 'Don't be disingenuous, Daniel. Nothing surprises you.'

'How did you spend your day?'

'Roland came to see me.'

'He did?'

'Yes.'

Daniel waited for her to continue. The firelight danced shadows on the wall behind him. She watched the patterns forming.

'He's a slippery one,' she said at last.

'We know that.'

Anna examined her hands. The nail of her little finger was broken. She continued: 'I don't know why. He didn't ask me anything. I don't know why he came.'

'What did he say?'

'He seemed very pleased with himself. Reckoned they would find the woman and child quite soon.'

'What do they know?'

'Who knows, Daniel? Who knows?'

'Didn't you ask him?'

Anna did not immediately reply. She was studying a spot to the left of him, a coffee table on which there was a vase of daffodils newly cut from the garden and a framed portrait of Alex. 'I didn't want to sound too interested,' she said quietly.

She turned to him and looked puzzled. 'Why have you come, Daniel?'

'I came to see you.'

He stood up, walked across to the cabinet by the window, and poured himself a small malt whisky. Then he returned to his seat, the same seat in which some ten hours earlier Roland had been sitting. A briskness came into his manner.

'I've decided to close down the operation.'

'When?' There was a spark in her eyes. It flared up and died again almost immediately, like a match not holding a flame.

'Tonight. They will have left on the evening tide.'

'Oh,' was all she said.

'You're surprised?'

She gazed directly at him, then shook her head. 'Not really. It had got out of control. You're right. We overreached ourselves.'

'You never did like it, did you?'

'It's too late now.'

'What's too late now?'

Anna closed her eyes momentarily, and with her thumb and forefinger squeezed the bridge of her nose. 'It's too late to think about me.'

His calm examination of her continued. The clock in the hall struck a quarter to ten. 'So,' he said quietly. 'Alex won't be home tonight. He and Wolf will go to the safe house in Tottenham until we see how things are settling.'

'And the woman and the baby?'

'They will be taken care of.'

She looked at him. She did not ask the question and he did not volunteer the reply.

She sat up. There was a slow, almost langorous quality to the movement. Then, closing her eyes, she put a hand on the back of her neck and moved her head, once clockwise, once anticlockwise. It was a lonely, private gesture, as if she were suddenly unaware of his presence. She opened her eyes and blinked a couple of times dully.

'I'm terribly sorry, Daniel. I think I'll have to go to bed.'

He acknowledged this with a slight nod. She stood up and left the room, not looking back at him. He heard her footsteps go up the stairs. He sat for a while watching the fire eat its way through the dark logs, splintering them with seams of red. The night silence grew heavy. The clock struck ten. He went over and poured himself another drink, then sat at the desk and picked up the phone. After a moment he dialled a number. He waited for thirty rings, then replaced the receiver. He sat for a few moments, sipping his drink. Then he tried again. Again no reply.

He got up abruptly and walked over to the stereo in the alcove. A few seconds later the opening notes of Mahler's Fifth exploded into the silence. He looked up sharply and reduced the volume. From his pocket he took out an automatic pistol, cocked it and slipped the safety catch.

Then, with deliberate strides, he was out of the door and into the hall. The strains of Mahler followed him into the silence, covering the sounds of his foot fall as he climbed the stairs. Outside the bedroom door he paused for a second, then slowly, silently turned the handle. From the window cold shafts of moonlight slid across the room, revealing the bed and the shape of the reclining figure under the covers. He walked softly across the thick pile carpet until he was standing by the bedside looking at her. Her dark hair was splayed out against the pillow. Caught in sleep there was a kind of innocence about her face, a hint of a pout around the corners of the mouth as the muscles slackened, a soft babyflesh quality to the skin. The man seemed unaffected by her vulnerability. He moved the gun to the back of her skull. It was an almost matter-of-fact gesture. But even as the muzzle touched her hair her eyes flicked open, alert immediately. He put out his free hand and touched her cheek. It was almost a caress.

'Close your eyes, Anna. Go back to sleep.'

'You shouldn't do this.' Her voice was clean and steady, without fear. 'You shouldn't do this. It can't change anything.'

There was the sound of a shot.

Daniel pitched forward, his head striking the wall with a crack. Where his ear had been there was a rough red circle. A line of blood flowed down his cheek and neck and began to saturate his collar.

For a moment there was silence in the room. Then from behind the curtain a man appeared, tall, with a moustache, wearing a dark blue polo neck and holding a pistol. He walked across the room and crouched beside Daniel's body to examine it. He and Anna looked at each other. Without a word he leaned forward, picked up the telephone by the bed and dialled a number.

Epilogue

The gravel leading up to the house was strewn with dead leaves. The chestnuts had shed during the freak October storms and the wind had swept their harvest over the path. No one had bothered to clear it up.

A man in his mid forties, dressed in a suit and a grey trench coat, was walking up the side path from the road, the stones crunching under his feet. As he approached the front door he passed the large For Sale sign hammered into the ground near the garage. When he reached the main porch he stood for a second, then rang the bell.

A short time elapsed. The door opened a fraction, hitting a chain and sticking a couple of inches wide. Through the crack he saw the face of a woman: full lips, big dark eyes, a shock of dark hair. She looked ill.

'Mrs Weston?'

'Yes, who are you?'

'The name's Cranley. Jeffrey Cranley. I believe Norbert and Norris, the estate agents, called you this morning. I made an appointment with them to see the house.

She frowned slightly. 'Oh yes, I thought Mr Norris was coming with you?'

'He was, yes. But just as we were leaving the office he had a call from the hospital. I gather his wife is expecting a baby. So of course I told him I'd come along by myself. I do hope that's all right.'

She sighed, a gesture more for herself than for him. 'I see. Do you have any kind of identification, Mr Cranley?'

'Of course, of course,' he said eagerly, his hand flicking inside his jacket pocket and re-emerging with a wallet crammed with credit cards – Access, American Express, Diners' Club.

She did not respond to this display, but simply closed the door again to release the catch, and then opened it wide. He went in smiling, fumbling with his wallet, pushing it back inside his suit. The woman stood by the door waiting, then closed it behind him. She motioned to a room across the hall and he went in.

It must have been a lovely place once: light, big, full of a sense of age, with French windows looking out onto a sprawling garden which reached out to the fields beyond. But it was desolate now, sparsely decorated, with pale patches on the walls where there had once been paintings. The floor was bare and echoing under their feet. The only furniture in the room was a desk at the far end and one armchair near the huge open grate. The room was cold. The fire had not been laid recently. The man looked round appreciatively, noting the far door out into the kitchen and pantry and the side door to the drive beyond.

'What a lovely room,' he said, smiling.

She did not reply. She stood, patiently waiting for him to finish his inspection so that she could lead him elsewhere.

'And such a magnificent fireplace,' he said, going towards it, away from her. 'May I ask, Mrs Weston, why are you moving?'

Her voice was quiet, almost too quiet to hear properly. 'The house is too big for me. I am taking a flat in London.'

'I see.'

He was almost inside the fireplace now, running a finger up along a dark beam, black with soot. He pulled a handkerchief out of a pocket to wipe his hand clean.

'Have you been here long?'

'About five years.'

'Living alone?'

The remark was thrown politely over his shoulder while he crouched with his back to her, staring up into the further reaches of the chimney.

'No, I was married. My husand died last spring.'

'Oh, my goodness. I'm so sorry.' He straightened up, turning slowly towards her. 'I really am very sorry, Mrs Weston.' He had approached to within a couple of yards. Now he stopped. 'Or should I call you Anna?'

Only her eyes reacted, first in shock, then fear, and finally pain. In a sudden, sharp movement he reached out and grabbed the front of her sweater. As she lurched forward his boot landed crack on her left shin. She piled head first onto the floor, landing awkwardly, half on her side, with her right cheekbone taking the splintering impact on the bare floorboards. Behind her the man went down on one knee, right arm outstretched, his revolver jabbed hard into the fold of skin below her ear. 'Count to three, Mrs Weston,' he barked.

One.

In her head she started counting. Then from somewhere a line of poetry.

'Slowly the poison the whole blood stream fills.'

Two.

'The waste remains, the waste remains and kills.'

Three.

No one resigns from terrorism. It is a contract for life. MI5 might have protected her, but not when, hearing of Alex's death, she refused further co-operation. This had always been clear. She knew the comrades would never let it rest there, that when they were ready they would come. She did not recognize this man; he must have been sent by the Swiss group, despite the London accent. What was he waiting for? Was this merely the start of some obscure ritual of revenge?

She waited. He waited. But for the scratched skin and the aching bones she might have been already dead.

Finally it was the man who broke the silence. 'You have a chance,' he said. 'There is something you can do for us.' He spoke slowly and carefully, pausing between each sentence. 'If you help us, the account is settled, and you will be free.' She felt his body relax. The gun was no longer pressed into her head. She had no doubt, however, of his continued vigilance. Anna painfully shifted over onto her back, where she could see him. When she was still again he uttered the single word: 'Luis.'

'Luis? Is that a joke?'

'Somebody's joke. Not my joke. And not even funny.'

She continued to stare.

'You don't know?' His tone was lightly sarcastic, as if he pretended to disbelieve her. 'Luis is the source of all knowledge.'

'Roland?' Anna could not have disguised her incredulity.

'Jarvis!' He was delighted by her naive response. 'Jarvis is certainly well-informed, but I'd hardly call him a "source". No, Anna, for better or worse, Roland is exactly what he seems.'

'I knew there was a traitor.'

'Apart from yourself?' He waved the gun in a way which might have been expansive or threatening. 'Expound.'

'Apart . . . from myself.' She shook her head, trying to collect her thoughts, then she continued: 'When Roland interrogated me, he already knew. He implied he'd got it from Mike, but he knew much more than Mike could have told him. He only needed one thing – the island, the location. He had the rest. My telling him was purely a formality. Why, then, was it necessary to ask?'

She put this to the man as if she really expected him to respond; he shrugged, disinterested. She answered it herself: 'So I should be blamed for revealing it. No one would look further. In that case, I wonder, who was the other, the real traitor, the one I became a scapegoat for?'

'You thought it was Daniel?'

'I thought it was Daniel. But then . . . I knew it couldn't be. MI5 wouldn't hit its own man.'

'Why not? It's been done before.'

Anna paused to consider this remark, but found it meaningless. 'Anyway . . . that's why. It wasn't just because of . . . because of —'

'You're lying, Mrs Weston.'

'I don't give a shit what you think.'

'Prove it!'

'How?'

'Kill Luis.'

'I don't even know Luis.'

'All the better. No one would suspect you.'

'Who is Luis?'

'Name of Gerald Halliwell. MI5. Counter-Subversion. A sleeper. Friend of Daniel's from way back. They turned him. He was the one that betrayed you.'

'How can you know that?'

'How do we know? Come now, Mrs Weston, how long have you been out of it? Don't you know better than to ask questions like that? Let's just say Luis wasn't the only one to change sides.'

'But how do you know your convert is telling the truth?'

'Mrs Weston, please!' He rapped three or four times sharply on the floor with his pistol. 'Your suggestions are illogical and irrelevant. You have our offer. You're blown, you're retired, you're clean. You can do it in perfect safety. And then you can live your life in peace. What about it? You lose nothing, and you can gain . . . everything.'

It was true, in a way, all that he said was true, but on another level it was a lie – not vicious, not deliberate, but a lie none the less. As he said, she owed it to them. And they would look after her, in their fashion, as well as they could. But it was not good enough. Nothing she could do could possibly buy her safety. Sooner or later there would be an infiltration, or someone would be indiscreet, or would break and turn (as she herself had done, before). Or MI5 would simply put two and two together. And if somebody had to be thrown to the wolves, why not Anna Weston? What good is an ex-terrorist? That was why she had been offered this, she was no good for anything else. It was happening again, she was always being offered things, in the belief that she could not afford to refuse. She knew without thinking about it, because she had not ceased to think about it for the past six months, that there would never be any life for her without trouble, there would never be an end to the matter.

It was enough. She made her decision. She had made it long before this thug jarred his way into her life. She turned her head and looked at him direct. 'No,' she said. 'I'm not interested.'

'No?' the gun wavered in the man's hand. The pale autumn light picked up the sheen of the barrel and sent sunlight crashing round the room. Anna watched its flickering movements on the wall before her. She remembered the shadows of the long summer evenings in the dormitory at boarding school. She thought of what she had learned then, that no matter what they did to you there was one thing you always had: the sense that you were you.

The bullet hit her in the chest, directly below her left breast. The force of it knocked her over, flat on her back. She was immediately still.

The man stood up and walked quickly to where she lay. He kneeled on one leg over her body and felt the main artery in her throat. Her eyes stared up at him. In a movement that looked almost tender he closed them. Then, without looking back, he walked out of the room, out of the front door and along the gravel path towards the road. A few moments later he was gone from view, the sound of his car receding into the distance.

Around the house a wind gusted suddenly through the branches of the chestnuts, scattering the last few leaves onto the ground. After the wind there was silence.

OTHER BOOKS FROM PLUTO

NOT A THROUGH STREET
ERNEST LARSEN

Emma Hobart drives a New York taxi. Her lover, Hoyt, is investigating a mysterious death. Emma's cab is involved in an accident that causes Hoyt's death. Student anti-war politics and political corruption block her search for the killers. One question too many and Emma is driving for her life.

A feminist cabbie invades the Chandler tradition – the result is stunning.

Ernest Larsen was born in Chicago and went to Columbia University. Since then he has worked at a variety of jobs, including being a house painter, a department-store Santa Claus and a taxi driver. He is currently Editor of the film journal *Jump Cut.* He lives in California.

'Something decidedly new in the author's style, which is sensitive, compassionate and even poetic.' *New York Times*

240 pages
0 7453 0039 1 £2.50 paperback
0 7453 0041 3 £7.95 hardback

THE ANVIL AGREEMENT
KEN BEGG

Cytogerm is a miracle drug with deadly side effects. Its manufacturers are intent on eliminating everyone connected with it. Its discoverer, Dr Sean MacLean, is on the run. He attempts suicide. His failure has terrifying consequences. A medical thriller of *Coma* standards.

Ken Begg works for the Medical Research Council of Great Britain at Edinburgh University.

160 pages
0 7453 0030 8 £2.50 paperback
0 7453 0031 6 £7.95 hardback

WATCHING THE DETECTIVES
JULIAN RATHBONE

In Brabt, trains run on time and the bags you lose end up at the lost-and-found. Suddenly, the clockwork state is interrupted – by police brutality and terrorist violence. Headlines and news bulletins put the blame on 'left-wing violence committed to the overthrow of the state'. Commissioner Jan Argand agrees, until an anti-nuclear demonstration turns into a near massacre and Argand himself narrowly escapes an attempt on his life.

'Julian Rathbone is a highly original artist whc uses the thriller form to comment on the increasing violence and absurdity of the post-industrial world we live in.' *Literary Review*

240 pages
0 7453 0011 1 £2.50 paperback

DAYS LIKE THESE
NIGEL FOUNTAIN

The routine of John Raven's life is interrupted by the purchase of photos not meant to be for sale. The shop desperately wants the photos back. Heavies lean on him. His flat is ransacked. Why?… Raven witnesses a bomb attempt on the house of a MP. He is dragged deep into a whirlpool of fascist thuggery. *Days Like These* sardonically captures a seedy world of political violence and bitter-sweet personal relationships.

Nigel Fountain lives in North London. He is currently an editor on the London weekly magazine, *City Limits.*

0 86104 796 6 £2.50 paperback
0 86104 797 4 £8.95 hardback

DANCE HALL OF THE DEAD
TONY HILLERMAN

A young Zuni Indian Fire God disappears – and is then found murdered. His Navajo friend is running for his life. Lt Joe Leaphorn, also a Navajo, stalks a killer whose trail is crossed by archaeologists on the make, a Federal narcotics agent and hippy dropouts.

'Hillerman has created an altogether believable set of characters… He knows his background well.' *New York Times.*

The reputation of Tony Hillerman's Indian reservation thrillers is growing fast. *Dance Hall of the Dead* won the prestigious Edgar 'Mystery Novel of the Year' when published in the US. This is its first publication in the UK and Australia.

0 86104 692 7 £2.25 paperback
0 86104 693 5 £7.95 hardback

MORBID SYMPTOMS
GILLIAN SLOVO

Feminism grapples with murder in this pacey thriller set in the alternative London of Marx and muesli. This first novel by a young South African writer is a welcome intrusion into the male world of private eyes, mobsters and random violence.

'A thriller in which neither are the villains crazy reds nor the hero a macho bully… And the sleuth is a socialist feminist.' Elizabeth Wilson

160 pages
0 86104 745 1 £2.95 paperback
0 86104 773 7 £6.95 hardback

MURDER IN THE CENTRAL COMMITTEE
MANUEL VAZQUEZ MONTALBAN

The first appearance in English of a Spanish writer whose crime novels are international best sellers and have won both the Planeta Prize (the Spanish Booker) and the Grand Prix of detective fiction in France. Set in the fratricidal world of the Spanish Communist Party, this is the perfect political thriller.

'At last a thriller worthy of the name; a taut, intelligent tour de force set in the shadowy minefield of post-Franco Spanish politics.' Julie Birchill

224 pages
0 86104 747 8 £3.50 paperback
0 86104 771 0 £7.95 hardback

THE CHINA OPTION
NANCY MILTON

Superpower politics, love, and work come into conflict in this atmospheric thriller set in China, as an American journalist discovers a perilous escalation in the Sino-Soviet conflict.

'Milton has every detail right, from the garlicky smells of Peking's courtyards to the gauzy chiffon scarves women wind round their drab Mao tunics in a bleak nod to femininity.' *Los Angeles Times*

320 pages
0 86104 746 X £3.50 paperback
0 86104 772 9 £8.95 hardback

OCTOBER HEAT
GORDON DeMARCO

A page-turner in the hard-boiled tradition, *October Heat* is set in the world of graft, payola and corruption of West Coast USA politics in the 1930s. Upton Sinclair, a socialist, is poised to win the election for governor of California – big business and the mob are out to stop him.

'*October Heat* moves as fast as a speeding bullet. It is without rival the first left-wing detective story. Dashiell Hammett himself would stand up and uncover for DeMarco's Riley Kovachs.' *San Francisco Chronicle*

192 pages
0 86104 744 3 £2.95 paperback

FRISCO BLUES
GORDON DeMARCO

It's 1947. San Francisco. The war is over and the boys are coming home. America is changing. Jackie Robinson has just broken the colour bar in the national game and baseball has been 'integrated'. Or has it?

Chet Jones, a promising young black baseball player in the negro leagues, has fallen to his death in a racially troubled shipyard. Was it an accident, as the company claims, or murder? Riley Kovachs finds himself in work once again.

Gordon DeMarco lives in San Francisco. Before becoming a full-time writer, he was a student striker, a dishwasher, a chauffeur and a docker. His hero, Riley Kovachs, also appears in *The Canvas Prison* and *October Heat* (Pluto Press).

'Mr DeMarco makes his points without sacrificing his excitements in what must be the most innovative publishing experiment of the crime-story year.' *Guardian*, reviewing Gordon DeMarco's *October Heat*

128 pages
0 7453 0040 5 £2.25 paperback
0 7453 0042 1 £7.50 hardback

JUNK ON THE HILL

JEREMY PIKSER

To avoid being a customs officer, Joe Posner was prepared to do a lot of things – including becoming a private eye and moving to New Jersey.

Business is slow. So slow that Posner is reluctant to turn down sixteen-year-old Melanie Gold's offer of work. Gold later turns up dead, and Posner is left without a client but with a lot of unanswered questions. His search for the answers takes him to the affluent suburbs – 'the human potential movement', therapy, and heroin consumption. For sure, Posner's New Jersey looks nothing like the covers of *Time*, *Life* and the *Saturday Evening Post*. Still, what can one expect of a state where the delis run out of strudel.

224 pages
0 86104 786 9 £3.50 paperback
0 86104 787 7 £8.95 hardback

THE WASTE REMAINS

JUDITH COOK

The body of a young journalist is found on a Suffolk beach, close to land owned by the Ministry of Defence.

His death marks the beginning of a nightmare for Janet, one of the women he was involved with. Unhappy with the police investigation, Janet's attempts to uncover the truth bring her into direct confrontation with the defence establishment, determined to cover up anything in the name of national security – even murder.

A sleepy Suffolk town, a washed-corpse, and a nosey librarian: ingredients that make *The Waste Remains* an east-coast fast page-turner.

'Intelligently alarming debut.' *Sunday Times*

128 pages
0 86104 779 6 £2.50 paperback

THE LIFE OF THE AUTOMOBILE

ILYA EHRENBURG

Translated by Joachim Neugroschel

Increasingly recognized as a great twentieth-century classic, *The Life of the Automobile* is an exemplary 'non-fiction novel', a genre which includes such recent works as *In Cold Blood* or *Schindler's Ark*.

Ilya Ehrenburg, renowned Russian author and journalist, gives a panoramic overview of the world the automobile made. The globe was scoured for oil, rubber and other raw materials; the assembly line was invented to tailor the worker to the production of the car; and the automobile moguls have fought it out on a world stage.

Ehrenburg takes us behind the scenes, to the rubber plantations, to the assembly line (as a witness to the first automobile death), into boardrooms and governments. In trenchant, witty and fast-moving style he recreates for us the fever and the frenzy of the modern consumer revolution.

First published in Russian in 1929, *The Life of the Automobile* was not translated into English until 1976.

'A Futurist-Expressionist masterpiece, superbly translated.' *Sunday Times*

192 pages
0 916354 07 5 £4.50 paperback

WIDOWS
A Novel
ARIEL DORFMAN

The 1940s. The setting, ostensibly, is Nazi-occupied Greece. It could, just as well, be Argentina, El Salvador, Chile, or a host of other places round the world today.

Ariel Dorfman was a professor of journalism and literature in Allende's Chile and is the author of *The Empire's Old Clothes*.

'*Widows* is a political novel written in polished and unlaboured prose. It recounts what can rarely be spoken: the horror of being "disappeared" and the ingenious and implacable courage of those who insist on knowing who is alive, who is dead.' *Washington Post*

Ariel Dorfman's 'beautifully understated tale is as powerful as it is moving.' *Publishers' Weekly*

160 pages
0 86104 723 0 £7.95 hardback

Pluto books are available through your local bookshop. In case of difficulty contact Pluto to find out local stockists or to obtain catalogues/ leaflets (telephone 01-482 1973).

If all else fails write to:

Pluto Press Limited
Freepost (no stamp required)
105A Torriano Avenue
London NW5 1YP